THE SHINING FACE

THE SHINING FACE

A NOVEL

HAROLD MYRA

ZondervanPublishingHouse

Grand Rapids, Michigan

A Division of HarperCollinsPublishers

The Shining Face
Copyright © 1993 by Harold Myra

Requests for information should be addressed to:
Zondervan Publishing House
Grand Rapids, Michigan 49530

Library of Congress Cataloging in Publication Data

Myra, Harold Lawrence, 1939–
The shining face : a novel / Harold Myra
p.   cm.
Sequel to: Children in the night.
ISBN 0-310-58771-9 (pbk.)
I. Title.
PS3563.Y7S48   1993
813'.54—dc20   93-12262
CIP

Cover design by The Puckett Group, Inc.
Cover illustration by Marilyn King
Interior design by Anne Cherryman

Printed in the United States of America

93 94 95 96 97 98 99 00 / DH / 10 9 8 7 6 5 4 3 2 1

Contents

—— PART ONE ——

CHAPTER 1. 9
The Lion   The Blind Princess
The Festival   Daybreak

CHAPTER 2. 33
Night Things   Toads
Morning Child   Dark Energies

CHAPTER 3. 65
Old Askirit Culture   Kelerai
The Summons   The King's House
The Cleft   The Chosen   The Procession

CHAPTER 4. 107
The Rooster   Legend   The Void

—— PART TWO ——

CHAPTER 5. 133
The Lamp   Sierent   Culmecs
Enre   Keitr

CHAPTER 6. 151
Slave   Interrogation   Rycal   The Wounds

CHAPTER 7. 165
Mud   The Center of Camp
Salamanders   Sand in Aliare

CHAPTER 8.   181
The Boat   A Young Woman
"The Roundup"   Dawnbreakers

CHAPTER 9.   199
The Path for Two   Mela and Geln
The Scent of Life   Fire

—— PART THREE ——

CHAPTER 10.   219
Audience with the King   The Planet Shudders
Many Hands   The Weight of Darkness   Desert
The Greater Weight

CHAPTER 11.   241
The Tree   Seeds in the Dust   The Pendant

CHAPTER 12.   251
Birds in Flight   A Little Lamp
Delin's Skills   Other Worlds

Part One

When the world was judged—
when it was split and scorched—
our ancestors fell into darkness.

That was long, long ago;
now we have escaped the night.

But deep below us,
nations still live
in the nightworld
of beasts and chaos.

Soon, someone will go down to them.
Down to lead them up into the light.

—A CHILDREN'S LESSON

Chapter 1.

—— The Lion ——

Sunlight shone from white and red blossoms in Mela's long hair; it brightened the streams of petals into bits of sunrise. Three years old, playing on a grassy hill, she was like a mobile flower herself, with cascades of blossoms tumbling over her shoulders and down her back.

Her father, Steln, had plaited them into her hair, his skilled fisherman's fingers weaving Mela's thick black strands around the long stems and between the flowers.

Flowers in the hair of little girls was traditional among her people, the Askirit, but not in such volume. "What's this, Steln?" her father's friend had asked, then had whistled appreciatively. Laughing and slowly parting the aromatic blossoms, he had demanded, "Mela, where are you under there?"

"I got carried away," Mela's father said, admiring his handiwork.

The men grinned at each other when she bounced down the steps of the cave. "Never saw so much color tumbling off one little girl," the friend said. "Looks like she has white and red hair soft as goose down."

Little Mela had been oblivious to the talk, but her older sister, Ashdel, had heard it and resented it. She was six, too old for such an extravagant display. Girls her age wore a blossom or two over the ear. Now she watched Mela running, twisting, bending in the grass nearby, flouncing her long hair and bright petals. Ashdel puckered her face and repeated with disdain the common saying: "Tiny girls are tiny blossoms."

The previous day Mela's father had brought home a little bag and had opened it in their cave. It had filled the space with an unusual perfume. Mela had bounced up and down, saying, "Put some on me! Put some on me!"

"You wouldn't smell like my little girl," her father had said.

"It smells wonderful," Mela insisted.

Finally her father agreed to put one drop on the little carving of an osprey in flight that dangled from her neck.

"I'll do it," Mela exclaimed, and before her father could object, she squeezed the bag against the wooden osprey. Liquid gushed over her hands and the carving.

"Phew!" Ashdel snorted. "Makes my eyes water."

They stepped to the outside air, Mela clutching the pendant in her fist. "Not a subtle scent," her father apologized, laughing. "I traded a boy three little crabs for it."

Little Mela stood her ground. "It's wonderful."

Now the scent-saturated carving bounced against her bare chest as she suddenly ran toward a flash of yellow feathers darting into branches. Her leather skirt caught on a bush; she yanked it free, straining to see the bird. Her vision was very poor; the yellow blur sped into the tall grass.

At her feet she saw bright green. She bent down and peered at an emerald frog; it hopped and she blocked it with her hand. Its head rammed into her palm, its legs jerking out between her fingers. She squinted and lifted it close to her face so that her weak eyes could see it. The frog glared back, its eyes like wet pebbles, its white throat thumping.

Ashdel resented having to work, especially when Mela could run free. At six years of age, Askirit girls started sanding the handles for various weapons, getting them ready for skilled artisans who would do the intricate shaping. She had five of the rough-cut hardwood lengths in a neat, gray-brown pile beside her; off to the side were two off-white lengths of bone. She always saved those for last. The oak and birch gave off a sweet woodsy smell when sanded, but she hated the odors from the bones.

"Why make bone handles?" most people said. "Wood is easier and better." Yet some insisted on them, for Ashdel's people had come from below, from the nightworld where trees did not grow, where weapons were made of the only material possible— bones from their prey.

Those who insisted on bone handles for spears and daggers dreamed of their ancestors' exploits below, where they had mastered the underground seas and deep caves. Therefore the Askirit who had come up, though they hunted grasslands and woods, preferred the net and the hook and the stout little boat.

The sun had moved, putting Ashdel in the shade. She gathered her handles and carried them past several cave entrances to a grassy knoll at cliff's edge above the sea. The wind shifted, blowing briskly from the grasses. Ashdel faced it, sniffing its scents.

A man nearby shouted, "I smell it!"

She turned, understanding instantly. Lion! For days the village had been abuzz with talk about it.

"It killed a man down the shoreline," a woman said.

Another woman contradicted her. "I heard he fell onto the rocks—then animals found him in the night."

Men and women were scrambling to gain height above the lower cave entrances, and those inside had emerged to look at the grasses. Ashdel started gathering her handles.

A roar sounded in the distance.

"I told you I smelled him!" the man said.

Ashdel had dropped a bone handle and was stooping to retrieve it when a man shouted, "Hey! What are you doing down there, girl? Get up here!"

She dropped all the handles and fled. Reaching the base of the Askirit dwellings, she grabbed at the handholds in the steep rock face looming above her.

The crowd stood nervously, staring and listening, sniffing the air. A man shouted, "Look on the far side of the grass! See it moving?"

Far off, Ashdel did see movement. She wished her father were here instead of out somewhere in a boat. She wished—

Then she remembered Mela. Where was her sister? "Mela!" she exclaimed, "Where's Mela?"

A friend of her father's said, "Where did you leave her?"

"I didn't leave her! She wandered off!" Ashdel was straining to glimpse movement where she'd last seen the child.

"There she is!" a woman said.

Ashdel looked where she was pointing. Mela was not too distant, but she was at the edge of the grasses, almost into the woods.

"Mela!" she shouted. "Mela! Come here! Lion!" Ashdel's stomach lurched. Mela's tiny figure was stooping over something and she appeared oblivious.

A man shouted, "Mela! Come here! Lion! Lion!"

A woman then called to her. Another observed, "At least the lion can't smell her. The wind's shifted."

The man called again to her so loudly his voice cracked. But Mela had gotten up and was chasing something, the blossoms spilling over her in festive waves like little red-tinged whitecaps.

Mela heard her sister shouting her name, but Ashdel had yelled for her before in that shrill, panicked voice. It simply spurred Mela on. Ever since their mother had disappeared a year ago in the earthquakes, Mela had mostly run free and was always escaping her sister.

She sensed a strange scent in the wind. She sniffed to catch it again, her remarkably sensitive nose a heritage from her Askirit forbears who had lived in the darkness below. She caught the musky scent again and was rather taken by it, not connecting it with the lion's roar.

The scent disappeared; she walked out in the open on the meadow trail. The wind shifted again, and she faced into it.

Ashdel saw her sister below emerge from the grasses, far from the lion, but both of them in the open field. "The wind's shifted again," a woman said. "See, he's caught her scent."

"He's starting to stalk her!"

Several men picked up their spears and the atlatals that launched them.

"She's moving *toward* him!"

Ashdel's throat was pumping with fear as men clambered down the cliff face. "Don't know if we can reach her in time," one said, his voice fading from Ashdel as they dropped down to the lower ledges. The big lion was moving at a steady pace, intent on the little figure ambling toward him.

Mela lost the lion's scent again. A bee buzzed past her and lighted on a flower. This danger she understood, for she'd seen a boy stung. She stopped and warily watched it gathering nectar, wondering if the bee might land on the blossoms in her hair.

When she looked up again, the lion was close enough that if she had sharp eyes, she could have distinguished his stealthy form on the slight rise. But to Mela, the grass and sky were blurred.

Then she smelled him, that tantalizing musk, now strong and full. She stood facing him as he moved toward her. The lion hove into view as a growing nimbus of dried yellow and slowly focused into a face and shoulders and swishing tail.

He stopped and looked around as if disinterested. Then he looked directly at her, as if evaluating an oddity, his skin rippling away flies on his coat.

Mela stared cautiously back, as she would at a stranger from the next village. It was a curious beast. He stood on tremendous legs, a yellow-brown mountain of fur piled high above her.

She wet her lips and said in a small voice, "You are bigger than horses!" She moved closer to him.

Ashdel saw Mela closing the gap left between her and the lion as the spearmen were racing toward them. She screamed as the white and red blossoms on her head and shoulders, and the spindly legs below the little skirt, kept moving closer and closer to the great cat. She stamped her bare feet hard against the rock, angrily saying, "Mela! Mela! Stop, you fool!"

Mela's left hand was on the osprey carving, pungent with its odd scent. The blossoms in her hair were lifted by the breeze and rippled above her forehead and beside her cheeks. The lion stood impassive, studying the scents and the tiny creature before him. She stood close now, looking him full in the face. His eyes were large, intent. When she saw his skin ripple against the annoyance of the flies, she let out a little laugh.

The spearmen were close now, coming in groups from several directions. They saw Mela standing right below the lion's nose and heard her laughter, as if there were some joke between them. Before they could get into position, the lion turned, raised his head, and then loped off toward the hill grasses, quickly disappearing into them.

—— The Blind Princess ——

For the next two years, Mela was defined by those moments with the lion. "What saved her was the smell of that carving on her neck!" a woman said, wrinkling her nose in disgust. "The big cat figured she'd taste as bad as she smelled."

Another said, "She looked like this strange, audacious, spindly thing—" and another interrupted, "How could he tell what she was? A moving, blooming stinkweed bush."

Mela's father laughed with the others, then added, "Poor lion. The meal walks up to him, looks him straight in the face and assaults his nose. Then it laughs at him."

Mela sensed the pride as well as humor in her father's voice. The story grew. One of the spearmen swore he'd heard the lion laugh with her, and others said she'd not only talked to the lion but also touched its face as she laughed.

But Ashdel confronted Mela. "You didn't even know what you were doing! You were just curious, that's all. You nearly got yourself killed, and then you laugh about it."

But Mela hardly understood all the fuss. She liked it when the children teasingly called her Lion Blossom. It was far better than the new nickname they were starting to use: "Clumsy." Her eyesight was getting much worse, but she wouldn't reveal it to anyone.

Now five, she sat in the middle of a little pool, playing with turtles and lizards. The Askirit were fond of filling depressions with water and putting in harmless creatures from their nets. Mela enjoyed touching them, but she could barely see them unless she brought them very close to her eyes.

She stepped away from the pool and cautiously started climbing the rocky trail home, squinting down at the sounds of ducks flying past. As several older boys loudly roughhoused past her, she pressed herself against the rocks.

Only when she entered her own cave did she move

confidently, sure of the wedge-shaped cabinet for tools, the furs for sleeping, the racks for drying meat and fish. But she didn't realize something had been altered in her ordered space. Her father had placed a rough-hewn ladder between the work and sleeping areas. He was standing atop it, looking at a space that might be enlarged for net storage. Mela came briskly around the corner and crashed into it, tipping one of its legs off balance.

As Mela's face and shoulder smashed into the wood corner, a blaze of pain-filled greens, reds, and blacks exploded in her brain. She never heard her father's shout or the sound of his loud clawing to regain his position above her. She crumpled and lay gasping as he grabbed wildly and finally fell all the way down to the stone floor, his knee smashing into Mela's calf. She cried out, but her voice was unheard beneath his roar of pain.

Her father was moaning. People ran toward them. "Something's broken!" her father moaned, but his voice was a dim noise behind her pain. The left side of her face was numb and swollen; she touched it with her fingers and felt wetness. Her leg throbbed the way it had when she'd wrenched it in a rock fissure.

Men were checking her father, who groaned when they touched his right side. Finally one said, "Nothing broken, Steln, but you won't be working any nets for a while."

Her father jerked his head to the side and groaned, "Mela, how could you crash into that ladder?"

The men stood above her like great shadows, her father a sad, accusing hulk lying beside her. A vague understanding of what had happened started to assemble itself in her mind. A ladder. She'd crashed into it. What ladder? Why was her face wet and hurting so much?

"The ladder was right there in front of you," her father said, raising himself up on his left elbow.

She tried to think of something to say. She felt like one of those birds that sometimes got caught and tangled in the nets, all drenched and disoriented.

Ashdel was standing above them both, staring at Mela.

"How could you crash into it?" she demanded, in the same tone her father had. "It was right there! Couldn't you see it?"

"It wasn't supposed to be there," Mela said in a quiet, small voice.

"It was right there," Ashdel retorted. She said again, even more vehemently, "Couldn't you see it?"

Mela pulled her throbbing leg under her, reached for the rock wall to steady herself, and shakily stood. The others could see, now, the ugly bruise on her face and the blood that formed a streak below her eye. "I couldn't see it," she said.

Ashdel snorted, "How could you not see it? You didn't look."

Mela appeared dazed. Her mouth became a thin slit—a tight line beneath a puffed eye and a glazed one. But her voice suddenly came out with indignation. "I couldn't see it!" she shouted. "I can't see anything. I can never see anything!"

She had never said that before, even to herself. The words broke against her spirit like the violent storms of the nightworld, blasting at her resilience.

Ashdel cleared her throat, about to say something, when one of the men held his hand in front of Mela's face. "Do you see my hand?"

"I see something moving."

He bobbed it back and forth, then suddenly thrust his open palm at her eyes. She barely moved. "The girl's nearly blind," he said. His voice was a curious mixture of amazement and awe.

"She is not!" Mela's father declared. "I've seen her face light up at the sight of a friend. I've seen her chase gophers in the sand. You can't do that if you're blind!"

"How long ago did she chase gophers?" the man asked.

Steln was silent. A woman had begun dabbing gently at Mela's face to clean it, making birdlike, gentle sounds.

"I know when it's day and when it's night," Mela said softly, defending her father. "I see movements. . . ."

"She was not born blind," her father explained, "but she has weak eyes. They've always been weak."

The man reached over and touched her forehead with his fingers. Careful to avoid the bruise, he gently traced her profile down her forehead, over her nose and lips, slowly to the slight cleft of her jaw. "Blind Princess!" he pronounced, as if the two words were part of a holy rite.

Everyone knew that Mela, though not in line to receive the queen's intaglio, was distantly related to the royal family.

"She's of Asel and Yosha," another woman said. Then she repeated, slowly, "Blind Princess," as if it were an omen that affected all the land of Asta. A woman at the entrance to the cave then also said, her voice filled with wonder, those two words: "Blind Princess."

People listening in the growing crowd whispered to each other about the wondrous prophecies that went with those two words. "All the nation will converge on our village," someone said.

The woman who had been comforting Mela and cleaning her face said quietly and kindly, but with firmness, "She is a princess, and she is blind."

"She is not blind," her father insisted again. He took her from the woman into his arms, mindless of the dull pain in his chest as he hugged her. He could hear the words "Blind Princess" around him and outside, spreading like startled birds scattering into the wind. Even little children were picking up the news and scampering off with it. He wanted to grab the words and pull them back into his little dwelling and alter them, or at least explain them. But they were loose out there, on every villager's lips.

—— The Festival ——

Mela sliced the cleaned fish into many pieces, then slid them into a huge pot. The old woman, Grelsa, had added several small logs to the fire beneath, and Mela felt its renewed heat as she leaned over it. Normally a twelve-year-old would feed and stoke the fire herself, but Mela could not, for she was now totally blind.

A young mother entered and handed Mela yet another small child; that made five under their care that night. As the mother left, Mela said, "She's late—she'll miss the beginning. I heard the signal."

The drumbeat announcing the start of the Askirit festival came at midnight. The villagers would already have gone far into the largest, deepest caves to experience total darkness as their ancestors had lived in years before. Many would enter the caves as early as sunset, striking flints as the first Askirit peoples had, producing sparks in the blackness, reveling until the midnight signal was given to emerge under the stars. They would then come out in high spirits and lie on their backs in the grass, reliving the exodus of their ancestors who, on a bright, starry night long ago, had emerged from the nightworld of Aliare to wonder at the tiny, bright lights above them. Their people had lived for millennia below the surface in a world of total darkness, a world of warfare and clashing religions.

"Hear them?" Mela asked. "They're making the 'sounds of wonder.'"

"Those aren't the only sounds they're making in the grass," Grelsa said dryly. "There's more than religious reasons people go deep into those caves soon as the sun is set. You notice none of these young women want their babies out there with them."

Mela didn't care about that. But she did resent being forced to cook and tend babies instead of joining the celebration. Two years before, when she'd been with them in the caves, everyone equally unable to see, it had filled her with a sense of belonging.

For once she was one with her people. It was the only time she felt on equal terms with them. But now she was shut out.

"I should be there!" she said bitterly.

"Why?" Grelsa asked. "You can't even see the torches and the sunrise, let alone the stars."

"I should be there," Mela insisted, slashing with her knife at a piece of meat. Into the pot went fish, sea herbs, snails—selected foods available to their ancestors deep in the caverns, each with a symbolic meaning. The sound of two babies fussing irritated her. "You've been to these all your life, Grelsa, so you don't care!"

"The sunrise is what always inspired me," the old woman said. "Never cared as much for that darkness stuff, but it does set you up for the sunrise!" Grelsa picked up one of the babies and made soothing sounds. "Imagine how Yosha and Asel, who'd never seen light all their lives, must have felt when they first saw that sunrise, the brilliance of it, the colors!" Grelsa told once again the traditional tale of their wonder at their first moments in the light of day.

"I'll never again see it," Mela said in a soft voice. "But I can go down in the caves and feel the damp. In the darkness I'm more alive than the others! I sense more. I feel their reactions as they walk out under the stars. The night sounds, the feel of dew on grasses, the heat of torches when they light them. I can sing the songs and listen to the tales."

The old woman sighed. It was true girls her age usually went to the celebration, the great national and religious event of the year. But it had not been her decision to trap the girl here with the stew and the babies. "Here, Mela," she said, "clean off your hands and hold this baby. I'll get the other one."

Mela silently complied. She rested the baby's head in her palm, its back on her forearm, moving easily with it. She stirred the pot; aromas of meats and herbs and roots filled the room and roused her appetite. She ladled herself a bowl and ate it quietly, patting the baby's head with her fingers.

"Up to the time I was your age," Grelsa said, "I always

participated in the celebration as an Enre. I was being trained in everything—everything." The old woman's badge of distinction was her selection and years as a novice to the Enre—the elite, deeply religious cadre of women trained from birth in their own unique warrior arts. "Asel, our queen—she was Enre. Still is!"

"Asel's not queen now."

"Queen mother—just as good. She's very, very old," Grelsa said, as if defending Asel's decision to step down. "She was queen, and she was Varial, leader of all the Enre in the Askirit kingdoms during the unthinkable wars below."

Grelsa spoke with enormous pride. Yet given the opportunity extended novices at age twelve, Grelsa had chosen to leave the Enre to work at ordinary tasks like shaping weapons and making boats and nets, to marry and have children. In spirit, Grelsa would always be Enre. Yet Mela wondered if she'd had the spiritual intensity, the physical skills and boldness required of that select corps of women.

"Asel and Yosha, king and queen of all Asta," Grelsa was saying in a familiar litany. "Your great-great grandparents. Makes you a princess indeed."

"There are hundreds of great-great grandchildren," Mela retorted, angry that a third baby had started fussing. Mela put down the one and moved toward the other. She had mentally mapped her surroundings, the pot and fire being the center, with everything in precise paces from it. She picked up the other child and easily moved back into position. Outside, youthful, exuberant voices were coming closer. She heard their footsteps nearing, and before she had quieted the baby, their loud chatter was entering and filling the cave.

The newcomers were girls Mela's age and older, giddy with their nightlong freedom. The custom was for young girls to prowl around as a pack rather than to dally with the boys, though this was often the subject of their conversations.

"Smell the food!" one girl exclaimed, throwing her hands joyously into the air and inhaling deeply the odors of the stew.

She reached for the ladle by the pot with one hand and a little bowl with the other. All night the celebrants were free to come in and help themselves to one dipper of stew.

Mela recognized many of the voices as the girls chattered giddily and dipped out the stew, slurping it into themselves. She listened for Ashdel's voice, but decided she was not among them.

She heard her name whispered, then a giggle. Several dropped their empty wooden bowls on a side table with a clatter as one said just loudly enough for Mela to hear, "She apologized to a goat!"

"What?"

"She must have thought it was a man," the girl explained in a low whisper. "She bumped into it on the trail—and, I swear, she said, 'Sorry, Sir, I didn't see you.'"

Another girl said, mocking, "Sorry, Mr. Goat!"

The new explosion of giggles were like ice particles striking the emerging sweat on Mela's forehead. She shouldered her way into the knot of girls and said in a loud voice, "I did not say that!"

For a moment the girls were startled into silence. Then one said, "Lion Blossom? Hah! If you're so brave, why do you always deny you're the Blind Princess? Scared to go into the night-world?"

Another said, "You talk to lions. You can talk to poison things in the pit." Then the girls made bizarre sounds of monsters.

Mela declared hotly, "I'm less afraid of the dark than you!" She thrust the baby into the arms of the girl making the loudest sounds, then turned away and stalked into the night air.

She tramped to a lip of stone jutting out above the sea and stepped to its edge, letting the breezes blow at her face and hair. Her hands were shaking; she pounded her right fist into her left palm, then dropped both arms to her sides. Behind her in the darkness, voices drifted from all directions, shouts from young people chasing one another, cries of wonder, and youthful mocks of traditional exclamations.

Then the drum sounded a second time, signaling the lighting of the fires. Mela turned her face toward them. Years before, when she could see, she would watch them ignite, scores of them appearing red and yellow, alive in the darkness.

People began shouting the traditional words, "Fire! Don't touch! Light brighter than stars!" She thought again of how fire must have appeared to these people coming up out of darkness. Mela's ears were hearing the same exclamations and shouts her ancestors had as fire penetrated their darkness. But unlike them, she saw nothing.

Slowly she returned to Grelsa in the cave. By the time she entered, the old woman had quieted the babies and was welcoming a group of older women, offering them ladles and bowls. Mela was surprised at how strongly the aromas now filled her nostrils; before, while stirring the pot, she had gotten used to them, but now they soothed her and whetted her appetite again. As the women were finishing, she filled her own bowl and sat in a corner, eating quietly.

"Every time I go down to one of those caves," a woman was saying, "my skin crawls and my throat gets thick as grease." She turned to a companion and said, "Why'd you have to drag me so far down anyway? Just barely inside is deep enough." She made a shivering sound, shaking her shoulders as if she felt terror, yet at the same time savored the danger. "When we got deep down there, I swear I heard gurglings and creepings beneath and felt hairy tentacles and lizard wings."

Her companion laughed. "We struck flints—a few sparks to keep us sane." This woman also shivered deliciously. "That's all Asel and Yosha had down there."

"But they knew how to defend themselves in the dark. What if one of those things somehow crawled up on us?"

A boy's voice asserted boldly, "Those caves are nothin'! Just little dead ends. You must have heard bats or something."

Several boys and men had just entered, and another boy said, "I've been to the caves at Korbas. They go down—all the way down—and there, *anything* could come up after you." He made sounds of being strangled and then chewed on by a horrifying predator.

The first boy said, "Yeah, but you didn't go down those caves, did you?"

"They don't let you."

"But I've heard things in Korbas come out after you and drag you all the way down to the pit. I'd never get near them."

Mela's father was among the men and boys entering. He greeted his daughter as the women left and he started ladling his stew. She returned his greetings in icy tones.

The men and boys ate hurriedly, anxious to return to the tales around the big fires and the anticipation of the pageants to come with the dawn. They soon left, but Mela's father remained, sitting beside her, fingers absently tapping the empty bowl in his hands.

"Wonderful Daybreak Stew," he said. Grelsa thanked him for the compliment, but Mela remained silent.

"Someone has to watch the babies," Steln finally said. "I'm sorry it was you this year."

"This year? Yes! And last year. Next year, too? Because I'm blind, does that mean I'm a total drudge?" She banged her bowl against the floor. "No matter how often you explain, I don't know why I'm here with the stew pot! Other girls are off in the caves celebrating."

Grelsa said, "You might as well tell her."

He stood slowly and put his bowl on top of the stack of dirty ones. Then he carried them all to the bucket of water and slowly lowered them and began washing. It wasn't his job, and Mela knew he was trying to say something to her by doing a little of her work.

"It's not everybody, Mela," he said apologetically, "but some people don't like you in the caves during the Daybreak festivities."

Mela walked over to him and dropped her own bowl into the water. "Why?" she demanded.

"Fear," he said, picking up her bowl to wash. "And guilt."

Grelsa was humming to an awakened three-year-old on her lap, but she stopped to say, "You must understand how your blindness affects people—especially our people. You remind them we're supposed to take the light down to Aliare, to carry truth to the darkness. That's wonderful to chant about—but not to be close to actually doing it."

Mela recited the fateful line: "A Blind Princess will lead her people to the light." She jerked her head back. "Just one line in all the rituals—that's it, just one line! Who knows what it means? Who says it's me? I'm not going anywhere down. My world's dark enough and nasty enough."

Then Mela added, "I don't care if I wreck their biggest night of the year."

Her father hunched down his shoulders, as if he were very cold. "I don't want them angry with you."

"But doesn't anyone stick up for me?"

"Your father speaks up for you," Grelsa said. "He always does. But he is a wise man who does not want you hurt."

"Hurt? Not hurt?" She heard the sound of her last word echoing back at her from the depths of the cave. She could smell a snail on the wall next to her face, and she flicked it into the air with her finger. "Remember, Father, when you led me from tree to tree, and you said, 'Feel the bark, the leaf, the branch. Smell it. An oak.' You asked if I remembered seeing the height of a poplar? This smell, this bark, the shape of this leaf? And you did that with each tree for me. 'Oak, beech, and pine,' you said. Green. Remember green? Brown bark but green needles. Every season you had me smell and touch flowers so I could remember. 'You can tell a laurel from a rhododendron,' you said, and you told me how to feel the difference. And all this time you were saying, 'You can live fully, Mela. You can make up for your eyes. You can feel and smell and play instruments and sing and listen to what we'll miss. You have a life ahead, Mela.'—But here I sit with the stew pot!"

With her bare foot, she had found the snail on the floor and picked it up between her toes. She tapped it against the stone. "Does Ashdel stick up for me?"

Her father took a long time to answer. "They sometimes tease her because of you," he said. "Lion Blossom. Blind Princess. She's always hearing talk and teasing—but she never joins in the laughter."

"But does she stick up for me?"

Her father finished washing the last bowl, put it down, then pulled his daughter to him. "She probably wishes she could. But let's not worry about what people say. You and I, the two of us— we'll go to the fires right now. We'll tell some tales. We'll even go down to the caves, if you want. The sunrise is almost here, and the pageants will be starting with explosions and songs."

—— Daybreak ——

Something skittered across Mela's wrist; she jerked her hand away and shook it hard, envisioning many legs under a rippling body.

"Spider?" her father asked.

She answered with a grunt.

He placed his hand on her shoulder and patted her hair. "Something from one of your nightmares?"

They sat in the depths of their village's deepest cave. She hunkered lower, silent, rocking a little to the rhythm of his fingers on her hair. For this year's Daybreak, he had brought her to the caves, but they huddled in the black depths like outcasts. Other men and boys were in big groups, swapping tales and laughing loudly; other girls Mela's age were together noisily shuddering and giggling as everyone began the evening watch in total darkness.

Steln knew his daughter wasn't welcome with Ashdel and the other girls, and he was determined she not be left with the stew pot again. Ever since that night a year ago, she'd steadily become more withdrawn, morose, resentful.

"Remember when you wore blossoms in your hair?" he asked. "You would pull them out to sniff them and stare at them." Not too long ago, he could draw her out with such reminiscences of the days when he took such delight in her and she'd responded with a beloved child's vivacity. But she no longer reminisced with him about that world they had once shared.

"Mela, I thought you wanted to come down here. You said that in the darkness you were in your element—more than anyone else, you could identify with Asel and Yosha before they first saw the light."

She scuffed her feet against the damp cave floor and blew air through her teeth. "Celebration? Daybreak? It's not meant for me."

She took two thick pieces of flint and struck them hard, creating a few sparks. "The sparks and the flint are dark for me, and the stars will be dark when we emerge from the caves. When the shouts to greet the rising dawn start, its rays will be dark for me. The people who see it all and laugh and sing don't know anything—not anything—about living every day of your life in darkness! Let them really live what Asel and Yosha did, the darkness I live every day."

"None of us can know," he admitted. His arm was around her shoulders, and they sat huddled together as merrymakers stumbled around them, quoting the old tales, singing ancient songs that had been created in the subterranean worlds beneath them.

It was nearly time for the signal to emerge under the stars when they heard a voice calling, "Steln! Mela!" It was a man's voice, but unfamiliar.

"Here! Deeper down," Steln called back.

Soon they distinguished among the many movements around them a man's footsteps approaching, with lighter footsteps behind.

"Glad Dawnbreaking," the man said formally as they rose to greet him. Mela was surprised to hear the old greeting. They soon learned he preferred all the old terms. "I wanted to find you before the signal," he said, "to share the dark with you for a few moments." He spoke with such enthusiasm Mela pursed her lips and began edging away. She thought she might as well just go to the stew pot, eat a bowlful, then sleep.

"I am Leas," the man was saying. He then introduced a boy and a girl about Mela's age. She returned the children's greetings but said nothing further. The sounds of celebration, instead of making her feel on common ground with others, deepened her feelings of isolation. She resented this stranger's patriotic and religious fervor, and now these children's happy little voices. She moved away from them, sidling along the wall of the cave, her blindness making her relatively surefooted and quick in the darkness.

But not, she realized, quite quick enough. She heard other young feet directly behind her. She stopped; they stopped with her, and she heard only their breathing. "Why are you following me?"

"You're Mela," the boy said. "Leas heard about you all the way in Kelerai. We came to see you."

Kelerai, Mela knew, was where vast geysers erupted from below in the daily cycles of the planet. If they lived there, they had come a long way. What did they want with her?

She made a popping sound with her tongue. "I'm nothing to see. I'm the one they stick by the stew pot and try to keep out from under everybody's feet. Didn't they tell you I'm blind?"

She felt fingers touching her cheek, then heard the girl's voice. "We know," she said. "We're blind, too."

The girl's fingertips lightly explored Mela's face, tracing the contours of her forehead and cheeks, her eyes, the line of her jaw and back up to her hair. "You're beautiful," she said. "You truly are a Blind Princess."

The lingering scent and feel of her fingers had been like unexpected spray on Mela's face.

"May I?" the boy asked. Mela did not answer, but he, too, lightly explored her face with his fingers, saying, "In Aliare, this is how all our ancestors saw each other. It's the way we too can know our faces." When he finished he said, "It's true. Your face, Mela, is beautiful." He had touched her lashes when he was planing over her cheeks with his palm. "Your eyes are wet. Why are you crying?"

Mela cleared her throat. "No one calls me beautiful," she said. "Everyone says I've made my face into an ugly frown."

"Mela!" Her father's voice was calling, and Leas began calling the others, who responded cheerfully and started moving back toward the men. Mela followed, unable to stop the flow of tears as she thought about these children her age who were blind, who actually shared her world as none of her other companions could.

Leas was striking flint, spraying off showers of sparks in the darkness. "It's in the wrist," he explained when Steln complimented him on the rhythmic, wide sprays of light falling at their feet. "This is all they had in Aliare to sing to and dance to." He want on describing how he was studying many of the old arts from below, trying to master them and pass them on to others before they became lost forever. "And who better to master the crafts and all the old ways than children who are blind?" he asked. He explained that he had started a school near Kelerai, that vast split in their world where the waters blasted up from below in the most spectacular wonder on the planet. "There, where the waters from below shoot toward the skies, we listen, and touch, and sing, and learn of our remarkable ancestors who built a culture in darkness. They speared and hooked prey and cooked and stitched and created magnificent liturgies and sagas without ever seeing one shaft of light."

Mela was amazed at the way these blind children and Leas's enthusiasm were affecting her spirits. He was saying nothing about Aliare she did not already know, but his passion for it penetrated the dull dread that had been building in her this past year.

The great drum in the village reverberated through the cavern walls. They started moving up toward the entrances and soon found themselves lined up behind others to receive the priest's blessing before stepping out under the stars.

"My goal," Leas was telling Steln, "is to help these blind children delight in what the Askirit had in their nightworld— what they too can have: the touch of a loving face, the aromas and the taste of many foods, the scents from the old masters, the thrill of combat skills, the songs and stories and rituals. These blind children, of all people, can imagine it. And they can reproduce so much of it. They can help our culture bring back the ancient skills before they're lost forever."

It was Mela's turn before the priest at the cave's entrance. He touched a trace of yellow pollen on her closed eyes and said, "Open your eyes to the wonders of light."

"We have escaped the darkness," she responded in the traditional words.

They emerged under the night sky. The two men and three children walked to the near meadow and, with scores of others, rolled onto their backs to look upward. As Mela listened to the expected exclamations of wonder and the buzz of voices and laughter, she wondered at the irony of her lying on her back, imitating her ancestors getting their first glimpse of stars, but seeing nothing.

The drum sounded again, and all around her she heard the lighting of fires and torches, with the traditional exclamations.

"Fire!
Light for your eyes!

Warmth for your hands!
Watch out! It burns!"

Leas kept talking about the wonders of the subterranean civilization that had birthed their little nation, explaining his methods of teaching the blind to use their techniques. Mela listened until she heard the murmurs around her that the sky was becoming alive with the sunrise. Soon came traditional exclamations of wonder.

But Leas said, "Here in Asta we think we have everything. But we don't have the little birds of hope announcing the dawn as our ancestors did. We don't have the challenges of leviathan and keitr. The wars below were terrible, but they were glorious too for those who sought the light." He was holding a lighted torch and handed it to Steln. "Wouldn't you like Mela to go with me to Kelerai? To learn? And to hope?"

Steln said, "You must ask Mela."

Leas turned to the girl, who was seated in the grass, and said, "Mela, would you go with us? Your father would visit you, and you'd be with many other children like yourself."

She didn't answer his question but instead asked her own: "Why did you call me the Blind Princess?"

"Because that's what's on everyone's lips. But what it all means is known only to the Maker."

Chapter 2.

—— Night Things ——

The eyes of Geln's five-year-old sister, Delas, were wide and darting from face to face as she said, "Then the night thing dragged the girl down tunnels, down and down to piles of gnawed-up bones." She lifted a piece of boiled fish and held it under her chin, then raised it delicately with the tips of her fingers and savagely bit into it. "The night thing ate her up!"

Their mother grimaced while chewing grel roots and fish. "Who told you that, Delas?"

"It happened last night," the little girl said indignantly. "She went out in the dark to get wood."

"How would you know?" Geln demanded. He was four years older than his sister, and his voice was full of condescension. "Did you follow them? Did your friends? People who snoop around night things get their own bones crunched." He held up a fish bone and cracked it in half.

"Stop snapping at her," said Bek, Geln's older brother. "You don't know anything more about the rifts than she does."

Geln glared at Bek, the distinct burn scars on his cheek growing red. More than most, Geln's thoughts were constantly on the rifts. Just thinking about them would race his pulse.

The earthquakes on the unstable planet had created great gashes, then had ground them shut again. Except here, near Geln's little village of Korbas. Here, great rifts still gaped open in the sandy hills—frighteningly open to the nightworld beneath.

Generations before, quakes had sealed off the cracks through which their ancestors had emerged. The rifts of Korbas were a startling phenomenon. From the many cities and villages of Asta, thousands came to peer into the rifts and, with daylight close on their backs, venture a short way down with torches.

Lately, visitors had been telling of persons who'd disappeared during the night—always during the night—and these reports were fueling many explanatory tales.

Delas was repeating one she'd heard that day: "A huge, hairy thing lurched out of the night. It caught a woman who had come from the city to see the rifts. It dragged her off screaming, and they say she saw the rifts real good that night. Some say she'll be a beast-wife down there and will turn into a thing herself."

Their mother, an Askirit widow and a very religious woman, said wearily, "Delas, all we hear are stories of things crawling out of those awful rifts. They divert us from the real battles ..." She began vigorously pointing to her own bosom as she pronounced, "... inside you! That's where the night things whisper. That's where you have to seek the light."

Geln slipped away from the table, hoping to avoid the evening cleanup. He sidled along the rock-and-dirt wall but was barely outside when some of his mother's hens started clucking at him. A resplendent, green-white-scarlet cock cast a baleful look at him and began escorting the hens away.

"Stupid rooster. Stupid hens," he muttered. "Stupid clucking at me all the time."

Geln scrambled down a hill and headed for the hut of a man he loved listening to. Among the Askirit were those whose ancestors had belonged to the far tribes. They followed the Askirit religion but happily called themselves barbarians nonetheless, forming little enclaves of huts.

Tesken was a man who lived alone, who hunted and did odd jobs and never seemed to care for anything but reviving the old superstitions and stories. But for Geln, it was more than just the stories. Tesken liked Geln's company; no one else seemed to and, for that matter, few liked Tesken's company, either.

At his knock, the old leather flap was flipped open and Geln darted in. Tesken was short and wiry, with a white stubble of beard. They sat down on old sacking, chewed on spicy roots, and Tesken commenced talking. A big flat toothpick bobbed on his lower lip as he grunted and gasped through stories of nightworld horrors.

He described nightstalkers who could sniff out warriors and grasp them in their talons, cracking leg bones in their jaws. "But they were only beasts," he said. His voice suddenly hushed, as if no longer conjuring old stories but confiding truths about terrors just outside the hut. "Worry more about those that are beasts possessed. Like sand shriikes."

He paused for effect. "They're slow and clumsy," he said. "But possessed." He pulled at the sacking tangled under his haunch, straightening it. "And they're here. They've risen from the abyss."

Geln was also adjusting the sacking under him, his hand jerking at it. "How do you know they've risen?"

Tesken chewed slowly, ignoring the question, staring at his visitor. "They've put eggs from the abyss into the sands of Korbas."

Geln wrinkled his face in disgust. Their ancestors, finding their way out of the night, had encountered sand shriikes deep in the abyss.

Tesken said, "They hatch small as worms. They wriggle through the sand in packs, devouring anything, feeling and hearing every vibration in the sand. They feed and grow, then split their skins and become a pack of larger shriikes. They keep growing, keep splitting, always ravenous, always sucking prey into the sand, wriggling over them with a toxic slime. They grow and split until . . . ," and here Tesken bit down hard on his toothpick and pulled his lips back over his teeth, "they change!"

He contorted his entire face. "No one has seen what they become, but it's said they're as possessed as the wings that brought them here."

Toads

Nearly a year later Geln bolted off after supper full of determination and plans. He moved quickly over the dry, sandy ground, entering a small opening in the hill. Like Geln's family's dwelling, the storage area had been dug out by hand. He found in the semi-darkness a coil of rope and yanked it up from the clutter. "I'm not afraid of the night," he muttered. "I like the night." He hefted the coils over his shoulder.

"Why are you taking the rope?" Bek demanded, towering over him.

Startled, Geln jerked his head up and glared at his brother.

"Look . . . ," Bek said, hesitantly this time, as if inviting him into fraternal secrets. "You don't need to prove anything—"

"Who said I was trying to prove something?"

"Why else do you keep going out at night? Why tell people those crazy stories?" Bek stood ramrod straight, like their military father always had. Geln sensed he was being commanded to shape up, to stand erect, to join his brother in practicing with blades and spears, to shed these dangerous compulsions. Bek's words were an invitation to camaraderie: "Just forget the night; join us during the day."

"How can I—with this?" Geln retorted, his hand rising to the scars on his cheek. They looked like a fat, three-fingered hand clutching toward his eye. His face was flushed, and the thin, burned skin once again revealed the redness beneath.

"People will forget it if you do," Bek said. "It's time to grow up."

Yet Geln knew he couldn't possibly forget it, nor, in a strange way, did he want to. It was part of him, part of who he was.

Bek raised his chin like a commanding officer and said, "You can't always be Mommy's little burnt baby."

This was not the first time Geln had heard these infuriating words. He still remembered the day they had first come from his brother's mouth, hot as the coals that had burned his face. At the sound of them, humiliation seared his throat and he couldn't speak. Instead, he darted away from his brother and into the darkness.

Geln had been just barely five years old when he'd gotten burned. He had responded to a late-night call of nature and had noticed firelight in the distance. Curious, he'd stalked it. He had seen no one near, so he'd gone closer and closer till he felt the fire warm on his face.

A voice had boomed out, "Hey, boy!"

Little Geln panicked, turning quickly. Seeing a dark shape before him, he wheeled around, slipped, and fell into the hot coals at the fire's edge.

He screamed and ran in terror. Behind him, he heard footsteps heavily pounding after him, which sped him forward more quickly. He ran, it seemed, though the entire night, the terrible pain in his face, until he fell exhausted on the sand.

They had not found him until midday. He told them about the fire and the voice, but no one knew of a man with a campfire that night. Most ignored his story, for Geln had been found at the very edge of the rifts. Tales of evil spirits and night creatures spilled into their conjectures. The stories spread, stories of why the creatures from below had burned him at the edge of the nightworld. Worst of all, people said they had already claimed his soul.

After the incident, night after night after night Geln would awaken from the agonizing burns, whimpering on and on until his mother came. She would take him into her arms and soothe him, rocking him gently and saying, "My baby, my poor burnt baby. It was only a campfire. Don't fear, I love you. Don't fear, sleep, my poor, poor, burnt baby."

Bek, who slept nearby, at first tried to be patient but grew very tired of it. One night when Geln started whimpering again, Bek exploded in a sarcastic mock of their mother's soothing voice. "Poor burnt baby!" he said, accenting the last word. "Poor, poor burnt baby." He'd stood up above Geln, said yet again with dripping sarcasm, "Poor burnt baby," then hissed loudly, "shut up!"

Geln had never whimpered again. He'd rammed the terrors deep down, the humiliation cauterizing his voice. The face of his dead, heroic father loomed over him, saying as he once had while instructing his little boys, "Ignore the pain. Soldiers march through it!"

Now ten, Geln purposely faced the night terrors, determined to confront them. He gripped the rope coiled securely over his shoulder, ready to accost the mysteries and stalk the night.

Two boys his age were waiting for him in a culvert. One of them, Kel, stood up, holding three unlighted torches. Geln sensed his nervousness as Kel, his voice high and cracking, said, "Let's go. It's dark enough. Nobody will see us if we crawl along the gully."

"Not yet," Geln said, jaws clenched tight as he sat down beside the other boy. He kicked at a dirt-encrusted boulder and watched the dust rise in the squint-gray air. "It has to be darker. They're still watching."

Once, thousands of visitors had come to Korbas to gaze at

the rifts with a mixture of terror and fascination. But no longer. The rifts had been declared off limits, and a military detachment patrolled the area, watching the sands for anyone foolish enough to climb over the heaped-up barriers. But no guards patrolled at night; a torch heading toward the rifts would be seen from far off, and who, it was asked, would go there in darkness?

"But we'll go without torches," Geln had said when he was persuading the two boys. "We'll get to the rifts unseen, then strike fire when we're in them."

Kel and the other boy, Parn, had listened to Geln's schemes and thought them wonderful adventures to talk about. They even thought up many ways to fool adults as they hid torches and told stories of what they might find in the rifts. But when it became clear Geln was serious, they'd quickly backed away. "Who knows what comes out at night? And you know the wild dogs out there on the sands—they're huge!"

Geln had shamed them as cowards, cajoled, nagged at them day after day. He told them how everyone in the village would view them if they had descended into the rifts at night. "We wouldn't let anybody know except when we'd tell them. And we'd bring back proof."

"What proof?"

"How should I know? Whatever's down there. If it's nothing, we'll know it's nothing! We'll know! Think of it. We'll have entered the unthinkable. Only the three of us."

Korbas was hot, dusty, remote—a month's journey from Mela's village, a week's desert crossing from Asta's capital city, Aris. Dwellings and workshops had been dug out of the sides of the desolate hills. One small river flowed through the village, sustaining some shriveled grass, dry bushes, toads, lizards, insects, and exactly eighteen trees. People in Korbas knew each tree, and Geln now led his companions out of the culvert, feeling their ways on all fours along the river toward the largest tree, a willow, which was closest to the rifts.

"Wait till we can see the stars," Geln said.

Someone in the distance was calling a child. "Let's go now," Kel said, hugging his unlighted torch near his chest. "It's dark enough."

They started creeping toward the hills, peering at the dim horizon. After topping the first rise, they rose to their feet and hunched forward, walking as fast as they could without stumbling. Winds blew; they squinted against the dust. A toad hopped in front of them; a bird cried as it flew past.

Parn tripped and cried out as he sprawled forward, skinning his palms on the sand. He cursed in a hushed, fearful voice. "Can't see a thing!" he said. "This is stupid."

Geln sat down beside him. "We're already past the barriers. Look how far we've come." With both hands he turned his companion's shoulders toward the fires of the village, which looked like little red beads on a distant shoreline. Turning to Kel, he said, "We've already walked into The Forbidden."

The wind stopped blowing. Another toad hopped in front of them, then another. One landed on Parn's foot. "It's making me wet!" he yelled, shaking it off.

Geln rushed over to him. "Not so loud."

Parn was shivering. "It got my foot all wet."

"Baby!" Geln mocked.

"Why'd it hop on my foot like that?"

"Forget the toads. Let's get into the rift and light these torches." Geln hunched forward, low against the horizon.

They moved over a rise, then another; more toads were hopping crazily in the loose sand. "Don't step on the things," Geln said. "They must be out here mating or something."

As they neared the rifts, Kel suddenly kicked at the air. "One got up my pantleg!" he exclaimed. He snapped his foot back and forth, then bent over and whacked his calf hard with his palm again and again until something slid down past his ankle into the sand.

"Good work," Geln said with a laugh. "A soft, squishy toad now squished. Yuk!" He bent down and looked at it; one leg was still jerking a little. But he also saw other movements; sand was swirling around the toad. Geln squinted and hunched closer. The sand was moving like water streaming around a rock, and the little body was sinking.

"Let's get moving," Geln said.

"I'm lighting the torch!" Parn declared, raising it in his left hand. With a quick move, he grabbed from Geln's pouch the tiny enclosed flame of slow-burning pitch and wax.

"No!" Geln grabbed at Parn's torch. "People will see you."

"I don't care." Parn jerked away and knelt to light it.

"At least do it down in this gully!" Geln said, grabbing his arm and pulling him forward. Kel came shivering behind them. They huddled together, and at the first flicker of light they saw all around them the eyes of toads.

Parn's voice sounded as if he was swallowing sand. "Why are they coming at us?"

"Stupid toads," Geln replied, but he thought, *They're not coming at us, they're being hunted. They're trying to get up on us to escape.* Geln spat, then said, "Hold your torch down at them."

Parn lowered the torch and held it at arm's length. The closest ones hopped away, and Geln could see swirls in the sand among the toads.

"Let's get out of here," Kel said.

"We're almost to the rift!" Geln objected. "Let's just go to the edge and look down."

"Are you crazy?" Parn lighted another torch and it flared brightly, showing the erratic movements of toads all around them. "Something's spooking them!"

"Probably those big dogs," Geln said. "Toads must be great dog food. But they won't bother us—not with these torches."

All three torches were lighted now, and Geln could see some

of the toads kicking and hopping frantically to get out of sand holes opening beneath them.

"It's not dogs spooking them," Parn said. "Can't you see the sand swirling? Can't you see those little wrigglings up over the toads' backs? Like white bellies of tiny snakes whipping around." He and Kel held their torches out low before them and, like the two sides of a crab, began sidling crazily toward the village, stamping with their feet and poking with their torches.

Geln followed, his mouth dry with fear, yet strangely exhilarated.

Halfway back, Geln heard the yelp of a dog. It was running toward them, and Geln felt for the handle of his blade. But before the dog could reach them, it became stuck in the sand which was swirling around it and sinking under him. It yelped repeatedly as it dug in a frenzy with its forepaws and kept trying to leap out with its hind legs.

"There's something big after it!" Parn said, holding his torch aloft. "Look at the way the sand is roiling, like an octopus underwater, coiling and thrashing."

"What's rippling up its coat?" Kel asked. "And what's that sour smell?" He lowered his torch to the sand around his feet. "I'm not standing here watching." He hustled away toward the village, Parn scuttling off with him.

But Geln did stand and watch. He saw white things thick as his wrist wriggling over the dog as it sank lower and lower. Finally the sands engulfed it.

"From the pit," he whispered. "The eggs have hatched."

The undulating waves of sand started to move toward the fleeing boys. Yet nothing was moving around Geln.

He thought Tesken had exaggerated about the sand shriikes, yet now a great churning was about to overtake Parn and Kel. But strangest of all, a voice within was saying to Geln, "You can stop them." Urgently it hissed, "Their lives are yours. You decide their fate. Let the boys be devoured, or let them escape. Choose!"

What were these alien thoughts? He saw in his mind sand sucking down Parn and Kel, white things wriggling on them. Or he saw himself saving them through complicity with the powers. What delicious power was being offered—to command the hideously roiling sands.

He was the chosen one, he who already was marked by the night.

For an instant he toyed with the idea of watching their devouring. The boys were running in a panic now, fully aware of the movements behind them. But before they were overtaken, he willed the sand to be still.

As quickly as he willed it, the turbulence ceased.

The boys shot ahead, their feet spitting up little spurts of sand. Geln watched them disappear and squinted at the few remaining fires in Korbas.

Now that they were gone, what about him? He felt power within, yet he was alone out here on the sands. What would his complicity cost him?

His burned and disfigured face made him feel at one with something out here. It made him feel enormously important, as if great things in the universe were at stake. He remembered that Asel and Yosha were said to have survived the shriikes and the abyss only through spiritual power, and he thought, *Yes, there are all sorts of alien powers out here.*

Dark powers whispered to him of remarkable deeds and the glories of dominions. Geln doused his torch, tossed it into the sands, and turned toward the rifts.

—— Morning Child ——

Geln looked down at the boys clustered in front of the ornate door to the village's holy place, a cavern dug deep into the side of the hill. It was high noon. Geln was late, but if he hurried, he could join them before the priest ordered them to enter.

He rushed limping down the hill, muscles aching. His mother had not detected his late return, but his brother had heard his shaking hand knock over his water cup. "This late?" Bek had hissed. "Out in the night with a rope?"

Now, as he saw Bek among the boys, he avoided his brother's eyes. Geln dreaded speaking to anyone, for all the power of the night had bled out of him; he had slept late and had hidden himself all morning.

He saw Parn and Kel staring at him. As their eyes met, they looked away. Then, their eyes darted back, furtively scanning Geln's face. They looked frightened, as they had when they'd fled in the night.

They're afraid of me, Geln thought. As he watched their timorous movements, his anxiety disappeared. Why, he asked himself, was he afraid to face anyone? He had gone to the dreaded rifts at night—he and he alone.

He studied the faces of Parn and Kel, feeding on their meekness and awe. Theirs were the looks Geln had braved the sands and the rifts to see. He pushed through the other boys and planted himself in front of them.

The two boys were wilted weeds. "Sand shriikes," Geln said. "They nearly got you."

Parn's face was like dried mud in the marsh. "Were they?" he said. "Then now we know."

"I walked to the rifts."

Kel grimaced, staring at his feet. "The rifts are death."

Geln cocked his face at a jaunty angle under the hot noon

rays. "Yes," he agreed cheerfully. "And, believe me or not, I saved you from the shriikes."

The boys had begun moving into the cool darkness, and as the three followed he did not say anything more about how he'd held their lives in his hand or what he'd felt in the night or that he'd looked for long moments into the darkness of the rifts and thought he had heard wings far below. He simply walked behind them as, without torches, they felt their ways down one level, then another, until far below, they bunched up against wooden walls.

He was fingering the graceful carvings of birds flocking toward the ornate door when the priest summoned them. They entered a lightless room, as their ancestors beneath the surface had done for centuries, ready to participate once more in the ancient liturgy.

The priest led them in their recitation: "In the beginning, the world was bathed in light. But the Maker, Eshtel, brought judgment. A sphere struck the planet, breaking apart continents, shattering civilizations. The world became void; a thick dust covered all.

"But Eshtel moved again, creating a new world. Waters rushed into deep fissures, gouging out canyons and peaks, shaping a new land in the dark hollows beneath the surface."

Geln's lips but not his heart were repeating the holy words. "Eshtel saw that many fell into the darkness below. On them he had pity. To those filled with longing and hope, he said, 'Out of the wreckage comes life. Seek the way to the light.'"

The priest then dramatically lighted a large torch, which illumined the room. "We have climbed out of darkness," he declared.

The boys responded in hearty unison: "Declare the ancient promises. Seek mercy and purity. Auret has fulfilled the prophecies."

"The cripple is made whole," said the priest.

"Those in darkness now see," the boys said, each lighting his torch.

In unison, priest and boys said, "Praise the Maker."

The boys lined up before the inner sanctuary. The priest jerked away heavy leather curtains and strode forward, the boys following to enter this holiest place in the village.

"What evil have you done?" the priest demanded.

The boys responded in one voice, "We have sought darkness."

"You must pay with blood!"

Geln wrinkled his nose at the smell of dried blood from other ceremonies rising from the damp dirt floor. He listened to the priest moving from boy to boy till he stopped in front of him, reached out to find his wrist, and gripped it tightly.

The priest held a small animal in his hand; he pressed Geln's hand against its face. Geln felt the wet nose on his palm. As he had done so often before, Geln ran his fingertips over the bony edges around its eyes, then touched the moving lashes and made a circular motion on the closed lids.

"Where is the light?" the priest asked.

"We live in it," Geln said. "But we do not see it. We have risen from darkness into light, but we shut our eyes to holiness."

The priest moved past him to the other boys, repeating the ritual, then killed the little animal with a knife. He cast a handful of blood at the boys. Droplets struck Geln's forehead as the priest said, "The guiltless animal dies, so that you—in purity and power—can face the terrors."

The priest moved from one boy to another, giving each a challenge. When he thrust his face against Geln's, he said, "When you're broken and ravaged, seek the light. Break the teeth of your enemies."

Though no response was called for, Geln declared in a strong, resonant voice, "And all their bones also!"

He heard a sharp intake of breath from the priest and many of the boys. Geln savored his dismay and the shock of the boys that he would violate a holy ritual.

Finally, after a long silence, the priest pronounced the

traditional instruction: "Eshtel's light nourishes your eyes. In his purity, never flinch—not from the jaws of leviathan himself."

The priest repeated the ritual with each boy, then cut up the carcass. When Geln felt the piece of raw meat being pushed between his teeth, he smiled and bit down, and when the priest declared them absolved of their impurities, he did not chew it to welcome new energies. He felt very different energies coursing through him and he quietly spat the flesh into the dirt.

The rooster stood as if waiting to confront Geln. He shook his orange-red cockscomb imperiously as the hens wandered behind him, pecking and scratching. The lordly fowl seemed particularly belligerent, threatening to accost Geln's legs as he walked toward the entrance of their home.

He heard his mother's voice within, then his brother's. He couldn't avoid them as he entered; she looked up and stared hard at Geln. "Have you heard?"

He stared back at her. "About what?"

"Gwellian and her baby." His mother's weathered, lined face was puckered about the lips and eyes. "The baby lived only moments, and Gwellian won't live out the day."

The young neighbor woman had just the day before stood among the chickens in their yard, arc-backed to support the weight of the child within. Geln had thought her inflated belly must have been a terrible burden, but the mother-to-be had talked and laughed as if it were a huge puppy snuggled up to her.

"We were waiting for you," his mother accused. "We're going over there to comfort the woman as she enters the light." She was fussing with Delas's hair, twisting a flower into it, as she always did when they went somewhere important. Geln wondered whether the dying Gwellian would possibly care about how his sister looked.

"I'll stay here," Geln announced. "Things I have to do."

His mother studied his face. "You scared of being around death? Or just don't want to go?"

He thought of telling her that the boy who climbed down into the rifts was not afraid of anything. But he simply said, "You won't need me."

"Yes, we will," she insisted. "All of us need to bring comfort to their family. You need to see her one last time."

"You and Delas and Bek go."

"Did you hear how he behaved today in the sanctuary?" Bek asked. "He interrupted the ritual with his own smart-aleck comment."

His mother whirled to face Geln. "What did you say?"

"I was only agreeing with him," Geln said evenly. "He told me I should break the teeth of my enemies, and I said, 'And all their bones too.'"

"You should have heard the tone of his voice," said Bek, "and how it echoed everywhere."

"No one adds to the ritual!" his mother shouted. "It's holy!" She grabbed his shoulders and dug her fingers into them like talons into prey. "What's the matter with you?"

She shook him, then flung him toward the entrance. "You're coming with us," she said, her mouth tight and her jaw shaking. "You'll respect the dying."

They had not far to walk. The young woman had asked to be carried near the river. Geln saw people gathered beneath Korbas's only willow tree, a great, green shock of hair by the river in the dun terrain. Many of the crowd were in the shade of the tree, but Gwellian, though the day was hot, was in the bright light. Her husband's hand shielded her eyes from the hot beams of early afternoon.

Her face has sunk, Geln thought, as he and his family stepped in among the little crowd. He remembered Gwellian's full face alight with stories and her fingers plaiting flowers into her hair. Now she seemed corpse-like, hair flat and disheveled and sweat-dried, as if a thousand days of dying had passed since he'd seen her yesterday among the chickens. A thousand days instead of one night and one day of agony and loss.

But then her face brightened a little. Her husband was reciting the psalm for parents in grief. As he finished Gwellian said, her voice surprisingly strong, "Say it again."

He hesitated, waved a fly from her face, and swallowed. Then he started anew, reciting:

"We prayed for a child,
and our seed grew large,
and we rejoiced.
But now we mourn.
He was to brighten our days,
but he's gone to the light.
We mourn, but he dances!
He laughs in worlds of wonders.
Why these tears?
Our mourning child awakens today,
He's gone before us into the dawn.
He's our morning child!"

Gwellian said through thick lips, "Our child plays in the flowers. He rejoices in the Holy One."

Geln grimaced. *He's killed you,* he thought. *The baby has killed you and you prattle about his being in the flowers.*

"He died on my breast," Gwellian said. "And soon I'll embrace him. Will he be a babe? Or a grown son?" She smiled through her pain.

Geln ground his teeth. *You smile,* he thought, *but your baby and your own body will be cast into the sea. You will be two corpses, and your eyes will not see light, nor will you ever smell the flowers again.*

Gwellian said in a changed, troubled voice, "Who is that boy over there?"

Geln's mother stepped toward the dying woman, whose hand was pointing at her younger son. "It's Geln. You know him—my son. Just Geln."

Gwellian tried to lift her head slightly, staring at him, her expression totally changed. "Go closer," Geln's mother whispered harshly, pushing him forward. "Comfort the dying."

He took a few hesitant steps forward, frightened that so close to dying, her spirit might have somehow entered his thoughts. He felt the scar on his cheek inflamed and hated it. Gwellian stared into his eyes and said in a whisper, "Shadows 'round you. Flickers of fire in your hair."

Sunlight sparkled off the droplets of sweat on her forehead and under the damp hairline, creating a look of delirium. But her voice was firm, controlled, accusing as she declared, "Geln! Geln!" The fingers of both her hands were tightly gripping her husband's wrists. "By you, Geln," she said, "by you, our world will convulse."

—— Dark Energies ——

Dusk. Geln walked beside a brackish marsh formed by a trickle that bled from the river. Here one of the eighteen trees of Korbas had finally died. For years, half the thick pine's branches had stretched out brown and dead, and this spring, the last of the needles had dried up. Its top third had toppled into the watery weeds, and some had surmised it had been hit by lightning. But as Geln poked at the dry punk of the tree's base, he knew inner rot had toppled it.

He smacked a cluster of spore puffballs on the dead bark;

brown dust rose in a cloud, then was quickly dispersed by the wind. He struck some more, watching the dust rising toward the mountains. He was waiting for the shadows, so he could explore under cover of darkness.

"What are you doing?" It was a little girl's voice. His six-year-old sister stood near the dead branches of the tall stump, a stick like his in her hand. Her fist was cocked on her hip; her chin was raised, and her pursed lips demanded an answer.

Geln struck more puffballs, and their spores drifted like smoke toward her. "Just messin'," he said. "You'd better get home before dark."

Instantly she asked, "Are you getting home before dark?"

He didn't answer.

"What's the rope for?" she asked, poking her stick at the long coils he had tossed under the tree.

He turned from her and knelt by the water. As she came to kneel beside him, he tossed a stone at some polliwogs, which squiggled away into the weeds. "Water's drying up fast," he said. "These may never get legs."

Delas poked at the water as he had, a skinny girl with black hair and dark skin. Geln could never feel as angry at his younger sister as he did toward his mother and brother. He didn't like the constant questions, but he enjoyed her fascination at the talk she heard about him.

"What's down in the rifts?" she asked, swishing her stick against the rushes poking out of the water. "What have you seen?"

She'd asked that innumerable times. He stood abruptly and began walking around the oblong marsh of seasonal life and yeasty decay that stuck like a wide thumb into the arid terrain. She followed him around it, pestering him about taking her with him tonight, just for a little while.

She whipped her stick across the rushes. "They say being out here at night's like looking for a live snake hole to sit on." She laughed, trying to draw him out. "They say night things are hungry."

"That's what they say."

"So why are you out here so much?"

How could he explain that at night, alone with the winds and seeking to witness and avoid the unspeakable, he felt alive, he felt a rush of energies? He had told himself he could withstand people's glares and taunts in the day if he came out of the silences of the night.

"They say you love the night," she said. "Love it more than the day." Her lower lip stuck out, her eyes intent on his face.

"Our ancestors had nothing but the night. It's where I belong." With three fingers he covered the fingers of his scar, pressing tightly on the skin beneath his eye. "I'm marked. And since Gwellian, everyone says the shadow's on me."

"But don't you love the light?" she asked abruptly, anxiously. "Mother and Bek worry that you don't love the light."

Mother and Bek. He thought of the two of them as upper and lower teeth in a giant jaw, always working together against him, always trying to crush his soul. *But,* he thought, *their teeth keep striking stone.* He smiled, pleased with the image.

Delas saw his smile. She brightened, smiling back at him and said, "I always share my secrets with you."

Her face is so young, he thought, *her little secrets so easily violated.* "My secret is this. I've been in the rifts only once—just once—and they scared me spitless."

As soon as he'd said it, he worried she'd repeat it to someone. But it seemed to make little impression on her, and she was soon pleading again, "Take me with you tonight. Just a little ways." She was holding onto his sleeve, twisting it back and forth.

He turned on her and said roughly, "You don't know what could happen to you."

Her small face looked boldly up at his. "Whatever happens, we have Eshtel's light within."

They were standing by the dead tree again, and he noticed

attached to the base a fungus as large as his thigh. It stood out boldly, like an off-white clamshell. He kicked at it, expecting it to fall apart. Instead, the thing felt weighty and hard, hurting his foot. Angered, he kicked again, this time at a sharp angle to dislodge it. On the third blow it fell with a substantial splash into the marsh.

"It's almost dark," he said. "You'd better get going."

She stood there silent as the rushes. The longing in her eyes resonated in him, as if his own eyes were staring into his own inner depths.

He gripped her shoulders. "It's almost dark now," he said urgently, squeezing her shoulders as if to press the words into her. "You know you can't be out this late. You've got to start home."

"Come with me!" she insisted, pulling at his forearm. "Mama's making chowder, and I'll get some bowls and bring it outside. We'll eat together, just you and I, out in the dark. She wouldn't mind. You don't even have to go inside."

No one but Delas could make him feel obligated. Of course he should go back with her. Of course he should eat the chowder with her and share the evening adventure of eating with her in the night. But this innocent child did not belong in the wild dark.

"I'll take you to the willow tree." As soon as he said it, her face turned sober and tears formed. She turned her face toward the vague shapes of the mountains.

He knelt and hugged her, hating the tears forming in his own eyes. "I'll take you to the willow tree," he repeated, grasping her shoulder and leading her along the river's edge.

Geln wanted to be angry at Delas, but he couldn't as he watched her standing sullenly under the willow. She was inviting him to camaraderie no one else offered. But he had left her; he watched her break away from the tree and run toward home, a darting figure in the shadows.

The incident upset him. He stared long moments at the

brightening stars, thinking of holy phrases about the powers of light and of that vast expanse of little lights. "Yet," he whispered, "all I've ever felt from the stars are cold, bright specks of judgment."

It was the night he both hated and loved that warmed his blood and fired his passions. He wanted to return to the rifts, yet when he thought of the powers out there, he kept hesitating. On the night of the sand shriikes, might he have misunderstood everything?

As he ventured onto the sands, he realized he was far more fearful than the night he'd peered into the rifts. Yet he forced himself to keep moving, saying to himself, "Welcome the dark," even as he studied the sands, looking for movements. He kept imagining being swirled into a hole and sinking into the sand, smothering. He braced himself, listening to birds and the distant bark of a dog.

At the edge of the rifts, he squatted above them, listening. He whispered to himself again and again, "Welcome the dark."

Suddenly, full of reckless resolve, he anchored his rope and started lowering himself. He was thinking not only of the shriikes but other creatures Teslen described with relish, things that crawled and oozed and sucked up prey from the crevices of the nightworld. But as he descended, hand over hand, he heard and felt nothing except one little quivering thing that raced across his neck.

Just before his rope ran out, he found what seemed to be a trail, and he followed it till he came to something unexpected: wide shapes of ancient, polished stone. As he explored them with his hands, small pieces crumbled away.

A statue, he thought, *a man's back.* But it was so old it was almost worn away. Could it have been made by his ancestors' ancestors, long before judgment rent the world? Long before the only survivors were those buried in the great hollows below?

Slowly, his hands discovered the crumbling, chiseled backs of four men shoulder to shoulder, life-size, muscular, bending forward. Connected, around the other side and facing them, were four women completing the circle.

Like all Askirit boys, Geln had been taught to explore carvings and statues with his hands the way his ancestors had in the darkness. He'd been bored with the lessons taught, but now his hands eagerly sensed the shapes coming alive under his palms and fingers. He found a ridge of sharp teeth divided the men from the women on each side of the semicircle. Each was gripped firmly by both a male and a female hand.

Geln circled the eight men and women huddled toward each other, exploring their muscled, crumbling limbs. He wanted to touch their faces, but the sculpture was compact. He would have to climb into it. Grabbing two men's shoulders, he hoisted himself up, hoping the ancient structure would not fall apart under him. On hands and knees, balanced atop the stone heads and shoulders, he found that, indeed, there was an open space in the center.

Carefully he slipped down into the sculpture, holding a man's arm for balance. When his feet were steady, he followed the arm's contours until he felt the wrist and the taut, strained fingers arced fiercely downward.

As he followed the man's fingers to their tips, he was stunned to feel that they were plunged into a woman's eyes. Geln's own fingers jerked away. He hesitated, then gently explored the woman's face. It was contorted in agony.

He touched the other women's faces. Male fingers raked furrows into their stone flesh. Beefy hands grasped and twisted mouths and noses; knuckles chopped into teeth and jaws. Geln's fingers explored with terrible fascination the details of this hideous mutilation. Did the sculpture depict some tragic, historic event?

As he faced the violated women and wondered at the statue's meaning, a bizarre sensation penetrated him. The men behind him seemed to be radiating their rage through him and into the contorted faces of the women. His mind became filled with venom and words: "Women! Betrayers! You manipulate and destroy us."

Geln wanted his own fingers to ride the stone ones into those female faces. He felt fury at his mother, thinking, "How you smother me!" But the thought of his hands brutally assaulting his mother's face made him turn the other way.

As soon as he faced the men, rage toward them radiated through his body. He followed a woman's arm which thrust into a man's face, her nails ripping into a cheek and an eye. He traced another arm and found its hand clawing and twisting a mouth and jaw. The enmity coursed through him: "Men! Liars! Rapists! You use us and discard us." As he covered the avenging fingers thrust into male faces, he thought of Bek and men in Korbas who despised him. The women's rage lifted him like a spark from a fire.

Something was under his leg. He reached down to find a small, round object beside a woman's foot. It was the stone figure of a cowering child.

Geln's fingers traced its terrified posture. It was a little boy. His mouth was a grotesque O, ridges of skin like ripped earth circling his broken teeth. His throat was quivering in a scream.

Suddenly the feelings of rage became a chaos within, tearing at him, making him one moment want to strike the child and the next to lift him out of this cell of stone flesh. His hands, trembling as if they had been stung, were poised above the child's head. Jerking them up, he grabbed a woman's head in each hand and kicked up his feet, scrambling his way up through the opening in the center. Gaining the top, he slid down backs and then rolled a short distance. He lay breathing heavily, then shakily stood and began searching for the way up.

Geln did not return to the rifts for a long time. He hated the statues, yet their enlivening, terrible energies fascinated and lured him. He began returning to the rifts' edge, traversing the sands at night without fear, sensing the night had chosen him. He would peer down into the darkness, listening, wondering.

Finally, he again began to explore the depths, avoiding the statues. Night after night he would descend into the rifts, and night after night he would open himself further to dark mysteries.

He discovered a tunnel very far down. He followed it until it dead-ended in a pile of shattered boulders. Exploring the blockage with his hands, he brushed across something odd, something surging with energies.

Slowly, he reached out and touched its edge again. It was something carved poking out from the debris. He tried to free it, but it wouldn't budge. He yanked away some of the rocks around it, gave another strong pull, and it tore loose.

It was a bone carving, a simple little thing, yet radiating power into his hands. It depicted from the waist up a man and a woman leaning over a game. Geln traced with his fingers the man's elbows thrust out on the game slab. Then he touched the man's face and found part of it broken off. The woman's face, he found, was also gouged, the nose torn away.

When he discovered on the far side of the game slab the carving of a newborn baby, he took a quick breath of recognition. The three figures completed the description of the famous carving king Yosha had left below in Aliare.

As he ran his fingers over the carving, he sensed the powers that had disfigured the faces. The same dark feelings he'd felt from the statues coursed through him. The infant too was crushed on one side.

Geln was torn between wanting to drop it and wanting to dig his fingernails into the figures and revel in the forces permeating it.

He thought of Gwellian and her husband and her dead baby and their treacly joy against these radiating dark powers.

"Take the carving," something dark within him said. "With it, you stand alone. You have the power. You need never again fear man or woman."

Said an opposing voice, "Drop the carving and flee."

"Take it!" the first voice insisted. "Didn't Gwellian admit that by you the world would convulse?"

—— Aris ——

Though he would be gone a full season, Geln had said only curt goodbyes to his family and now strode, lockjawed, into the yard. He adjusted the carving he carried under his jacket. Increasingly these past three years, he drew from its power.

The dog slunk away, tail drooped. The hens, at seeing him, stopped their clucking and moved away. But the cock, shimmering in iridescent greens, belligerently stepped out from among the hens and strutted into his path, balefully gazing up at him.

Time and time again this creature had accosted him. Time and time again Geln had resisted his urges to retaliate. This time, coldly, Geln calculated the distance, backed up a half step, tensed, then shifted forward and kicked the rooster with the full force of his booted toe.

Feathers and rooster flew into the air as hens scattered loudly. The rooster landed heavily and lay on its side, its legs scratching sideways in the dust.

"Geln!" It was Delas's voice. She ran to the cock and knelt beside it.

His mother stormed outside and accosted him with her eyes, saying nothing, but standing rigid as a tree.

Geln hid his smile as Bek emerged also. He locked eyes with his brother, observing his ineffectual dismay. He shifted his gaze to his mother, then to the eyes of his shaking sister. He stood absorbing the heat of their estrangement, then strode away, the smile on his face like a bold, dark pennant.

The new city of Aris, named for their ancestors' capital in the great caverns below, stood nestled in mountains by the sea. The Askirit were working mightily to establish a new City of Light in Asta, with a great temple in its center. Not yet completed, it was patterned after all they could remember from the past.

Their worship had in some ways changed the least since emerging from the darkness. None of the ancient liturgy had been changed. Instead, new lexicons had been added, celebrating their emergence into the light and praising Auret, who had shown them the way.

Geln stood with other initiates at the temple entrance, smelling the sea air, staring at a thick white birch in front of majestic green hemlocks. The branches of the birch rose like arms outstretched to the sky, its airily moving leaves like light-green garments. The trees, the bright blue sky, and the forested mountains in the distance contrasted with Korbas's sere environment. Geln felt a troubling discomfort, an unaccustomed longing as he looked at this white tree flinging its arms up as if voicing a praise out of the liturgy.

The line moved into the temple, unlighted to symbolize the ancient worship. Geln followed, far more used to moving in the dark than his fellow initiates. He thought of all the lies he had told in so many rituals in order to enter this temple.

The initiates were stopped at the stairs. Geln ran his fingers along the wall's carved faces—men, women, and children with eyes upward, expressing worship and joy. He dug his fingernails into the face of a young woman, mouth open in song, and slashed his nails across her open lips.

A priest's voice loudly intoned,

> "We stand in darkness.
> We climb to the light."

The priest then struck a tiny torch, mounted the steps, and

started climbing. They followed the little firefly of light above, circling ever higher on the great staircase with its intricate carvings and symbols.

As they entered the sanctuary amid a great crowd of worshipers, they heard women with stringed instruments playing and singing. After a time, male singers began harmonizing with the women, shaking pevas and striking percussion instruments.

Abruptly, the tempo increased, the signal for the worshipers to join in. Around him, enthusiastic voices in the darkness began singing praises about the light.

Another priest stepped forward. "Who is the most holy person in the temple?"

"The person beside us," said all the worshipers.

"Why is that one holy?"

"Because of the holy light within."

Men and women throughout the sanctuary began touching each other's faces in holy respect. Geln stood motionless. Then he felt a young woman's fingers sweeping over his eyes. She said the expected words, "Holy is the one who loves the light. Holy are you." She moved her fingers over the contours of Geln's face in gentle motions of awe and appreciation for Eshtel's creation.

When her hand touched Geln's scar, she hesitated. He grabbed her wrist and pressed her hand flat against the scar, fingers splayed up with their tips against his eyes. "Don't you recall Auret's tale? He was mutilated for you and me." He said this ritual statement derisively, then reached out and touched her face, placing his fingers in the same position as he had imprisoned hers, tips pressed tight against the flesh under the eyes.

For several moments he held the woman in that awkward grip as the congregation spoke to each other about holy neighbors and touching Eshtel's glory in their midst. Then he said flatly, "I was disfigured for me," and he released his grip and walked away from her.

A priest's voice boomed out, reciting liturgy and exhorting his listeners to faithfulness. Geln stood alone on the perimeter, smiling about how thoroughly confused the young woman would be about her holy neighbor.

The priest declared the ancient promise:

"Hope will come.
The Hope of Aliare.
He will invade the world.
He will afflict his enemies with light;
He will nourish his friends with light."

The congregants stood in silence and darkness to wait with their thoughts about their ancestors worshiping for generations in endless night with these same promises on their lips. Another priest broke the silence by declaring the new words:

"Yes, Hope has come!
The Hope of Aliare.
He has invaded our world.
He transcends Aliare.
He hurls fire from world to world.

"Hope has come!
Auret has brought us the light."

Hundreds of torches flared in celebration. They lit the sanctuary amid shouts of acclaim. But Geln stood to the side.

On the appointed morning for their initiation into Askirit manhood, the young men climbed past the sanctuary and up to the highest levels of the temple. Like their ancestors, they wore robes of woven sea fiber and human hair, repeating words about the clothes' symbolism and the light toward which they climbed. Guards required passwords at every level, for only those who had come through strenuous and dangerous tests and had convinced the priests of their spiritual intensity could climb and enter the highly restricted Tolas.

One by one, priests led the initiates through the darkness to assigned places in the Holiest. Sparks signaled the beginning of the ceremony as the High Priest began the Rite of Inclusion, saying, "The Tolas is holy. Here, you are received into righteousness. Bring no impurity. Here, you cannot hide your thoughts from the light."

He led the throng through the ancient ritual. No one could see in the darkness that Geln stood silent when the initiates repeated pledges of fealty. Then the priest recited:

"Hope has come,
Auret has come.
He afflicts his enemies with light.
He nourishes his friends with light.
He hurls fire from world to world!"

And then he declared in a loud voice,

"Askirit, receive the light!"

At those words, high windows were slid open and light poured in from the side and above, causing a shout of exclamation. Young men next to Geln wept joyously at their moment of being declared an Askirit. The High Priest then said the ancient words,

"Young men,
Let your joy ring out!"

It was traditional to respond with hearty laughter, for so Auret himself had laughed when he had passed through initiation in the Tolas of Aliare. The young men's laughter was an odd mixture of exuberant sounds and shouts. But Geln did not join in until the sounds had started to ebb. Then he too laughed, but it was not a joyous laughter. It was laughter without mirth, laughter that disdained, laughter that was not Geln's but the laughter of the dark. It reverberated throughout the Tolas just after the others' voices faded away.

Chapter 3.

—— Old Askirit Culture ——

"Show her, Jesk," Leas said. "Show Mela how you gather keitr."

The boy, half Mela's age but blind like her, reached out and found her arm. Mela and Leas were stooped over in the low cavern, but the boy was just tall enough to reach the winged mammals hanging upside down. Each had been painstakingly carved from bone, replicas of the living creatures used below as deadly weapons.

The boy's fingers found their way down her arm to her hand, then lifted it high. "Gathering keitr," he said by rote, "is often fatal. It takes just one slip of the hand."

Mela felt foolish, for the boy was attempting to cup her hand as he raised it with his and he was tipping her off balance. "Your fingers should be straight up, but loose." Jesk let go of her hand. "You listen and listen. You listen for the keitr to move, you listen to it breathe. You pinpoint the head, no matter how long it takes. Only when you're sure—then you grab!"

She barely heard his instantaneous motion and the equally quick movements at his belt as he deposited his catch in one of the belt's pouches. "The head has to be down. Keitr will hibernate in there, but not unless they're straight down, wings folded back."

Mela laughed. "They're already folded back. They're carved that way."

"But not live ones! In Aliare, no one could gather keitr

unless he'd practiced for years with carvings just like this." He removed his keitr belt and proudly handed it to her. "With a live keitr, you grasp the wings firmly, and you cache it quickly." He put her fingers on the bulging pouch. "Feel how snug it fits? Otherwise it chews through and bites you."

Mela smiled. "Which would make me very quickly dead." She was determined to be positive, to not start out wrong at this school.

"We're trying to keep all the old skills alive," Leas explained. "Everything here is authentic—we even have guano on the floor."

She had already been repulsed by that malodorous fact. "Obviously, though," she said, "not from live keitrs."

They moved to another tunnel, this one high and spacious, where several girls were fashioning weapons. He introduced each one to Mela. "They're producing authentic weapons already, which helps expenses for the school." He asked one girl to pull several spears and blades from their bins; she placed them carefully into Mela's hands. "The skilled touch of women. We use bones—only bones, as in Old Askirit culture."

"So I understand." Mela remembered Ashdel's dislike of sanding bone spears instead of sweet-smelling wood.

"We try to be thoroughly authentic," Leas said, leading Mela down stone stairs.

"But I hope you don't eat your meat raw."

"Not yet. But maybe you could start us off," he said lightly.

They entered the bone-cutting grotto. Here the odors were heavier and, in their own way, as unpleasant as the guano. Boys were sawing and hacking at bones of all sizes, but it was the setting vats that gave off the strongest smells.

Mela stepped back and explored the wall's perimeters, edging away from the vats. "You'll grow to love the smells," Leas said. He took a thick, flat shape a boy had been rasping and hefted it in his hands. "You could lay the keel for a small boat with one of these. We're not ready for boats yet. But someday we will.

Someday!" He touched another boy's hand which was gripping a large saw. "Right, Ket?"

"Someday we will," the boy said heartily.

Leas raised his voice and said to all of them, "Let's hear the song Yosha sang when he was a boy like you cutting bones down in Aliare!"

The boys started singing to the rhythm of their sawing and rasping:

> *"Would you be a master craftsman?*
> *Come and work.*
> *Your fingers must be clever,*
> *to form the blades of Tarn,*
> *the spears and tools and wheels.*
>
> *"Bones, bones, bones,*
> *a thousand bones;*
> *each becomes a perfect shape*
> *beneath your fingers.*
>
> *"Come and work.*
> *Your hands must grow strong,*
> *to split thick bones.*
>
> *"Work and work and work.*
> *Become a master craftsman.*
> *But first now, learn your bones.*
> *Niroc bones for tiny nails,*
> *Osk bones for benches.*
> *Bones of a peshua to pick your teeth!*
> *Ah, what would you do without bones?"*

They sang it through several times, and Leas said, "Think of it—all they had down there was bones. But they made everything—boats, spears, beautiful carvings ... and, like you, they could see nothing. Nothing but sparks."

Leas led Mela up a steep incline until they emerged at an opening far above the entrance to the caverns. "I call this Kjotik's Jaw—a lookout the same as Yosha's opening far above his village. He'd sit and listen to the winds and dream of facing leviathan. I sit here and listen for the roar of kelerai. I watch the people who come to see it, to see what poets and singers call the most beautiful sight in all creation." Leas turned Mela a bit to her right and cupped his hands behind her ears. "Tomorrow you'll hear it. And you'll feel it—even some of the spray. We're close enough, but not so close we're in danger."

Mela was fingering the oval opening, wondering how far she might fall if she slipped. She wished Leas weren't showing her so much so quickly, before she could orient herself.

"We call all these caverns—all the school—Wellen, after Yosha's village," he explained as he led her back down to a large, open area. Suddenly a great mass of fur panted into Mela, pushing her backward. A slender arm quickly pulled the dog away from her, and the voice of a girl about her age said, "She never bites— except people who need it."

Leas laughed. "Meet Lysse. She can't sculpt or sand or sew, but she loves to care for the animals." Mela heard the girl limping as she led the dog away. "That's right. A tree fell on me," Lysse said cheerfully. "Caught in a storm, and they said I was dead. But I was only blind and useless."

Again Leas laughed. "She's useless no more. Mela, you'll find yourself coming here every time you feel down. Lysse and the animals together are a sure cure."

Leas left, and Lysse helped Mela into the pool so she could sense the motions of fish and eels. "In Aliare, people did this all the time," she said. "They loved pools. They climbed in with luminous eels and fish, so they could stare and feed their eyes." She draped an eel over Mela's shoulders and its tail splashed vigorously.

After Lysse had shown her all the animals, Mela decided she was the most cheerful, humorous person she'd ever met. The entire time Lysse had said only one sad thing. It was this: "Auret was a cripple too, you know. He was a lot more crippled up than me." Yet the way she said it wasn't full of sadness. Her voice was, rather, full of wonder.

That evening all the students sat around a fire singing. Leas didn't mention the rumors about Mela's being the Blind Princess, only that they should welcome her.

"I have to be careful about fire," Leas explained to Mela as they listened to its crackling and felt its heat. "Many blind children know only its pain, not understanding distance makes it safe."

"The sounds of a fire are wonderful," Mela said.

A boy was strumming an instrument and singing a ballad. "Especially wonderful as a background to Delin's singing." Leas said, then leaned over and whispered, "He's only twelve. Delin's our only genius. Music. Stories. Sculpture. Fortunately, he doesn't know he's a genius—he simply loves to create."

The boy was singing well-known songs about the founders of the Askirit kingdom and about those who had climbed up out of Aliare and into the light. Then he began his own songs about Auret, about hope fulfilled and the children he loved. Delin sang as if he had met him, and it made Mela feel very strange, as if the boy were actually very old. When the heat and the sounds of the fire were gone, Leas said, "I wonder if Delin would show you his clay sculptures. Each one is like a ballad."

The boy led them to a small room where the sculptures were kept. As they approached it he said to Mela, "My name's not really Delin, you know. But they let me call myself that. He was Auret's friend." The boy felt his way past sculptures set high on a natural ledge until he stopped. "Here. I made this just a few days ago." He carefully guided her hands to it. "You can keep this one with you if you like it."

She at first had trouble deciding what the shapes were all about. She touched a steep flatness and a series of elements set against it. As she explored the rounded shapes, she sensed stylized figures. Touching shape after shape, she realized the figures were in motion. They were children, one above the other, linked by gripped hands. Their expressions and the fluidity of their bodies reminded her of cats' skins rippling, or figures melting and moving under her hands.

She continued to touch the distended shapes, murmuring her approval, her spirits lifting at the force of its message. "Climbing to the light!" she said. "The one lifting the other. Escaping the darkness, hand gripping hand." She was thinking of the times so long ago when her very young eyes had seen leaves and flowers and insects in bright sunlight. A great longing came over her.

"You're right about the light," Delin said. "But they're not climbing up. They're descending. They're taking the light down—down to the abyss."

Mela stiffened. Her hands moved away from the sculpture and hung in the air. Delin said, "Perhaps our generation will be the one to take the light to Aliare. Think of all the Askirit people down there, still longing for light, still singing all the songs we do but not knowing the way out."

Mela grunted an indistinct sound. Genius or not, Delin had gotten caught up in all this talk. She sensed the little boy was waiting for her to say she wanted to keep the sculpture, but she simply thanked him and said she needed to rest.

When Leas led her to the girls' sleeping area, she turned on him. "What are you trying to do? Shame me into becoming the Blind Princess?"

Leas clucked sympathetically. "Mela, I didn't know what he'd show you. I was as startled as you were." He put his hand on her shoulder. "I will never, never pressure you about your future. But I can't shield you from all the talk. More than ever, the songs around the fires at night are about how dark it is down there, and how nobody up here cares."

——— Kelerai ———

Mela sat in the high opening Leas had named Kjotik's Jaw, feeling the morning breezes and listening to shouts of people below assembling to view the phenomenon of kelerai. As the planet turned on its axis, water plunged into the great hollows beneath the surface, creating gigantic storms beneath. Each day, as the planet rotated, waters roared up and out in spectacular geysers of massive proportions.

Mela had been at the school for a year. Meeting kelerai here each morning had become a ritual and a passion. First its powerful rumblings reverberated through her, and then the mighty roar burst through the ground and above, lifting her spirits. She exulted in every aspect of kelerai: The people's exclamations of wonder; the spray that, when the winds were right, misted her face; the triumphant sounds of birds rising to greet the upward rush. Now she understood how in the darkness of Aliare people would shout with great longing and praise: "Kelerai! Kelerai! Kelerai!"

This morning, for the first time, she would be able to share this, her most powerful experience, with her father and sister. Filled with anticipation, she was already fretting about their not yet arriving, for she was determined they should miss nothing.

In the corridor below, Mela heard Lysse's slow, distinct movements. The crippled girl shared her passion for kelerai; nothing needed to be said as she came and sat beside her. Lysse broke the solemnity by placing a small bird on Mela's knee. She pressed some seeds into her hand. "It will go anywhere with you, if you have some of these."

Mela opened her hand to the tiny bird. Its pecking for the seeds tickled her palm and she laughed.

"See," Lysse said, always trying to convince Mela of the wonders of touch contrasted with sight. "A person who sees would have just flung the bird off when it pecked on her palm. But you," she said with merriment, "you just experienced a small delight!"

Lysse often spoke of "experiencing a small delight."

Mela reached over and in Yette—the ancient tactile language from below, which all the students were learning—she playfully raced the signs for wriggling toes all the way from Lysse's fingers to her elbow.

"An impudent small delight," Lysse responded. The bird flew off, and she added, "Hear those wings explode? I love the sounds. Now, if I could see, I doubt the sounds would affect me much. And music! And all the scents and things to feel. When I push my face into the fur of a kitten or a rabbit . . ." She snorted happily. "Oh, the feel of a puppy trying to squeeze all of his body into my little hand! I love coarseness and softness, warmth at the belly and the coldness of a nose. Even a slimy, clammy snail tracking across my palm is . . ." She paused and then declared decisively, "a small delight."

"And kelerai is a large delight."

"Yes! The sounds. The shaking of your bones. The tangy scents and mists." Mela dusted the seed husks from her hands. Lysse's thickened, stiff hands reached out and gripped Mela's. "Even your sad, sad voice is a small delight."

Mela took no offense and squeezed Lysse's fingers. "And even your hands are full of whimsies—like your voice. You are always luring me out of my little morbidities!"

Mela said it as an attempt at humor, and it had its desired effect. Lysse burst out laughing. "Little morbidities! Well, we'll just drive all of those out."

Mela's father and sister arrived in a rush, barely in time to sense the first rumbles beneath them. "Feel it?" Mela asked. "Just the slightest shift, like an insect sound?"

Her father waited a moment. "Not yet."

Soon the slight motion became a rumble they all felt, and then a powerful reverberation that set them making remarks about how strong it was.

"It just keeps getting stronger," Mela said, her face flushed with excitement. The thought came to her that perhaps this was the only prize she'd shared with them since she had lost her sight.

Ashdel said, "It's shaking everything! Even my elbows and feet!"

"You'll hear it suddenly roar out there, and then it just gets louder," Mela explained, standing now, her bare toes kneading the stone floor in rhythm to the vibrations.

"Oh!" Ashdel exclaimed, and their father gasped. "Look!" Ashdel shouted, "It's roaring upward! It's as big as the sky!"

Her father, who had seen it before, said, "Magnificent! See the blues—all shades of blue, with white foam merging with the clouds. It's a liquid mountain of cliffs that keeps changing its shape."

Ashdel said, "Those winds blowing spray off to the sea make the edges look like snowstorms."

Both her father and sister kept pointing and describing until Ashdel shouted, "A rainbow! See the rainbow?"

She pointed until her father said, "Yes. I see it."

Mela's toes had stopped wriggling to the sounds and her face was no longer flushed. She could not describe sights. Her world of sounds, scents, and touch seemed irrelevant to theirs. After all, she thought bitterly, when the poets described kelerai, they said it was the most beautiful *sight* in all creation.

As kelerai settled down to its great steady flume high in the distance, her father said, "You didn't say anything. Truly, it was magnificent."

"It always is." Mela tried to keep sadness out of her voice

and turned to Ashdel. "I'm glad you got to see it." But the experience had shaken her, and she fought to keep her spirits up as she led them on a tour of her school. As they stood before the large display of ancient warrior figures made by the students, her father asked her why they all faced the shoreline.

"I don't know."

"Well, is this the Laij invasion? They have keitr belts and spears, but I notice—"

"I don't know anything about this," she interrupted. "I've never touched the figures. I'm just not interested in how they killed each other down there."

Yet Mela couldn't avoid thinking about dangers and death in Aliare, for so much of what they did at the school explored these aspects of Old Askirit culture. At the clay sculptures, she was alone with her father and at first had him look at ones done by others. But finally she said, "These, on the end, against the wall. These are mine." He stood with her a long time not saying anything and she decided he was unable to figure them out.

"You have to touch them, feel them," she said, picking up her vague shape of a woman with a rounded hump at her side representing a baby.

"Good," he said lamely. "A woman with a baby." He hesitated a moment. "I can see the nose, and you made a crease for the mouth." Then he asked hesitantly, kindly, "But no eyes?"

"No. No eyes. They have no eyes." She heard him reaching back against the wall for another. "Is this also yours?"

She said yes, and he felt it with his fingers. It was large, mushroom-shaped, with six thick legs extended. He picked it up. Almost all the underside was a deep mouth and teeth made of wood splinters she'd stuck in the clay.

He studied it for a time. "Did you mean it to be hideous?"

"You've heard of what's down there."

"Yes."

She took the carving from him and hurried him down to the pool and the animals and to Lysse's sense of small delights.

The Summons

When it was heard the blind children were entering the city for the Festival of Kelerai, people started standing and soon hundreds and then thousands were cheering as they filed in.

Lysse, with her usual edge of humor, said, "Now these people have a fine attitude." Mela smiled. "None of us ever got cheered before."

Behind them they heard Leas grunt. Mela was surprised that he was embarrassed by the crowd's reactions. As they sat in the crowd facing a high promontory, the chants of appreciation for them had barely died down when Lysse asked Leas, "Why didn't you like that?"

"You know why they cheered? They think because you're blind, you're magical. That you have special powers."

"We do!" Lysse snapped back happily.

Leas did not banter back as he often did. "Dangerous superstitions that corrupt the nation. The old barbarians venerated four: Leviathan. Sierent. The blind. The crippled."

Lysse made a whimsical gasping noise. "So I'm doubly magical?"

"It's pagan," he said severely. "People here don't realize how many pagan ideas creep in."

People cheered singers and other performers mounting the promontory.

"If it's pagan, why did we come?" Mela asked.

"Because the entire pageant is about Old Askirit culture. They can't stray too far. You'll love the music, the ballads, the stories. . . ."

They did. Even Mela liked the songs of facing dangers like leviathan and the storms of sierent, the humorous romances and the heroic battles against invaders. However, when they started singing ballads depicting men and women longing for the light and crying out for someone to come down from above to rescue them, she shifted uncomfortably and tapped out in Yette on Lysse's wrist, "If this is all about how heroic life was down there, why all this guilt?"

"Because," she whispered, as if Mela had asked it in jest, "we all love to wallow in guilt." But Mela didn't take it lightly.

On stage, a woman sang about her longings for her baby's future. She raised her arms and with great emotion sang, "Will he be born in the light? Born in the light? Born in the light?"

Bathos, Mela thought with disgust. By the time the festival was over, Mela's mood and Leas's had reversed. He had gotten caught up in the production, feeling the emotions deeply, saying, "Some pretty thin stuff—once they made a mishmash of Askirit faith—yet wonderful tunes! The tale of the Enre was very, very good—and the parts about Asel and Yosha and Auret—even that was fresh."

But Mela wasn't listening. She had lagged behind, unable to share the feelings of her friends whistling and singing in front of her.

Ten days later she and Lysse sat in Kjotik's Jaw waiting for others to arrive for a class. Lysse said something about the Blind Princess and Mela exploded. "Fifteen commands in the liturgies to take the light back down to Aliare. Fifteen! But only one about a Blind Princess, and no one knows what it means!"

"Sorry. I promise I will never again say the word 'princess.' It's just exciting, that's all. Everybody knows the prophecy, and that you're blind and have royal blood...."

Mela said in Yette, pounding out the words vigorously on Lysse's palm: "I am not a princess. I'm a very, very distant relative."

Others arrived, and Leas had them all sit in a circle. He was forever attempting new ways to inculcate Old Askirit culture and the news of Auret's triumphs. To Leas, the circle of twenty children was both family and sacred trust. He had them sing a psalm, then he approached the first student in the circle and grasped his hand. He placed a seed in it, saying, "You are eternal. You will be transformed, life to life, world to world, joy to joy, forever. Auret is here. Auret will be there."

He repeated this with each child until they all held seeds. He carried a tray of soil to the center of the circle. "Come." They all moved toward him to press their seeds into it. "You are more than the trees. You are more than sand or sky or deer or birds. You will see wonders in many worlds."

He had them pass around wood carvings of animals, ships, tools, and other things they had made. "Think about this. Is anything like you? If so, why?" He got the children to describe themselves as birds, animals, trees, even the sounds of thunder.

Delin said, "I am the ocean. I am sometimes loud and frothy and sometimes quiet, and I'm always changing—but I'm always the ocean."

A little girl said, "I am Yette. I don't speak out loud, but inside I race like fast fingers and have a thousand things to say to myself."

Lysse said, "I'm the spicy scent of a sliced apple!" but she did not elaborate.

"I'm the apple itself," said an older girl. "Slippery and smooth and trying to get along with everyone, soft but easily bruised and easily skinned."

It came to Mela's turn and she waited so long to speak the children started fidgeting. Finally she said, "I am that beetle you hear buzzing on the floor. It buzzes and kicks its feet and spins in a circle on its back. It'll keep struggling till someone steps on it. Or picks it up and tosses it into the trash. Or maybe it will keep buzzing forever."

Delin stood to his feet and walked over to her. He took her slender hands in his smaller ones and said, "Or someone picks the beetle up and carries it out into the light." He then reached up and touched her cheek in the affectionate Old Askirit sign for friendship.

Years later, in winter, Leas sought Mela out one evening and found her working on clay figures. He stood for a time watching her shape and lift and press three round lumps stuck each above the other. She sensed he was there and, grasping the top one, held two fingers slightly apart and shoved their tips into the clay. When she pulled them out, they left two holes.

"You know I'm watching, don't you?"

"I know your breathing very well." She rounded the eyes she'd just made till they were very large.

"You don't have to do eyes. Now you're making them look silly."

She turned to him. She was eighteen now, and she had begun to fully speak her mind. "There's something you haven't told me, isn't there? I've sensed it in you all day." She jerked her fingers upward nervously. "Tell me quick, because I know you've got news."

She felt him pressing into her hand an octagonal shape a thumb's width thick. It was smoothly polished wood, etched on one side with a hawk in flight, on the other a field of stars. She fingered the royal seal for a long moment, first one side, then the other. "I had many terrible images of what you would tell me. But this is the worst."

"You haven't even heard the message. You don't know that it's bad at all."

"No," she agreed, "I don't have the message. What is it?"

"You've been summoned to Aris. To the King's House." She could tell Leas was trying hard to keep the excitement out of his voice as he made that pronouncement. The octagon frightened her, but his enthusiasm angered her.

"Isn't being summoned to Aris the worst?"

He hesitated. "I don't know what it means. You're of royal blood—"

"Lots of people are of royal blood!" She clenched her fists in front of her. "You can find plenty of them in Aris; they'll point themselves out."

Mela reached with her right hand and grasped the head of her sculpture with the new, big eyes. She squeezed it, obliterating the eyes, making a fist so that the clay squirted out between her fingers. "I won't go."

Leas stepped close, putting his arm around her shoulders. "You have to go. This is a royal seal. But your father will come, and I will go with you."

"And you'll bring all the little blind children?" She snorted with anger. "They talk as if they can merrily skip into the depths, down into Old Askirit culture—like attending a pageant. They love talking stories and heroics and my being a Blind Princess." She rapped her knuckles sharply against the potter's wheel. "But they know nothing about the hungry night."

Leas touched her fingers wet with clay. "You're right. They do not."

Her eyes felt as if they were swelling in their sockets. "I can understand, Leas, why you want to go down there. Old Askirit is all you think about. Well, you and Father go to Aris. Tell everyone I'm deranged—" She broke away from him. "You're cruel to let children think they'll someday take the light to Aliare. You fill their heads with illusions."

He stepped back as if slapped. "I'm not cruel! I weep for every blind and crippled child. But I won't take away the dignity of choosing great challenges. Not even when they're too great to achieve."

She reared back, then thrust her face toward him. "But Aliare's your dream. Why should I choose it?"

"No one will ever force you!"

She leaned heavily against the potter's wheel; her hand began aimlessly spinning it. She quickened its pace more and more, then stopped it suddenly. "Yesterday I found a flower in the snow. A sad flower. Limp petals. Stem drooped into the ice—like a woman weeping. It was like me. It couldn't break loose, and it couldn't move. It just drooped there."

* * *

Leas, ever wanting to recapture Old Askirit skills, had set up two scent-making rooms. Mela stirred sea essences into a small pot in the room reserved for women. She and Leas were waiting for Mela's family to arrive; she looked forward to the reunion but not the trip to Aris. To lighten her spirits she said, "You aren't supposed to be in here. Men in Aliare never spied on the women's scent-making."

"Only wedding scents were secret."

"That's not what I heard." She sniffed at her developing creation. "Maybe it's just as well those old scents have disappeared. Maybe we'd hate them."

"Unlikely!" Leas said. "Women today know nothing about making the erotic perfumes of Old Aliare the poets spoke of. Now it's all airy flowers—" He stopped abruptly, then added, "So I hear."

"Ha!" She loved being old enough to tease him. "Now we know why you're not married yet. And why you're so desperate to get down into Aliare." She laughed. "You're holding out for a woman who can provide authentic wedding scents."

Leas popped air from his cheek in the Old Askirit way of saying her talk was foolish. "You keep talking as if I'm planning to go down myself. But I've never said that. Who would keep this school alive? Who would keep the vision before the people?" He rhythmically struck his bent fingers against his palm, making a sound meaning something was inevitable. "I long for Aliare. But I'm not called to go down."

Mela's hand had slowly fallen into the pot of scent. She was stupefied. Always she had thought his excitement about the Blind Princess rumors stemmed from his longing to descend with her.

She absently raised her hand and the pot fell off, crashing on the floor. Leas rushed to pick up the pieces; the scent rose strong in the air. When he had picked them all up, Mela said, "You mean you would let me go into the rifts by myself?"

"I never said you should go into the rifts! The king hasn't said so either." He was arranging the broken pieces on the table, and she sensed he was flustered. "The king didn't summon me, he summoned you."

His defensiveness amazed Mela as much as his words. Her hand rose slowly to her face and brushed away a shock of hair; the strong smell of the solution on it made her blink. She reached for the basin of water to wash it.

As she dried her hand, she heard the breathing of others and realized her family had entered the room and had been listening.

"Welcome," she said.

"Mela." Her father's voice had a tremble in it. He walked to her and tightly embraced her. "If the king commands you, Mela, I will go down with you. You'll need someone."

Ashdel made a noise like an injured bird. Mela clamped her hands on the table and braced her feet. "Dear Father, neither of us will go. But if I were sent, I would surely not ask you to come." She paused, then added bitterly, "If the king sent me to the gallows, it would do me little good to ask him to let my father join me."

The King's House

Mela sat upright in the wagon, startled awake by a loud cheer. She and her father and Ashdel had been riding all day; behind them were four more wagons filled with blind students. The cheers grew louder amid sounds of many feet running and joyful exclamations.

"Aris has gotten the word," the driver said dryly. "Blind children come to save the kingdom."

Mela didn't realize it was already dark until Ashdel exclaimed, "Look at the sparks thrown up. And lanterns coming from every direction."

The wagons were slowed by the crowds, even though they were on the outskirts of the city, skirting it to proceed directly to the King's House. When they finally arrived, they were rescued by the king's guards and escorted into a vast hall. At that first cheer, Mela had felt disoriented and threatened. But the other children were acting as if they had arrived at the most glorious pageant imaginable. As courtiers and matrons welcomed them, they giggled and whispered and kept their fingers moving among themselves in hasty Yette messages. But Mela was quiet and very relieved to be shown to her sleeping room.

Next morning she awakened early and felt breezes moving over her. She lay and enjoyed them for a time, then forced herself up and moved toward them, stepping over a sill and into a garden. She felt grass under her feet and cautiously made her way toward the sound of birds. As she walked, she wriggled her toes in the plush grass, but then she nearly stumbled against a low bench. Bending over, she explored its shape with her hands. She sat down, pointing her face toward the breezes.

"Hello." It was a young man's voice, cheerful but intrusive. "My name is Cheln." She returned his greeting, and though she did not want to talk, she politely told him her name. He sat down next to her. "So you're the Blind Princess."

"I am not!" she retorted.

"Oh?"

"I'm blind, but I'm not a princess."

"Hmmmmm." Cheln stretched out the sound, as if he were very sure of himself and more than a little amused by her answers.

"Actually, I'm a royal myself. If the right sixteen people die, I get to be king. But for you, I suppose it would be more than sixteen."

"Hundreds," she said instantly. "Thousands, more likely."

He laughed. "You're still some sort of cousin of mine. They explained it to me." She liked the warmth in his voice but thought him flippant about what she was facing. "The children were certainly giddy last night," he said. "Weren't you even a little excited about being a celebrity in the capital?"

She gripped the edges of the stone bench till her fingers hurt. "How could I be? You know what the Blind Princess is supposed to do."

"Hey," he said, snapping fingers against knuckles, "enjoy the attention! They can't make you do anything. The king only summoned you to solve a political problem." He clicked his feet together. "Enjoy the feasts, dance a little, then—" he paused to laugh—"walk away."

She stiffened. "Don't be flippant! How do you think the crowd would act if I did that?"

He shifted on the bench and his voice came back a bit more sober. "The crowds are what the king worries about. They listen to those who say he may be Yosha's grandson but he didn't inherit his courage. They say he grows fat in the palace while civilizations below wait in darkness."

"It's true the liturgies command us to go down."

"That's why every time a storm kills someone, it's the king's fault—he's brought holy wrath on us. They say every disease and pestilence proves we're defiled. And they sing ballads about the king's trembling in the dark."

The sun's rays were warming Mela's face; she brushed hair from her forehead and lifted her chin toward the warmth. "I've heard them. And they sing that the glory of Aris is gone." She lowered her voice and asked, "What if they're right?"

Cheln leaned toward her and whispered, "Everyone in the court asks that."

"Then he should do something! That's what kings are for. Send a battalion down there."

He sighed. "Until the quakes, no one could go down. Now, it's only the rifts of Korbas."

She flinched at hearing the word "Korbas."

"The king's troops are loyal, but not loyal enough to go down into the rifts."

"Yet," she said, her breath coming in quick bursts, "the king could lead a select band of patriots."

"The king is old," he said, shaking his head at her urgency. "And even patriots are only filled with childhood fantasies. A few brave souls went into the rifts but came bolting out in terror."

"And they expect *me* to lead thousands of them into the depths?"

His head jerked back in surprise. "Oh, not at all! Not at all." He touched her chin and turned her face toward him. "Why do you think last night they cheered you? Believe me, if they thought you were here to lead them into the rifts of Korbas, they wouldn't have cheered!"

Her brows knit tight as a knot. "But all the songs say so. The Blind Princess leads a great throng down to liberate all Aliare, bringing whole nations to the light. Have you ever heard a ballad that's different?"

Cheln assumed a fake voice, mimicking pompous authority: "The high priest has declared a new, convenient exegesis. The prophecy must be viewed with its proverb. Therefore the logic of the text—" and here Cheln squinched his nose theatrically— "clearly indicates the Blind Princess leads only the blind." He paused, then added in the same pompous voice, "You know the proverb, of course: 'The littlest. The weakest. The blind and the broken will confound the powers.'"

"I know the proverb. I know it well."

Cheln resumed his normal voice: "So do the people. No one wants to follow a princess into the dark." He blew air through his teeth, indicating she was taking all this too seriously. "Look, cousin, the king won't go. The army won't go. The priest and the people won't go. You don't have to go either." With a finger, he flicked a tear off her cheek. "Be wary. Be strong. You'll figure it out."

The King's House, like all Askirit dwellings, was hollowed out of the cliffs. Large, natural caverns had been enlarged so that strategic openings cast light deep into the intersecting tunnels. Courtiers coached the children for their audience with the king.

"Your school specializes in Old Askirit culture?" said one. "Remarkable! You must want to experience it, since darkness is your natural element. Think of it. Everyone—everyone!—in the dark like you."

No, Mela thought. *I don't want to go down into the bowels of this planet any more than you do. We wouldn't last a day.* But she said nothing.

They were led to the great vault where shafts of light poured down on them. Mela walked at the rear, annoyed at the way Ashdel kept whispering excitedly to her father, keeping his attention on her. The smaller children, all atwitter, were holding on to Leas, gripping his clothing and stumbling over each other's feet. The group strained toward the king, who stood majestically on a colorful mosaic representing the sun. One wide ray of light fell directly on him from an opening above.

Mela hung a bit behind the rest, directing her acute hearing to whispers behind her. "Truth is," she heard one man say, "the king doesn't know what to do with these children. The crowds love them; how can he send them down into the rifts?"

Formal statements were being made ahead of her and children were bowing at Leas's instructions, but Mela's mind was elsewhere. She felt that in this one day she had been forced to mature many years. A crushing weight was refining her even as she stood listening to the courtly prattle.

Be wary, she told herself. *Be strong. Listen.* When she was finally in front of the king, her mind was still churning. She forgot to bow. Her father put his hand on her neck and gently pressured her downward.

She did not feel embarrassed. Instead she was still thinking of the king's predicament and her own. The king talked to her like a small child, in extremely simple words. She wondered if he thought she was simpleminded, especially in light of her father's cueing her to bow and the common equating of blindness with stupidity. Ordinarily, standing before her king and realizing such things would have filled her with shame. But desperation had obliterated those feelings. She kept thinking of the proverb that had been used so callously: *The littlest. The weakest. The blind and the broken will confound the powers.*

The king obviously did not know how to talk to her. He asked awkward questions about her school and her interests. She mumbled answers, not caring that she was reinforcing his impressions about her slowness. "So you study Tarn and Aliare in school, and how they survived in darkness." He patted her cheek. "Do you like Old Askirit ballads?"

Abruptly she said in a strong voice, "If you send us below, more than the crowds will laugh at you."

The king's hand fell to his side. "I never said anything about sending you below. What do you mean?"

"Even if we reached the people in darkness, they would ask, 'What is light like?' We who are blind would have to say, 'We don't know. We cannot see.' They would ask, 'What is dawn like? What are the colors of forest and sea we have heard so much about? And kelerai, what is the sight of kelerai like?' We'd have to say, 'We don't know any more than you. We're blind.' And they would ask, 'Then why did you come?'"

A courtier quickly said, "Whoever goes down to Aliare would take a lamp. That would convince them. Then they could come and see the light for themselves."

She whirled on the man. "How about you? Will you take the fire down with me?" The courtier lost his smooth tongue and mumbled something. She turned to the king. "Will you go with me? Will your son?" She heard her father behind her take a quick breath. Leas cleared his throat to say something, but then he didn't.

The king did not answer her. Mela said, "Someone has to go. That's what everyone says. But who? Is there truly a Blind Princess?"

The king finally said something. "The prophecy is well known."

"Yes. And its weight grinds me to pieces."

Into Mela's mind sprang memories of an early childhood trip to Aris. She'd seen the venerable old presences of Yosha and Asel, so infirm they were propped up; as a little girl, she thought they would topple over dead if she'd touched them. Yet she knew Asel and Yosha were still alive.

"I understand there's controversy over what the prophecy means," she said respectfully. "Perhaps Asel herself could tell us its meaning."

"Asel couldn't help. You see how old I am myself, and she is my father's mother. Asel has no power. She barely moves. She cannot even see."

Mela stepped back. Though her throat was tightening and she felt as if a net were tangled around her arms and head, she forced herself to say in a quiet, humble manner, "Perhaps Asel will say or do nothing. But if I could only touch her. If I could pray for guidance with my hand on hers."

The king sighed and said, "You would have to speak to the Enre."

——— The Cleft ———

Despite tempestuous, icy weather, the four Enre launched their little craft. Mela sat centered among the women, wondering why, at Asel's age and frailty, she insisted on living on a remote island. In her prime, Asel had led the Enre, the devout corps of highly trained women. The leader was always named Varial, after the first Varial many centuries before.

"Will Varial be on the island?" Mela asked against the wind. "No," said Eln, leader of the group. "She's on a mission." Her tone and the weather did not invite further talk.

Mela bent her head into the wet wind and worried about what she would say to Asel, queen mother and, with her husband Yosha, founder of the kingdom. She dared not hope the ancient woman could actually explain the prophecy. But if she had any mental faculties left, perhaps Mela could find a way to use her words.

The energetic movements of the paddlers was like music all around her. "Is the boat's frame made of bone?" Mala asked.

Eln rapped the handle of her paddle. "No more than this paddle. The boat's design is original, but we use wood. We keep only the essentials of the heritage."

Mela couldn't stop herself from asking, "Is the command to go down with the light essential? Why don't the Enre do it? You have the knowledge, the power, the courage. What could withstand hundreds of Enre descending?"

"You exaggerate our powers."

The boat was grinding into a rocky beach and they leaped into the shallows to pull it ashore. As they dragged it under a stand of trees, Eln said, "We've discussed this many times. Ever since the quakes opened up the rifts, Varial has talked about whether we should obey the command to go down. But always the answer comes back: It is not yet time." Mela made a little sound she did not think Eln could hear, but the Enre abruptly turned. "Do you think we fear Korbas? Or Aliare?"

"No," Mela said lamely.

She was wet and miserable as they led her inland. They finally arrived at a lake where other Enre were camped. Mela stood close to the fire as a meal was prepared, then sat down eagerly when her portion was handed to her. She bit down on the baked grain mixture. "Is Asel here?"

"Asel is up in the high crags. In the Cleft."

Mela started to ask if she were coming down soon, but she sensed it was the wrong question. After the meal Eln said, "In the morning, we will prepare you." Then she showed Mela to a shelter with sleeping skins.

The women had risen long before dawn, and now on their knees in the darkness, they faced the horizon where the sun would rise. As she felt the air start to warm, Mela felt irritated that they were including her in this rite. Each of them could see the dawn and be uplifted by its colors, whereas she could barely feel the first weak rays on her face. They began chanting their love for the light and for Auret, but Mela brushed pebbles away from her knees and wished they'd hurry so she could eat.

After breakfast, Eln said to her, "Only the Enre visit Asel's refuge in the crags. But you may, if you are purified."

"In what way purified?"

"You must build a fire."

Mela flexed her cold, stiff fingers, then held them out palms up. "But I am blind. They do not let me build fires."

"I will help you." Eln led her to the lake's edge and helped her lay the fire. Then she handed her a small torch, saying as she guided her hand, "Light it."

Mela listened to it catch, then heard Eln stoking it. She moved back a bit from the heat.

"Open your hands."

Mela did so, and she felt rough pieces of wood tumbling into her palms.

"These are your rebellions. One by one, you must repudiate each one—and throw it into the fire."

Mela was nonplussed. "What do you mean?"

"We are all in rebellion against love. We all turn from the light."

"It is not I who have taken the light from my eyes!" Mela said sharply. But as soon as she'd said it, she regretted her tone.

Eln ignored her outburst. "Think of one person. Someone you resent, or someone who has not loved you well, or has failed you."

Or betrayed me, Mela thought. Leas! Leas with all his talk of Old Askirit culture and Auret and living forever. But did Leas care about her? Did he protect her? She cradled the small chunks of wood against her stomach and picked one out, drawing her hand back to throw it in.

"Say the name first," Eln said. "And repudiate what keeps you from love."

Mela's hand stopped. She said the name: "Leas." But she could not bring out other words. Her fingers worked over the rough edges of the wood. She became embarrassed at her silence and started digging her nails into the grain of the wood.

"Name how he hurt you. And cast your rebellion into the fire."

She felt forced to speak and said, "He has not loved me enough." Then she threw in the wood. The Enre waited. Mela grasped another chip, her thoughts on Ashdel. Her sister never put herself into Mela's place, never felt her fear and darkness and pain. She squeezed her lips tightly together, thinking of all the times Ashdel had preened, with no concern for her younger sister who had lost everything.

"Ashdel, for her callused heart." She threw the chip into the flames. Their warmth felt good on her cold fists. Another name came to her. Lysse. But why Lysse's name? She thought long and hard about her ebullient friend. She harbored no ill feelings toward her. Eln waited and Mela almost dropped the chip she was holding out. But finally she realized it was crippled, blind Lysse's happiness that bothered her. Lysse with the lively and lovely disposition everyone loved and which made her feel guilty for being morose. Lysse who indicted Mela's resentments and her feelings of doom.

"Lysse," she said. "For being Lysse, and for making me feel unclean."

Other names came, and she spoke them, until she had flung in many chips. And then a name appeared that she tried to blink away. It came again, and she raced her mind to seek others, but she could not avoid the name: Auret. She flushed. How could she resent love himself? But as soon as she thought that, she asked how love could let her go blind. It was an absurd contradiction. *Auret! Of course Auret has failed me! Here I am sightless and abandoned. Here he is supposed to love us beyond measure and yet taunts me with horrors.* She could not say his name aloud. As tears flowed, she realized that she had not been repudiating her rebellions at all. In some ways she had been savoring them like dark delicacies, pouring out her declarations against the others. Her life was so outrageously unfair! How could she discard the bitterness on which she had fed for so long?

"Auret," she finally declared, terrified at her saying the Holy One's name aloud, terrified at what Eln would be thinking. But she repeated the word: "Auret. For making my life a shambles. For giving sight to Ashdel and not to me. For saying he loves me, but loving others so much more!"

She was weeping copiously. "Throw in the chip," Eln said. "It is not Auret you are throwing into the fire, but your rebellions. And only Auret himself will enable you to do it."

She threw it in, repulsed by the fractures she sensed in her own righteousness. At the same time, as if flowing out with her tears, she felt the power of the resentments ebbing.

She laughed but felt startled by her laughter and quickly

wiped her face with her sleeve. Eln took a cloth to her face, then helped her stand. Mela heard the Enre gathering around them and then Eln saying, "Here are coals from your fire. Hold them at a distance." She placed in her hand the top of a hot sack of coals.

Mela swallowed. "Won't the coals burn through the sack?"

"Yes. Better hurry."

They guided her feet onto flat rocks leading into the lake. She was quickly up to her waist, and the coals hissed as they hit the water. Her feet kept following the submerged rocks as they went deeper. She took a deep breath as her head went under, Enre hands on each shoulder. Then she felt herself being lifted by their hands, as if she had suddenly become buoyant, riding forward and upward in the water.

Soon they all stood dripping on the shore. "You are purified by fire. You are cleansed by water. May your rebellions be ashes; may you soar, clean and lifted in his love."

They departed next morning for the crags. By noon they were high up a steep, winding trail cut into high rock formations.

"Asel loves these trails," Eln said, gripping Mela's wrist and pulling her over a rounded boulder. "They remind her of Tarn."

Mela slipped on the slick surface, but Eln pulled her up like a sack. "But how could Asel come up this trail?"

"When she was young and first found the island, she brought the Enre and she explored every peak, every niche. But that was long, long ago. For many years, we've carried her up in a litter."

Mela wished they were carrying her. Late afternoon, soaked by perspiration, buffeted by winds, she was relieved to hear Eln say, "We're here." Mela sat down heavily as the Enre around her dropped their packs.

"It's so windy up here," Mela said loudly, feeling she had to shout against the gusts.

"It always is. And we usually get a good storm at night." She said this as if she were describing a hearty dinner or wonderful music soon to come. Mela raised her eyebrows. "Asel loves violent storms, and this island has plenty of them. They remind her of sierent below—storms that could scour a cliff and suck boulders across a continent."

Mela grimaced. "I've heard the descriptions."

"Think of how Asel feels about it. If as a child you'd slept every night to the sounds of sierent, you'd miss them, too. And, unlike her years below—" and here Eln made a soft sound— "Asel has a fire to warm her as she hears the winds."

They entered tunnels that had been enlarged into a series of wide rooms. The Enre who served Asel had prepared a meal. They sat down and ate it next to her quarters.

"Asel slept a great deal today," an Enre said with an air of reverence. "She took a little food this afternoon."

"Perhaps she will be able to at least greet Mela."

They finished the meal, then Eln lifted a leather door hanging and led her into Asel's room. "Remember, you must have the right spirit before you enter. Nothing can happen in you . . . until you have come to your absolute limit."

The smell of the fire was heavy in the air; winds beat against a hanging on the opening. "She does not hear well at all," Eln said. "She insists on lying next to the opening with just the leather between her and the storms."

"How can we hear each other then?"

"Asel cannot speak. Only a little Yette at times." Mela felt for the walls, trying to orient herself. She had asked to meet with Asel, but now all she wished was to touch her, pray, and return quickly to Kelerai.

An Enre who had been tending Asel got up, took Mela's hand and led her to the pallet, as if to an altar. She said loudly enough, "She's awake."

Mela's mouth twitched. She had no idea what to say, and she wasn't sure she wanted this fearful woman awake so quickly. As she knelt beside Asel's bed, she was shaking.

"Touch her," Eln said. Mela moved her knees forward to the thick furs on which Asel lay, groping her fingers forward to find her shoulder. She worked her way down to her wrist and said both aloud and in Yette, "I am Mela."

The wrist turned slowly, the hand rising till it weakly grasped hers. Asel said in Yette on Mela's palm, "They have told me."

"I am honored you would see me."

Asel did not respond. Mela hesitated. Asel's arm and hand felt like membranes stretched over bones. What could she say to this frail wraith? Finally, aloud and in Yette, she slowly said, "The prophecy. The Blind Princess. What truly does it mean?"

Asel's fingers arced like tent poles above Mela's wrist, tapping out laboriously, "Auret said it. 'A Blind Princess will take the light to Aliare.'"

"Yes," Mela said urgently, "but what does it mean? Did he say anything else?"

Her response was the Yette flick of a thumbnail—"No."

Mela felt tears in her eyes. What good was this? If Auret had said anything more, her old mind had already set the story into the well-worn words Mela had heard all her life. But in desperation, she asked, "Am I the Blind Princess? Do you think I am the one?"

Asel's thumb and forefinger reached out and trapped Mela's little finger, a move which meant, "You are held by unseen wings."

Touched by the hope and gentleness of Asel's kindly message, Mela's tears increased. She dared not ask for more and even wondered if Asel might not be a bit senile. But then the old bones tight on her finger released it, turned and tapped out, "Only Auret knows. Wait for him."

Mela didn't understand. She was trying to think of a question that made sense when she felt Asel's fingers moving again. "Wait here," she said. "By the storms." Then the ancient fingers slid off her palm and down to her side. Asel's breathing changed and Mela realized she had returned to her sleep.

She sat beside the old woman for a long time, wondering if she would awaken. She did not. Finally Mela stood, and Eln held her kindly by the shoulders.

"What did she say to you?"

Mela's hand made a little jittery motion in the air, as if she were still communicating in Yette. "She said I should wait here. By the storms."

That night, Mela slept fitfully on furs Eln had placed for her beside Asel. Winds beat against the leather coverings, but no full-blown storm came. She was acutely aware of Asel beside her. Each time Mela would awaken, she'd wonder if Asel really meant for her to be lying here.

Asel slept till late in the morning, then ate only a little and went back to sleep. Mela meditated and prayed and spoke only a little to the Enre.

Late in the afternoon, Asel awoke again. She slowly lifted her arm toward Mela and planted one word on her palm: "Seek." Then she slept again.

Late the next night, Mela was awakened by a clap of thunder; rain was pounding the leather by her ear, and she realized it had entered her dreams. The storms of sierent had been tearing at her in a shallow shelter in Tarn. She tried to think of warm and lovely things to break away from the dread she felt from the dream, but the rain dominated her thoughts. She feared going back to sleep.

Two more days and nights passed. Only one more time did Asel say anything to her. It was early morning, when Mela did not expect Asel to be awake. Her old hand found Mela's under the furs and said simply, "Wait."

But Mela wondered, *For what? Once, as a little girl, I had sight. Now it is gone. After that, at least I had a life of music and touch and taste. But what's next? Am I to be driven into the rifts and lose what I have? Must the failures of the kingdom be weighted on my small back?*

The Enre led Mela in worship and prayer with a rite in which Mela had participated many times before. Eln sat opposite her and asked: "What is the weakest thing in the world?"

"A child," Mela answered.

"Who was the weakest child?"

"Auret. He descended into darkness. He was battered and crushed."

"Who is stronger than the stars?"

"Auret."

Eln placed in her hands the traditional pieces of dried meat. Then, before Mela was to eat, she asked, "Who is weak in the world?"

"Mela," she responded, and she ate all that was in her hand.

The nightmare came the fourth night. Mela had been sleeping through another thunderstorm, and the loud claps and pelting rain kept merging with her dreams. Suddenly the quakes that had taken her mother loudly split the ground at Mela's feet. She looked down into gaping darkness. Loose dirt crumbled beneath her and she felt herself sliding, then plummeting down and down and down. She struck something hard and jerked herself upright.

She stood quivering. Loose, wet dirt was sliding onto her shoulders, threatening to smother her. She struggled forward but felt trapped. Then her skin spasmed, for the loose dirt covering her was wriggling. In panic, she wrenched herself away, wildly brushing at herself. She heard water at her feet and began convulsively splashing it all over her body.

Ahead were floating colors. Flowers. Red and white

blossoms, thick, lovely, coming toward her, affixing themselves in her hair. The soft bowers piled themselves in great heaps on her head and flowed down her back. But then they began to get heavier. She felt legs forming in the blossoms, many, many legs stretching out, exploring, reaching down to her scalp and puckering the skin on her neck.

She was trying to scream. In an attempt to scrape the things off she leaped forward into a dense wall of thorns. She burst through on the other side, bleeding, but the red and white mass of squirming legs was still on her head and back and crawling now toward her face and belly. A broken rock jutted out of the formation. She thrust herself upon it, ramming the things against its hard surface, shoving her face and body against it, trying desperately to make air rip through her throat in a scream.

She collapsed. She looked up and the broken rock had a face, a man's face. The things were slithering over it. They were off her and on him, the horrible things crawling on his face. His expression was an agony, but his eyes locked on Mela's, as if he had come from all time to do this for her.

She was suddenly in a field, thick blossoms in her hair. She ran across it, buoyant. Freed. And she awoke. Mela lay, heart pounding, jaw clenched. The horrors of the depths that always haunted her had clutched her in embodiments more horrible than any of her conscious imaginings. She remembered all of the dream vividly. Yet its strange effect was a buoyancy lifting her and inviting her past the horror toward strong, astringent rays of light purging her repugnance and dreads.

She lay with both arms out in prayer. As she reached out to the light, she sensed the center was shifting. Something new, she realized, was being born. Joy was pumping a physical energy through her. *Clean!* she thought. *Clean! Clean!*

From one angle, she thought, nothing made sense at all. But from another, all that mattered had become clear.

When Asel stirred hours later, Mela was still wide awake. She reached over to the old woman's hand, and with a light dance of her fingers said, "He came."

Asel touched her palm with a light tap of the thumb: "Yes?"

"What is love?" Mela asked. "A sweet word? Or a roaring wind scouring putrefaction?" She held Asel's thin hand with both of hers.

"It's also light cleansing away death!"

Asel grasped her little finger as she had before, and Mela could not stop rushing with her other hand to say in Yette: "Auret took the horrors from me." She told Asel all the dream, and all the wriggling things that had been eating her soul. "He took them on himself," she said in wonder. She told her of lying through the night in prayer. "I kept hearing, 'You are my child. You are my child.' It vibrates in me now like the string of a bow."

Asel turned herself ever so slightly, then with a surprising energy tapped out, "You are a princess. Not because you are related to me, but because you are loved by Auret."

Mela smiled and said in Yette on her arm, "The loathsome things crawling on me—they were more than my terrors. They were also my rebellions."

The Chosen

After nearly half a year on the island, once again Mela rode with the four Enre toward an unknown shore. As the boat's bottom scraped, they leaped out and dragged the little craft over fat, round rocks till it rested with other boats from a little village.

Eln described the village to Mela, saying she could see Yosha's tent by the water. The village lay on a flat, rocky coast with no caverns or soft cliffs for tunneling. Yet it had plenty of trees for substantial huts. Not the Askirit way, Eln pointed out, but effective. The abundant food was Askirit fare: mussels, clams, fish of all sorts, and even sea otters and seals.

They had been told Yosha might be here. The last thing Asel had said before she left was that Mela must seek out Yosha. This was the fourth village they had tried.

A phalanx of guards stood sentry some distance from Yosha's tent. They allowed the women to pass, but at the tent itself, an old man challenged them.

"We are here to see Yosha," Eln said.

"Isn't everybody? You're a little late." He said his name was Kelse and he spoke in a kindly way, but firmly, as if he had been in charge of the king's details for a very long time.

"But no one is waiting to see him." Mela heard behind them sounds of men in boats and children playing on the shore.

"The villagers have already seen him. When Yosha comes to a village, everyone wants to touch his hand, to get his blessing. And he gives it to everyone. He can't lift himself off his litter, and his voice can't last the day. But he blesses them, every one."

"We were sent here by Asel. And we too would like his blessing."

Kelse thrust his head forward, studying Eln. "You will get it, I'm sure," he said respectfully. "But he has a custom. As each person in a village comes to touch him, he senses those with spiritual power. He invites them to stay. Maybe just two or three, perhaps only one. They stay with him—to wrestle with the powers."

Eln raised her chin and puckered her mouth. "Is that what they are doing in the tent? Praying?"

"It's Yosha's work. It's what he does every day."

Eln dropped to her knees. "Then we will join him." Mela and the other Enre knelt beside her and began praying for the village. Mela prayed for Yosha and those in the tent with him, and then for Asel and for Leas and her father. She gave praise and worshiped the Maker.

Still they remained kneeling. She started reciting psalms, one of which began: "Your prayers are one small wave on an ocean of prayers, and many waves move an ocean." *Yes,* she thought, all around her, rising in great swells, were the prayers of the Enre and others, rushing like surf toward the tent.

She remembered also, "Your prayers are one coal in a great, glowing fire." *Yes,* she thought, hot magma was now flowing from the tent to make her own heart burn with compunction.

"Your prayers are one quivering leaf on a mighty tree." *Yes,* she thought, she also felt her weakness. She was a quaking leaf, but part of a living, fruitful, mighty tree.

Mela was amazed that the day was nearly gone when they were finally led into the tent. Two persons were coming out and Eln said as they passed, "A young man and an old woman. Their faces are like ours—weary but exultant."

As they stood before Yosha's litter, Eln tapped Mela's shoulder, signaling for her to speak. Before she could, Yosha said, "Come, touch my hand."

She went to the sound of his voice, knelt, and found his sleeping fur, then his hand. It was old and bony, but strong enough to grip hers as he pronounced a blessing on her. "You have been praying with us," he said, breathing shallowly, as if each phrase were an effort.

"I didn't know kings did this. Such prayer is a wonder."

"It is the most important work of kings. And by far the most difficult."

He lay back as if to catch his breath, then rose a bit on his elbow. "It's no easier when you're old, you know. It's still a terrible wrestling with him who is hammering and gouging and shaping me into what he wants. Often I cry out for him to stop, but he never, never does." He eased himself back onto his litter. "It's an agony, a great work, the necessary work."

She moved closer to him. "I am Mela."

"I know," he said immediately. "You are the chosen." She shifted uneasily and her hand slipped away from his. "For generation after generation, I have waited. No one could take the light to Aliare, for it was sealed. But now comes the fullness of time. Now come the quakes and the rifts. Now comes one who is chosen."

Mela was amazed at his certainty. "The proverb and the princess," he said. "We have waited long."

She resisted simply accepting his judgment. "I am surely weak and blind. But I do not know who I may confound."

"That will be seen. You yourself must decide if you are truly chosen." Though his breathing was labored and he spoke in little spurts, resting between each sentence, she was amazed at his strength.

"You seem so much more vigorous than Asel."

He tapped in Yette on her palm, "Oh? Not so!" He laughed a tiny, weak laugh. "Asel has greater power. Perhaps she is already more into the next world, and I am lagging behind." His voice was full of affection as he said, "She promised to return from her island soon. But perhaps she will go ahead from the crags into the next worlds. . . ." His voice trailed off.

She sat beside him, listening to his breathing until he started, as if he had dozed. "What did Asel tell you?" he asked.

"She said you would go with me to the rifts, if I asked."

"I will. What else did she say?"

"She said hard things."

"Hard things must be said."

Her hands, flattened in front of her like taut wings, glided vigorously back and forth one on the other. "Asel said that I could not be shielded from the duties of royalty."

The old king took a deep, sympathetic breath. "Yes. You've heard the saying, 'We must all perform impossibilities!'" His hand crept toward hers, then trapped her little finger in the same way Asel had. "Every great venture, you know, is also a nightmare." She nodded assent, and then he said, holding her little finger tightly, "But didn't Asel say anything tender to you?"

She took his hand in both of hers. "Yes. The same as you just did. 'You are held by unseen wings.' "

—— The Procession ——

Hands cupped in the river for a drink, Mela thought she heard the sound of tiny bells. She paused, heard them again, and then the sound of horses.

"They're coming."

"I don't see anything," Eln said.

"The blind have an advantage with sounds." Mela lifted the water to her lips.

They were at the river near Korbas, having slowly traveled there with Yosha. Messages had been sent to Aris and Kelerai that Mela would carry the light to Aliare and that she was awaiting all who would join her.

"What desolation in these mountains," an Enre said.

"Majestic desolation!" Eln responded.

"I see the king is coming," another Enre said. "A great cloud of dust."

As they drew closer, Eln described to Mela the procession approaching. White and black horses, red plumes above their heads, carried ladies dressed in golden finery and men in blue and scarlet. But Mela did not need described the ringing of the belled bridles, the sounds of small harps and flutes. Behind the mounted leaders came wagons and then hundreds of walkers singing and shouting and laughing.

The horses at the front veered off toward Yosha's tent, but others came toward them until she heard her father's greeting. Leas called out exuberantly, "People for generations have waited for this! Half of Aris and Kelerai have come with us."

"It's remarkable!" Ashdel declared.

Mela walked toward them slowly, afraid of the horses. "You must look magnificent up there," she said.

"They are the king's mounts," Ashdel said, her voice like the little bells on her bridle. "We rode in the place of honor."

Mela grimaced. She could not resist saying, "Because you are going down into the rifts with me?" Ashdel did not reply.

"We'd better water your horses," Eln said, taking Ashdel's reins.

Mela turned from her sister as they dismounted. She felt as if she were Ashdel's possession, a thing to be used or discarded. But her father trembled as he embraced her. He again offered to accompany her, but she turned to Leas and said, "Perhaps Leas has changed his mind and you will both go with me."

Before Leas could answer, representatives of the king rode up. They greeted Mela with deference and made a great ceremony of presenting her with a regal lamp, not only ornate and beautiful but ingeniously crafted with special fuels to last a remarkably long time. Then they explained the calendar of events approved by the king. Solemn ceremonies, pronouncements, a night of singing ballads of old Tarn, a pageant presented by the finest musicians. The festivities would last three days.

A man proclaimed, "We want you to go with the national spirit within you."

"And how many are here to accompany me?" she asked. "All the songs, you know, have the Blind Princess leading thousands into the darkness of Aliare."

The man pulled back the reins on his horse. "That's songs, not prophecies. Perhaps some from all these crowds . . ."

His voice died out and Mela turned again to Leas. "With this great company, how many will go with me?"

He stood silent for a long time. Finally he said, "Only three. They, too, fulfill the prophecy. Jesk, Delin, and Lysse."

She felt as if all the blood had drained from her face, but she simply said, "Bring them to me." Then she stalked off toward Yosha's tent.

Kelse readily let her in. She knelt down by Yosha's litter and asked if they could dispense with the festivities and immediately go ahead with their plans.

"Now is an excellent time," Yosha said.

The king's courtier stood just inside the flap. When he heard Yosha's words, he stepped inside. "The king has approved a celebration, with solemnities and festal events—that this great crowd might inspire and assure these blind, brave Askirit youth. Perhaps, if it is well in your sight, King Yosha, we could proceed with them as the king has wished."

"Where is the king?"

"He cares for vital matters at the King's House in Aris."

Mela bent down and whispered to Yosha, "Asel said he wouldn't come because he'd be humiliated."

Yosha's voice sounded strained and very old as he said to Mela, "Tell the king's man what Asel told you."

Mela repeated it, then Yosha said, "Does the king wish to learn courage and humility? Tell him one learns humility through humiliations!"

The king's man had moved close to Yosha, straining to hear his words. The old man had fallen back on the furs and was breathing heavily. He lay quietly for a time, then finally added, "I'm just the old king. I don't decide things anymore. But do you know who decides this? Mela. She's the one who's going down. She decides."

At noon the next day, Mela stood at the edge of the rifts, her friends close by, a great company assembled below. Through the night she had prayed as much as she had slept, throwing rebellions into the fire and opening her spirit to the tasks for a quivering leaf.

That morning, she had spoken to her three friends. Neither

Delin, Lysse, nor Jesk could be dissuaded from taking the risks with her. She had also called Leas to her, and when he tried to apologize, she dismissed the attempt with a wave of her hand. "I am through with self-pity. Each must be called to his own task. Even the Enre, who don't fear the rifts, are called elsewhere."

And she spoke to her father, sharing with him all her fears and perplexities. "I am the chosen. I sense it, as if I am with child." She took his hands. "All through the night, I have been thinking of the wonders of birth. Have you ever witnessed a birth?"

"I witnessed yours. It filled me with wonder."

"Every birth is extraordinary."

"Yes," her father agreed, "Eshtel gives the miracle in its time, in weakness and blood and agony—and hope."

"And sacrifice," Mela added. "Even death." Once, she had been with a young woman who, after two days of hard labor, had died. "It is the mother's supreme moment. She takes the risk. She braves death, and others cannot do it for her. The great warriors stand mute beside her pain. Even the Enre cannot bring the child faster. From pain and blood and mucus and trembling limbs comes a great and holy event. An eternal—eternal!—soul is born."

Her father embraced her. "And what will be born of your faith?"

"A nation's redemption—if Eshtel wills."

At rift's edge, she asked Ashdel to recite a familiar psalm, which ended with the words:

> *"Eshtel uses the maimed*
> *when the strong avert their eyes."*

Then Mela declared, "I will not be battered by doom!" She pointed to the sun. "Instead, I will affirm the glory. You who have eyes—do you see it? Glory is crammed into every leaf, every crag."

She went over to Yosha, who was lying on his litter. The ancient king said to her, "It is clear as a struck bell. The call vibrates in you. You are the chosen."

She nodded. "I wish I could escape it. But it also lures me with new passion."

"Remember that you will not always feel the power. At times, you will be terrified, and you will wonder if all the prayers and affirmations were not wisps in your mind."

"I will remember."

"Remember also that many years ago, Maachah the priest spoke of the great absurdity. The absurdity that everything hinges on our little prayers."

Mela kissed his thin, bony cheek, picked up the ornate lantern which burned with a flame she could not see, and began to lead her blind friends into the rifts.

Chapter 4.

—— The Rooster ——

Dust blew against Geln and the other guards watching the procession at the rifts. Stiffly at attention, he blinked dust particles from his eyes as he watched the old king at the rifts' edge with brightly clad royals and the blind students' families.

Pathetic, he thought, *sending four innocents down into that.* Amused, he smiled and rubbed his thumb on the butt of his spear, his left palm nesting the atlatal that could launch it.

This high-spirited procession, which had brought him back to his village, had stirred Geln's passions. All the panoply—the impressive ranks, the colors and martial music—created images of where his own powers might lead. He knew the kingdom was vulnerable. Since the Askirit had first climbed to the surface, their enemies had been only hunger, lions, and storms; the military faced no threat and had grown soft.

Divided loyalties offered Geln many opportunities. All who long ago had climbed out of the darkness of Aliare had claimed they longed to follow Auret. Yet they had passed on to their children many tribal beliefs and customs. Geln had discovered which soldiers flew Askirit pennants and worshiped in the temple but did not believe.

The possibilities for intrigue raced his blood, but Geln bided his time. He took orders, coolly accepting others' authority. But now that he had gained a little rank, he started ordering others to do his bidding.

The king was coming down from the rifts; Geln's squad was ordered to escort him into the royal encampment by the river. He stood at attention as Yosha's litter was carried past. The royal face, wet from tears, looked impossibly old and frail. *The king,* Geln thought, *not flesh but legend.* Here, being carried past him, was the actual man who had once been as young as he and had entered leviathan's maw. *The man was born below,* he thought, *fought wars below, became king below.* The frail body passing him was an astonishment.

Yet Yosha was also his enemy.

He wondered what it meant that Yosha—the legend, the friend of Auret—had been peering into the rifts of Korbas. And what it meant that he who held his carving stood guard over him. What conjunction of powers was here?

At commands to follow the king's retinue, he spun around smartly and stepped forward. Scores of soldiers flanked the procession, and Geln saw Enre in strategic positions alertly scanning the crowds. The hundreds of trudging feet raised such a cloud of dust Geln thought it might choke the little river.

Children ran alongside, clamoring to see the legend.

They were let through the ranks, and one boy shyly touched him. "Are you Yosha? Really, really Yosha?"

The lined, aged face came alive with a smile and said softly that, yes, he was Yosha, and perhaps one of them would one day do greater exploits than he ever had.

"When you got swallowed by leviathan, what did it smell like?" asked a little girl. "I'd hate getting swallowed!"

Yosha started to laugh, and before he could reply, the children began singing a tune children had sung for generations:

> *"Kjotik! Leviathan!*
> *You make us tremble.*
> *We're just food for your belly.*
> *But Yosha said,*
> *'Eat this, Kjotik!'*

Yosha said,
'Choke on this, Marauder!'
He spiked your mouth with claws.
He twisted your tongue;
he stung it with selcrit.
Toothless Marauder!
Go back to the sea.
Go back.
Go back.
Go back to the sea.
Never return.
No, never return!"

The children kept repeating the chorus, "Go back, go back, go back to the sea," for it was a lively, happy tune. Yosha smiled, no longer embarrassed that the song stretched the truth. Years ago the king would have explained that he hadn't made Kjotik toothless, that the great sea monster had kept its many rows of teeth and had simply spat him out. But now he cared about correcting things far more vital.

"Children . . . ," Yosha said so weakly they strained to hear. "You know, little ones, I was spat out by Kjotik. But much, much greater, I was freed from darkness. Auret touched our eyes. He gave us light." Yosha held out his hand to a little boy. "He wants to touch your eyes too, and yours, and yours," he said, smiling at several little girls.

Geln couldn't keep from grimacing at this old fool prattling at children about light when they stood in the brightness of morning. But he was awed by Yosha's past, when in Aliare's darkness the king had worn a belt full of poisonous keitr, skillfully launching at his enemies the little messengers of death. Geln longed to trade his spear and blade for such a belt. Who wouldn't be awed by this ancient one whispering to the urchins of Korbas, this desiccated warrior who sang of dancing with the light, this frail monarch so weak and old and used up but full of strange powers?

Yet he's used up, Geln thought. *He's used up, and it's time for the legend to feel the weight of the powers he once defeated.*

It was expected of Geln while stationed in his home village that he would visit his family. To avoid talk, he was now walking briskly up the path to his home. When he rounded the corner, however, he was startled by the sight of a large red rooster pecking and scratching on the trail in front of him. He markedly slowed his pace. Another rooster—this one small but brilliantly colored—was imperiously leading some hens over the rise. In addition, the old cock he had kicked was near the entrance, moving with dignity and pomp, his head snapping right and left to evaluate everything in his domain.

In all, he saw six roosters and scores of hens scratching the ground, clucking and flapping their wings in flurries of dust. He slowly walked on and had come to a stop several paces from the entrance when his mother stepped out and confronted him.

"I heard the commotion out here." She waited for him to speak.

He stared back at her, refusing to say a word. The chickens had dispersed, though the roosters eyed him from their posts. His mother turned to look at them, as if in satisfaction at their stance. Finally she said, "You've been gone years. Haven't heard a word."

"I'm here now." He moved toward the home. "I'll stay here tonight."

"Why?" she demanded as he stepped past her. She moved briskly beside him, grabbed his shoulder, and spun him around to face her. "Why?"

He looked at her without expression. "I'm your son."

"Don't I know that! Don't I know it every morning when the cock crows. Don't I know that you are this great cloud over all of our lives!"

He twisted away as if to leave, but she grabbed his shoulder again and said, "No, you don't! Stay at home. Stay as long as you like. But talk to me about the rifts. Talk to me about what people say about you. Talk to me about the light."

He grinned at her. "We're standing here in the light. We worship the light because our ancestors could only dream of it. Now we're in it—and it's only . . . light. Only fire that burns, and rays that heat this dusty, miserable town at the edge of the pit."

His mother was breathing heavily, her lower jaw shaking. She restrained herself from speaking but kept her eyes locked on his.

The slight shaking beneath her mouth reminded him of a time when he'd been a little boy. She had stormed in at a group of older boys who'd been bullying him and had sent them scurrying. Then she'd lifted him into her arms and after a long time had gotten him smiling about something he couldn't remember. The memory triggered flashes of other moments with her, but his expression did not change.

"Don't criticize the town," she said. "It's not the town, and it's not the rifts, and it's not me or Bek or Delas. You've just given away your soul, that's all. Despite all my prayers for you, despite all the times you've heard of the Maker's love, despite everything, you've thrown it all away. And for what? For what?"

"You have no idea, woman. You know nothing of the powers in the world. Many powers, many truths. Powers to stifle, powers to energize."

"There is only one true power!" she declared hotly.

"You have dug yourself into a very little hill here, woman. Your kind of truth has always crushed those who wouldn't mouth your words. Think of the pit into which our ancestors threw their enemies. Think of the keitrs launched at their throats."

Geln was a tall young man, standing a full head above his mother. He turned abruptly, determined to step in through the opening.

"The way of light is love, not death," she said, reaching out and clamping him in a tight embrace. He felt her tears on his chest, but he did not raise his arms to hug her back. His mind raced with plans of visiting with Yosha, to let the king taste of the night.

Geln awoke wondering why his right arm felt numb. He tried to move it but found his wrists were fastened together behind him. He looked around in the darkness but could see nothing.

He waited, listening carefully, evaluating what might have happened. He was under a blanket, lying on sandy soil, the side of his face heavy on the dirt.

The sky began to lighten. Colors appeared on the horizon. As dawn broke, he made out the form of a woman beside him. She sat cross-legged in meditation, facing the light.

Geln studied her as the day brightened. She was not much older than he, tall for a woman, peaceful yet, he judged, tightly disciplined—like an Enre.

Enre! The Enre had taken him! They had come in the night, he realized, and had used their skills to carry him off. But how, he wondered, had they learned of his plans?

The blanket was jerked away, and he instinctively pulled his knees into his chest. "Sit up," a woman commanded. Her strong hands grasped his shoulders and pulled him upright.

Geln surveyed the flat terrain. Women were stationed strategically, each alert, watching him. All of them Enre, he thought—mostly young, none of them old, and all lean and tough and deadly.

An older Enre walked toward him and made a small motion with her hand. His bonds were loosed. She stood above him, studying his face. She seemed in no hurry, as if she might stand studying him till nightfall.

"How can you abduct me like this? I am a soldier of the king."

"And I am Varial."

He caught his breath, then hated his visible reaction. She did not have to explain that Varial did whatever she chose.

"What interest could the Enre have in a common soldier?"

"We know a great deal about you, Geln. You know how unstable the military can be."

The statement alarmed him. Varial had ears everywhere.

"It's not only your loyalty to the kingdom that brings us. It's your loyalty to the light."

Geln struggled to his feet. "You're listening to tales of old boyhood pranks in the rifts. How can you impugn my worship when I do all—all—that is required?"

She smiled and moved a half step closer, studying his face as soldiers do before single combat. "Every spy does everything required." She held his gaze, then made another motion with her hand.

A woman walked toward them. It was his mother.

Geln swallowed, determined to control himself, to take the initiative. He glared, then said, biting off the words and spitting them out, "How does a mother betray her own son?"

"Betray? You're a wayward son, but I haven't delivered you up to the judges." She held her hands toward him, palms up. "I am a widow. I am powerless. But I can ask for the Purgation."

He tightened his hands into fists. The Purgation was seldom used and often ridiculed, a ceremony to cast out furies from the possessed.

Asta's sun had become bright and hot. Varial motioned for Geln to sit down. She dropped down herself, facing him, and all the Enre moved into position behind her. They formed a V whose apex was Varial. "We are a tip of a spear," she said, settling into position. "We will not rest until light pierces your soul."

Varial quoted from the liturgy:

"Light!
Nothing pollutes it.

> *Light purifies.*
> *Light draws the waters upward.*
> *Light lifts you to itself."*

The Enre behind her all echoed, "Light purifies and lifts you."

Varial kept repeating the words, eyes locked on Geln's, hands tent-like in prayer like the Enre behind her. He listened with dull anger to these ritual words he knew so well and had so often mouthed.

It was noon before Varial stepped away and another Enre took her place. The new Enre gave Geln a drink of water, then recited praises to the Maker. He felt the spiritual force of these scores of women wedged before him, hammering at his soul.

Despite the hot sun above, another Enre moved into position and repeated holy words, then another Enre.

Unexpectedly, the face before him became that of Delas. Geln began to say something, but his sister severely shook her head no. She was a young woman now, with long, black hair and an intelligent face. She looked as tired as he felt as she quoted:

> *"Follow Auret.*
> *He breaches the darkness.*
> *Fear him!*
> *He conquers death.*
> *Choose him!"*

Delas repeated it over and over again, her face a blaze of perspiring determination. The words were a noisy buzz, all his childhood religion crammed at him. His emotions shut down; he was a stone under the hot sun.

As Geln watched the mouth of his sister moving up and down, something deep within was screaming in a barren, empty place. Why did they bring Delas here? He wanted to reach out and topple her, laugh at her, throw sand over this foolish wedge of women aligned against him.

Varial stepped into Delas's place. It was nearly dark, and she told him to rise. He did so unsteadily.

"You do not fear the rifts, do you?"

He did not answer.

"We do not fear the rifts, either. We will go there now."

By the time they stood at the rifts' edge, it was fully dark. The Enre lighted torches which flared brightly, illumining the steep, rocky descent. Small, dark figures of animals scuttled below into the shadows.

Varial held up a thick rod of flint. "The Varial who is now our queen long, long ago struck flint above the darkness of Dorte. She started liberation for that evil land."

With that, she struck one flint against the other, producing a spray of sparks, which fell away into the darkness. She continued sending off showers of sparks as she declared:

> "Did Eshtel make all creatures in Aliare?
> Things that crawl and walk and fly?
> Things with teeth in the darkness?
> Things with wings in the night?
> Yes! The Maker has made many worlds.
> Wonders of the Night world.
> Wonders of the Day,
> Worlds and worlds and worlds,
> Astounding worlds!
> Praise the Maker.
> He showers us with light.
> Praise the Maker.
> Flee from the pit."

She then led them down into the rifts. The Enre knew the terrain well, descending from ledge to rock and down narrow declines in a steady, determined pace. They moved steadily until Geln realized they were assembling above the statues.

Varial walked up to him. "We are not unaware of what was made here, of what brought the Maker's wrath on all the world. And we are not unaware of the rising darkness."

Many of the Enre had been carrying loads of dry brush and wood and now they made a great pile of it. Varial thrust in her torch, watched it flare up and declared, "Light extinguishes darkness. It destroys those who devour." The conflagration lighted the great cavern and Geln backed away from its heat as the Enre sang holy songs.

The fire subsided into red coals. The Enre pushed them into the void, watching them plunge brightly into the darkness. Then Varial raised her torch, and she and the other Enre descended to the altar and the ancient statues. Standing before the stone men and women, Varial said, "Before Aliare was formed, you were a stench to the Maker."

All of the Enre then smashed the statue until it lay in an uneven heap in the shadows of their torches. They flung the pieces into the void.

"The light is greater than the darkness," Varial said. They then cast all their torches into the void. Geln watched them flame wildly for an instant, then blink out below, leaving them in darkness. "We do not fear the dark."

Geln felt strangely disoriented, shivering in the night. The Enre led him up out of the rifts and left him there at the edge to find his own way home.

—— Legend ——

Geln stood in the firelight outside the king's tent, waiting to be summoned. It was not yet dawn.

He had fled the rifts in great haste. After racing home to retrieve the carving, which he found where he'd hidden it, he'd hurried to his tent. Despite aching joints and weariness, he had forced himself to bathe and don a fresh uniform. Then he placed the carving in a rich leather case.

He heard someone moving in the royal tent. Suddenly, an old man with long white hair in disarray burst heavily out through the flap. "What's this?" the old man demanded as he noticed Geln. He blearily looked him over.

Geln was taken aback, expecting a young orderly, not this hefty, disheveled man. "I was handed this carving by a courier," he said, repeating the story he'd used with the guards. "He had to get back to Aris—said I was to present it to the king personally. A gift from the royal family."

The old man motioned Geln closer to the fire and looked him up and down. His uniform was impeccable and he wore no weapons. "Stay right here," he said loudly enough for the guard to hear, then rushed off toward the latrine.

When he returned, he said, "The king won't wake until dawn." He made an attempt with his hand to straighten his hair, gazing sharply at Geln's face. "I'll call you when he's ready."

Dawn broke like a wide strip of fire on the horizon, accentuating Geln's chaotic feelings about his experiences with the Enre. *How futile,* he thought, *their hammering liturgies at me.* Yet they had succeeded in disconcerting him.

It was mid-morning before the tent flap was briskly thrown back and the old orderly emerged, now smartly attired, his hair carefully combed into place. "Give me the carving. I'll take it to the king." He stared coldly at Geln.

"I solemnly vowed I'd personally place it in his hands."

The man looked at Geln's shoulder patch, a burst of light over an arrow. "Come in," he said, holding open the flap.

Inside, a morning stew was bubbling. The frail form lying on the litter shifted position, and the old servant gently lifted the king into a sitting position. "This is the young man with the gift."

Yosha the legend, Geln thought. How could anyone be so old yet still alive? When he'd watched him at a distance with the children, his clear voice had carried some vigor; Geln was unprepared for how corpse-like he looked up-close.

The ancient king's eyes had trouble focusing as he turned his head toward Geln, but his voice came clear enough, though slow and labored. "Have you eaten?"

Geln was caught off guard.

"I hear you've been standing outside since before dawn. You must be hungry."

Geln had come to hand him the carving and leave, but he had to admit he hadn't eaten.

"Kelse, give him some stew."

The man ladled stew into a bowl and handed it to Geln. "Sit down, soldier," Kelse ordered.

Geln felt exceedingly awkward sitting in the king's tent eating stew as the two aged men silently waited. His hand trembled slightly as he spooned the food into his mouth, trying not to appear ravenous nor impolite, but wanting to get the ordeal over with. He finished and replaced the bowl, thanking his host.

"I seldom get to speak to a soldier," the king said. "I was a soldier, you know, long, long ago."

"Yes," Geln said respectfully.

"What is your name?

"Geln."

"I knew a Geln in Aliare. A fine man who launched many a keitr but never got scratched." He shakily lifted his arm toward Geln and turned his wrist. "See? This scar is from a keitr claw— when I gathered them in a cave. But Geln never got scratched."

At the king's insistence, the younger Geln touched the scar. Yosha said, "If you'd grown up in Aliare, you'd have found keitr gathering and launching them in combat a lot more challenge than your drills with spears and blades." The king spoke slowly, gathering force for every breath, and Geln wondered if his mind was much stronger than his body, the way he began rambling:

"Sometimes I envy the Enre. Most of what they learned below—their training, their mastery of the sea—they use it here in the light. But we old soldiers without keitr . . ."

He lapsed into silence. Geln was about to offer the carving to him when the king regained strength and began slowly, laboriously telling combat stories of the massive Laij invasion when he was a young man. He told of traitors and heroes, of visions and catastrophes. Kelse had slipped away quietly in the middle of one of the stories.

Geln could do nothing but sit and listen. His eyes wandered to the wardrobe hanging nearby, ordinary hunting and traveling clothes mixed with royal robes, with ribbing and flanges made to rustle impressively in the darkness. The king saw Geln's eyes on them and smiled. "The robes are silly up here. Below, in the darkness, they announced a royal personage. But up here I seldom wear them."

Geln looked through the tent flaps to the outside. It was already past midday. At the first pause, he held the carving out to him. "Here. It's a gift from Aris."

The old man turned his head and seemed to have trouble focusing. "Is it in a cover?" Geln tried to put it into his hands so he could leave, but Yosha said, "Take it out of its cover."

Geln's hands trembled as he slid the carving from the finely tooled leather case. He put it into Yosha's hands and stared, anticipating its power penetrating those old fingers and extending deep into his soul.

"It looks like something very precious to me long, long ago." He drew it closer to his face. "I once had a likeness like this of my mother and father and me." He was having difficulty seeing the details, drawing the carving to his face, then tilting it at an angle. "So long ago, in the dark. I saw it only by touch." He started his hand across the game board, and as he touched the elbow of the woman and planed upward toward her face, his motions were like a lover's caress.

Geln winced as Yosha's fingers touched her face and traced

the gouges across her left cheek and eye. The fingers stopped suddenly, then jerked back. Yosha's face remained impassive, fingers poised over the woman's figure. What was happening inside the old king? Geln's emotions, so long encased, were now splitting open. What would the dark powers do? He had brought the thing. Wouldn't it stop that old heart?

What if the king ordered Geln arrested? Why wouldn't he?

The gnarled fingers descended, slow as time, to the woman's face again. It touched her wounds carefully, as if assuaging them. Gently, Yosha traced each contour of her face, never flinching.

In the same manner, he touched the mutilated figure of the man, exploring his face. Then he stopped. "This disfigurement is not my father. Auret has shown me my father." He moved his hand over the baby with the crushed side and misshapen head. The process seemed interminable.

Without looking at Geln, without moving his fingers, the old king asked, "Where did you get this gift?"

Geln's mouth was as dry as the sands outside the tent.

The king, hearing no response, said, "How did you come by my mother and my father?"

Geln stood, twisted his fingers together and answered, "From a courier, from Aris." His voice emerged high and cracked, making the lie absurdly obvious.

The king tapped a little bell attached to his litter. "Sit down, Geln." Kelse stepped into the tent. The old servant glanced at the king, then eyed Geln sharply.

"Lay me down," Yosha said weakly, and Kelse lifted his thin body and placed it carefully on the litter, straightening the bedclothes. Geln thought of bolting from the tent, but the king said, "Kelse, this soldier will minister to me the rite of Death and Life."

The servant stared at Geln. Then he picked up a shrouded object and placed it on a stand by Yosha's head. He lighted a candle to place beside it.

"But I've never participated in that rite," Geln said, terrified. "I've barely heard of it."

"You need know nothing," Yosha said, his eyes closed, his hands on his chest. "Kneel beside the litter."

Geln did so. Kelse stepped outside, secured the flaps, then dropped the thick outer coverings, which plunged the tent into blackness except for the flickering candle. It threw shadows on the frail face lying so close and vulnerable.

Geln saw the shriveled king had few teeth; his old mouth moved oddly in the shadows as Geln looked directly down at it.

"Remove the shroud," the old lips said.

Geln pulled away the shroud to reveal a human skull mounted on an ornate base.

"Whose skull is this?" Yosha asked.

Geln looked from the old man's sunken face to the skull close to his nose. "I don't know."

"It is yours." Yosha moved his hands to his sides and gripped the edges of the litter.

Alarmed, Geln asked, "What do you mean?"

"The skull is yours. And it is mine. Put your fingers into those empty eye sockets." Geln did so. "How much do you think those eyes see?"

Geln did not attempt to answer the obvious. Yosha waited far beyond Geln's comfort, then commanded, "Ask the questions."

"But I don't know this ritual. What are the questions?"

"The questions in your soul will do. Ask them."

Geln settled back on his haunches, staring at flickering movements on the king's visage. Then he faced the great hollows of the skull's eyes. He had no questions except ones he could not voice. But, he thought, one does not refuse the king. He asked, "Why must we seek the light when we've already escaped the darkness?"

"Look into the emptiness of the skull's eyes. Look deep. These are your eyes."

Geln was unnerved by the quick response. He waited for him to say more, but Yosha lay with his lips moving soundlessly, until at last he said in a whisper, "What is your question?"

Yosha seemed almost to have stopped breathing. Geln hardly breathed himself as he asked, "Since climbing into the day, have you never felt again the weight of the powers you defeated?"

"I never defeated the dark powers!" Yosha said with surprising vigor. "Even when we came up from the darkness, even though we had kept our eyes alive by striking flint, still it was Auret who had to heal our eyes. Auret defeated the powers."

Then Yosha lay back and said, almost in a whisper, "The light is greater than darkness. Love is greater than hate." The old king turned his face toward Geln's. "Consider well the skull. I often do so myself. It has no flesh. It has no eyes. It is you. It is I, without the Maker."

Geln felt ensnared. The king seemed not at all senile. "What do you want of me?"

"I want nothing of you. But the light reveals you. Light streams down to illumine every beautiful thing, and every ugliness. Light is an awful thing, searing every vermin hiding in the dark."

The candle sputtered, then flared again. Geln felt he was going mad, looking down on this ancient face which uttered these terrible pronouncements. As he knelt level with the skull, he clamped his lips shut, determined to ask nothing more, his mind racing to develop a means of escape. He clamped both hands to his chest, pressing them tightly against the chaos within.

"I will ask you a question," Yosha said. "Who is Auret?"

Scores of ritual responses flowed through Geln's mind, but he said nothing.

"Auret holds together all that is made." Yosha spoke with great effort, rising on his elbows. "He flings the stars into the void, but he stoops to weep with a child. He is love. He walks through death and laughs in dazzling brilliance. He terrifies; he blazes in the center of all energies. He holds a seed in his hand, and his eyes are fire and ice."

Yosha spoke the last with such fervor that he sank back down amid the covers, his body trembling. Geln, still kneeling, dared not move, yet all his thoughts were on getting out of the tent.

The king's breathing grew slower and slower until Geln wondered if he were really breathing at all. He waited for a time, then held his hand above the old king's mouth. He felt no breath. Could he have died? He kept his hand there, and suddenly the king's chest shook, and he took another deep breath.

The king was alive. Yet into the maelstrom within Geln came the forceful insistence he should die, that when the king stopped breathing, Geln would be released. He would achieve what he had come here to do, he who was to convulse the world. It would be so easy to lift a cloth from the water pail nearby, a cloth heavy with water, and press it on Yosha's mouth and nose for a moment, to release the spirit of this ancient stick of a man.

His throat grew tight as his hand reached over to the bucket and slipped into the water. With his other hand he grasped the side of the carving, seeking its power which had so often coursed through him. He quietly lifted the edge of the cloth from the bucket and squeezed it, bit by bit, bunching it into his hands, keeping it low above the water line so the drips would not be heard.

Yosha slept, his mouth slightly open, his head to the side.

This is the only way, said the voices, *the only way out of this tent. The only way to regain power.*

He lifted the cloth higher, a few drips sounding in the pail. He began to move it toward the litter, his other hand on the carving.

As suddenly as a whip against flesh, he felt coursing through both hands, then through his eyes and all his body, an explosion of white light and a powerful grip on his wrists. Stunned, he called out to the old powers, to the energies from the carving. He dropped the cloth. Somewhere he saw a dense flock of dark birds rise with a raucous cry, flapping against wide streams of light slicing through dark clouds.

Yosha had awakened with a start. He lay breathing shallowly for a few moments, then turned to Geln. "Let me hold the carving."

Geln was afraid to touch it again, but the king repeated his command. Gingerly, he reached out and lifted the carving into Yosha's thin hands. Geln watched as once again the old man caressed the game board and touched the figure of the woman. He could see little in the dim candlelight—Yosha's fingers were a dark shadow moving over the woman's face.

He looked from the carving to Yosha. The frail king's expression startled him; it was serene, joyous, a smile broad and unmistakable.

After Yosha had meticulously explored every curve of the carving, he offered it to Geln. "Touch it. Feel the power of the light."

Geln reached out with one hand. He touched the face of the woman. It was smooth, whole, without a mark.

"Touch also the father's face." It, too, was whole, as was the baby.

The old king's eyes were closed again as he said, "You are Askirit. Didn't you know you were on holy ground?"

Awkwardly, raising himself on stiff legs, Geln got up. A cacophony of urgent voices screamed in his head, contrasting with a bittersweet longing in his chest. Geln felt like a piece of meat yanked by two hooks. The carving had betrayed him, and he longed to embrace its new form.

"Too late," a voice within urgently insisted. "You cannot touch that awful purity. It will destroy you like a weed in a fire."

He stepped back, staring at the carving lying by Yosha's head. "You are filthy," the voice insisted. "You are putrid. You would shrivel and die in that light."

Geln turned and pulled up the tent flaps. Night had come.

He peered into the darkness, then back at the candle now almost burned down. Outside, he heard something crack under a man's boot. Fear reached into him. He bolted through the flap and into the night.

—— The Void ——

Geln fled, stumbling through the night on the sand till he reached the dead tree by the tiny marsh. There he sat down heavily, his back against the decaying wood. Listening intently for pursuers, he heard nothing but a small animal at the stream and a faint voice in the distance.

He was utterly empty, except for the terror of the void.

He thought of the time Delas had tried so hard here to bring him back with her to eat chowder. But he'd felt driven to challenge the rifts. Now he could think of no destination at all. The forces of the king surely would hunt him down anywhere.

He sat stone-like, horrified, knowing he should get moving toward the mountains, but the void had swallowed his will.

A frog splashed behind him, then an odor assailed his nostrils. He bolted to his feet, recognizing the smell. He remembered the predatory roilings of the sands and the desperate motions of prey trying to keep from being smothered.

He sniffed and stared into the darkness. The terrain on both sides of the river was sandy, but away from the town, toward the far hills, was compact dirt and rock. He could scramble through the river till he reached solid ground, then bolt toward the hills.

Once, he'd lost his fear of the shriikes. They had been part of his power. But now the smell vividly brought back the memories of Kel and Parn racing away in terror.

He walked in the stream as quickly and quietly as he could,

cursing at every noisy splash. He slipped on a rock and fell in up to his waist, jerked himself up again and kept moving. He thought of getting out and racing along the shore, but visions of movements in the sand kept him in the water.

He stopped. He thought he'd heard a splash ahead. He stood stock still listening, hoping it was a frog or small animal, waiting a long time before moving again.

He heard a louder splash and a dragging of something heavy and then another splash, this one closer, and the snapping of a branch. Clearly, something was coming toward him.

Then he caught the scent again, the musky, sour smell.

He turned and headed as quickly as he could toward the town, cursing every reed that snapped and even the heavy sound of his breathing. He rushed till his breath came in painful gasps. What were the noises behind him matching his pace and gaining? He felt stalked like a hapless toad.

He looked up to the stars to pull down any faint rays of light to guide his way. As he stared, he saw directly ahead on a high knoll a huge, long form blocking the speckled sky. It stirred with a great whirring of insect wings. The mature shriike looked like a great, fat locust with extended head and a worm's body but stiff, jointed appendages with pincers beneath.

Suddenly, the thing rushed forward in a flurry of wings, turning its shovel snout and thick eye-stalks toward him. Geln bolted out of the water, heedless of the fact his feet were pounding across sand that could come alive any instant and knowing that the wings of that thing meant he was now nowhere safe. His legs pounded beneath him oblivious to direction until he realized too late that he was fleeing toward the rifts.

Forcing his legs to move yet faster, he raced in a wide angle so he could do a loop and recross the stream. When he'd made his turn, he started toward it but saw far off near the water what looked like another great bulk. The sour odor was now thick in the air. He realized with horror that not only was he being stalked, he was being herded by the things—herded toward the rifts.

Emptiness! All was emptiness and decay! The welcome of the dark had become the horrors of the void. The shriikes could play with him and the powers would have their revenge, they would satiate their hunger.

Another shriike whirred itself aloft toward him, then skidded into the sands, whirred up again, thin wings propelling its bulky body only so far till it hit the sands, squirmed forward, and struggled aloft again.

Blocked were the encampment, the town, the stream. He longed to meet an Enre now, to call out to Varial. How he wished they'd kept him captive!

Desperately, he tried to think of a place where people might be.

The huts of the barbarians.

Geln began running desperately through the night, hoping to reach one before he was intercepted. He plunged recklessly down a sharp grade, sprinted across a long clearing and grasped the edge of a hut where the skins came together over a post. He yanked at the thongs, knowing he had no time to waken the people inside. It wouldn't unlatch. He grabbed for his blade, felt an empty sheath and remembered his entering Yosha's tent weaponless.

The odors were near again. Were those the sounds of wings already? Desperately he bent down and bit hard on the thongs, chewing frantically, yanking his head back and forth. The thongs gave way; he spit out leather and slipped inside, pulling the heavy skin back against the posts.

He stood within, listening. The huts were long frames with leather stretched straight down in front, forming a triangle by angling down to the ground. He moved in utmost quiet toward the center, hunching down on hands and knees. The smell was unmistakable, and in the yard sounds of heavy bodies. He huddled quietly, scrunched down in a tight, compact ball.

Suddenly he felt strong fingers painfully gripping the back of his neck. "What are you doing here?" a man's voice hissed into his ear.

Geln could hardly speak. "Something's after me!"

"Sure!" the man said harshly.

"Can't you hear them out there? Things from the rifts. Sand shriikes. Can't you smell them?"

"Smells like you. You and your friends are here to pillage us."

At that moment came a great impact on the leather at the front, violently shaking the entire hut. The stocky man reflexively grabbed Geln by the shoulders, yanked him toward the hut's front, then threw him stumbling out into the yard.

Falling forward, Geln barely saw the large shapes around him, for his stumbling legs never hesitated but started churning in a dead run away from them. He was unaware of his direction until he realized he was moving toward, not away from, the rifts.

He kept running, sensing movements behind him. He wondered if he might get across the sand, then run in the gully along the rift's edge and somehow lose them in the hills.

Was it his imagination, or was the sand roiling off to his left? Did he sense movement in the sands behind him? His only hope was to reach a rocky ridge that could get him into the hills. Suddenly he was out of the sands and at the rifts, but confronted with a sheer rock formation too steep to climb. Wings sounded close by and the sand was clearly moving at his heels. Herded, he thought grimly, into the rifts, welcomed into the dark.

Jerking his head around, he searched the shadows for alternatives. Instead he saw above him, staring into his face, two oval red eyes at the ends of eye-stalks rooted in a gigantic snout.

He flung himself into the jaws of the rifts.

Geln stumbled and fell, scrambled up again. Damp air rose from below. He saw where they had herded him, toward the place of the statues. He darted in the opposite direction, plunging deeper into the darkness. He ran recklessly, not knowing his direction, and suddenly he was sliding nearly straight down. He was terrified of what chased him and terrified of being sucked into oblivion.

When he finally stopped to listen, all he could hear was the fast beating of his heart and his own heavy breathing. He dared not move but sat transfixed as time crawled slowly by.

He waited, it seemed forever, fighting sleep.

Finally, hearing and smelling nothing, he thought it at last must be morning above. He shakily stood in the darkness and tried to work his way back up. He began maneuvering the way he thought he had come but quickly realized he was disoriented.

He tried to ascend. For two days he tried every possible way to get back up, but he simply descended lower and lower.

Growing weak, he climbed a formation to reconnoiter but started slipping on slick rocks and into a muddy rush of water. He began tumbling down the wetness, clawing for a handhold, trying to dig in with his feet but speeding downward, rolling and flopping till suddenly he was plunged into a wide, running stream. It carried him along swiftly as he fought to keep his head above water.

The stream widened a great deal and kept rushing downhill. He continually thought he would drown, for this rush toward the depths of the planet bashed him against boulders and thrust him under the surface.

Why not drown? he thought. *I'm racing toward the underworld anyway, already shut out forever from the light.*

Suddenly he was flung out into the air, as if going over a waterfall. He flailed with his arms, clutching nothing, until his body splashed heavily into deep water.

Part Two

The littlest and weakest.
The blind and the broken.
These will confound the powers.

—A PROPHECY AMONG THE ASKIRIT

Chapter 5.

——— The Lamp ———

In the moist darkness just below the surface, the four young friends had already maneuvered themselves into an impasse. Tangled together against a mass of hard dirt and rocks, they groped with hands and feet to find an opening. Mela held the lamp tightly, its tiny pilot light hidden under thick flaps.

Lysse said, with exaggerated distinctness, "All those people above us—picnicking on the beautiful sands of Korbas . . ." She paused to accentuate her humor. "Every one of them really wants to be down here with us."

"Shut up," Jesk said good-naturedly. He was standing on tiptoe, hands stretched up high to locate a way over the blockage.

Lysse ignored his command. "I can hear them starting the festival up there. But they want to be down here with us. Jelna told me she couldn't stand missing all this."

"Here we are," Delin said, "blind and clumsy, carrying a lamp we can't see into a nightworld we may never find."

"You shut up too," Jesk said in his friendly, dry way. He was fumbling to find something in his multi-pocketed coat. They all wore coats that bulged front, back, and sides with food, clothing, weapons, and tools. But Jesk was a walking supply station, his oversize coat carrying ancient weapons and tools he had himself fashioned. He produced out of this expanse both a heavy little hammer and sharp little stakes. "We need to get higher." He drove a piton into hard dirt between boulders.

"Let me help you with that," Delin said.

Soon they had several tightly wedged and Jesk started up. Delin followed, then boosted Jesk even higher. Soon they heard Jesk declare, "Yes! It's open up here."

Delin came back down to boost up Lysse's crippled body. Mela gripped the ornate, octagonal lamp, climbing awkwardly with only one hand free at a time. Delin had offered to carry it for her, but she kept it tight against her, snuggled as securely as she had once nestled infants on long evenings with Grelsa.

They descended deeper and deeper until weariness forced them to set up camp in a deep cave. They spread out their gear and began eating.

"I wish we could make a fire," Lysse said.

"What would we burn?" asked Mela. She was leaning back against fibrous roots too moist to use as fuel.

"When we get down into Aliare," Delin said, "we'll find something. We have our flame to ignite it."

"Maybe fish oil would work," Jesk said, his voice rising. "We'll start the first fires they've ever seen! Barbarians, Askirit, Laij—they'll all see fire for the first time, and they'll have to believe! All the years of arguing over whether or not 'fire' and 'light' were just meaningless words from their ancestors—all that will be instantly over. They'll see it."

"Maybe," Lysse said. "Maybe not. Remember how they treated Auret."

Jesk had found small tracks and ridges in the dirt. He called Delin, who offered various guesses about their identity. Then he made one of his typical comments: "They're like the tracks of the Maker. Inscrutable. Little traces of something real that keep teasing our minds."

With water from her pack, Mela washed down the last of her meal, then numbly leaned back against the tangle of roots. "Even if sierent comes this high," she said, "it won't wake me up."

But something did awaken Mela. In her sleep she was vaguely aware of prickling sensations pulling at her hair and making her scalp tingle. She thrust a hand back at the nape of her neck, scratched and ran her fingers up like a rake into her hair.

Quick as a serpent's bite, something whipped around her fingers, entangling them, trapping them.

With her other hand, Mela reached behind her and grabbed at her wrist and yanked. But no matter how hard she pulled, she couldn't free her hand.

She dug with her fingernails into the thick mass, clawing for a grip. Her trapped fingers felt terrific suction from the tentacles—yes, she thought, they were alive like tentacles—and now they were grabbing at her other hand as well, trapping one finger and then another as she one moment pried and dug with her free hand and the next moment frantically tried to pull it away.

She screamed, twisting around onto her knees, trying to yank her hair and hands away. Yet her panicked wrenchings seemed to give the things more advantage, for they lashed her tighter, like a web snaring the struggling legs of a fly.

Her friends, responding to her screams, were shouting, trying to find out what was wrong. Finally a firm hand gripped her wrist, yanked at it, and then she heard a blade hacking.

"It's porsk!" Delin said, his voice close to her ear, his hand freeing one of hers as he sliced at the tenacious plant. "It's tough as wood—like Leas told us."

Jesk had gotten hold of her other hand and was also slicing away at the fibers. "Don't cut my fingers!" She felt the blows and pressures of the blades on both sides as she pulled to free her hands.

One broke loose, then the other. Delin bunched her hair in his hand and hacked at the fibers entangling it. Suddenly she broke free and tumbled onto the floor.

She sat up instantly, digging at the severed lengths still tangled in her hair. Her hands shook as they worked at disentangling the things, and when she spoke her voice came out quavering and high. "Porsk?" she demanded. "Porsk?"

"It's food!" Jesk declared triumphantly. "'Edible plant found in the highest ranges of Aliare.' It eats little things—insects, small mammals."

"And fingers!" Lysse said.

Mela grimaced.

"It was encasing your fingertips, like little sucking sleeves," Delin said. He took her trembling fingers in his hand. "Do the tips feel strange? It spreads a fluid that numbs and starts the digestion process."

She ran her thumbs over her fingertips; they were somewhat numb.

"Good thing Mela wasn't alone," Delin said. "She could never have gotten loose from that stuff."

"True," Jesk said cheerfully. "Just imagine the larger things awaiting us."

—— Sierent ——

Lysse was dangling above the others, trying to get down to them. "I feel stretched out like a hanging chicken up here."

"Then let go," Delin said.

She fell into his upraised hands and as soon as she got her feet steady observed, "Feels like we've been descending for years."

Jesk hushed them. "Do you hear something far below? Like faint, continuous thunder?"

A little further down and they all heard it clearly. But then, as they kept descending toward it, the sound became faint, and after a time, disappeared.

It was what they expected from sierent. Those who lived in

the darkness below called the storm times "night" and used the word "dawn" for when the winds died down and they could leave their shelters.

Hearing the storms, they were afraid they might reach Aliare's roof unawares and fall to the mountain peaks below. They descended cautiously until they found wide cracks but nothing beneath. It was like a long cliff edge, and when they threw rocks over it, no sounds came back.

They lowered their rope, dangled its full length and swung it everywhere, but it struck nothing.

They were perched in the cracks of Aliare's roof. Below was the great hollowness of the planet, the vast subterranean world.

They waited till they felt and heard once again the beginnings of sierent. At first they felt moist, gentle breezes. But before long the spray and biting winds drove them back up to shelter where they listened, fascinated by the horrific maelstrom below.

When they tried to sleep above the sounds, Mela concentrated on remembering the time she had been lying beside Asel in the crags, listening to other storms. She tried to absorb Asel's love for the sounds of this planet-shaking phenomenon.

When sierent finally ebbed and the dawn came, Mela awoke and again consciously turned her thoughts to Asel's faith, to brace herself for the improbable odds they faced below.

"It may be impossible to get down there," she said to her friends. "We're sitting here like wingless birds."

Lysse struck her cupped hand smartly against her knee to create a loud plopping sound. "One slip, and, *plop!*—that's us landing in Aliare."

Delin was affixing small utensils to the end of the rope, extending its reach a little. He shook them so that they jangled. "That'll make a sound if it touches something."

The air was still gusting and moist. All their lives they had heard about formations created by the storms. "They say the highest peaks are the most fantastic," Delin said. "Imagine—

sierent every night swirling and blasting and gouging spires and funnels and cones and bizarre and wonderful hollows."

They did not soon find themselves descending through fantastic shapes. For several more days they tried to locate something besides air beneath them. Then, as Mela was leaning far over an edge swinging the rope, it finally hit something with a resounding jangle. Quickly they all got into the position they had practiced many times, and Jesk started down.

At rope's end, knotted and noisy with utensils, he dangled until his foot finally located a thin shank of rock. He lowered himself onto it and felt it widen at his knees. He gripped the thing with his calves, the narrow rock rising like a spear past his chest, fragile enough, he knew, to break off from his weight.

"Lower me some more."

"Can't," Delin said

"Then I'll let go."

"Are you steady?"

"Yes," he fibbed. "Here goes."

Jesk shinnied painfully down, legs spreading wide as he landed on a substantial plateau.

On hands and knees he felt all around him and soon discovered a peak rising higher than the precarious needle on which he'd descended. From there, the distance to the others was much less and the others came down much more easily than he had.

As soon as her feet were steady, Lysse said to Mela, "Admit it. We've had our first miracle."

Mela was just getting up from her knees and said triumphantly, "I not only admit it, I proclaim it!"

But her triumphant spirit quickly ebbed as they descended the peaks. They slipped and slid down the wet curves of the crenellated, honeycombed configurations. They held on to each other, grasping for any kind of footing, always aware they might be at the edge of a precipice.

These formations may be fantastic, Mela thought as she clung to a slippery ledge, *but the experience of going down them is just a nasty, sprawling humiliation.*

—— Culmecs ——

The four friends slept in a huddle of legs and arms, scrunched into a deep cave's deepest corner. Sierent was over, but the first cries of birds outside did not awaken them.

A voice, however, did. At its sound, all four were instantly alert. It was the first voice other than their own that they'd heard since beginning their descent. It shocked them, as if the very air had erupted with Other.

The voice was masculine, the words foreign. It came from the cave entrance and was joined by another man's voice, and then footsteps coming toward them.

"Contact," Lysse said. She stood and stretched. "Are we ready for this?"

"We'll never be ready," Mela said, clutching the lamp and hurling prayers above.

Hearing her voice, one of the men shouted, "Askirit!" They turned and bolted from the cave.

Delin called out, "We have no weapons. No keitr! We come as friends from the light."

No response. Delin repeated his words, this time more loudly.

In heavily accented Askirit a man shouted, "Come out here!"

Mela shuddered. They emerged very cautiously.

"How many are you?" the man with the loud voice demanded. Delin and Jesk slowly walked toward the men, saying they were four unarmed friends from the light. Suddenly Mela heard scuffling and Delin cried out, "You don't have to do that!"

"Friends from the light?" the man said contemptuously.

Mela turned and hurriedly stashed the lamp inside the cave entrance. She'd barely turned away from it when the big hands of a great, wide slab of a man smelling of feathers grabbed her shoulders. Bird claws hanging from his necklaces scratched her arm as he searched her for weapons. Slowly, deliberately, he explored her face with his hands. "Definitely Askirit."

"This one too," said another man holding Lysse. "She's all crippled up."

"Askirit, yes," Lysse said. "But from above. We've brought you light—light from far, far above the peaks."

This statement made the man angry and he shook Lysse, but that only made her insist more loudly, "We were born above!"

Mela kept quiet, studying the men. They smelled of game and greasy eating, of blood and long journeys. Decorative stones clicked on the fringes of their sleeves. The huge one and his smaller, intense companion did all the talking; a quiet third man was eventually sent off. They talked of powers in the peaks and hungry gods, and she decided they were Culmecs, mountain barbarians she had learned about long ago. Mostly she sensed their fear. Dread of the light as an omen of doom. Dread of the peaks. Dread that made them talk of sacrificing prisoners and children up there.

Lysse again spoke urgently about the light and the Maker's power, but the men acted as if they had heard it all before.

Many more men came, evidently alerted by the quiet one. They spoke loudly among themselves. Mela began to identify names. Karssk was the big one with the booming voice; Luemuhs the smaller one.

Quietly she crept into the cave and retrieved the lamp. Walking right up to the men, she planted her feet firmly and said, "You murdering barbarians!"

The hubbub ceased. She waited just an instant, then said in a voice like driving hail, "You have murdered the innocent. The Maker hates the sacrifices on the peaks. He will destroy the evil powers with blinding light!" Then the tone of her voice completely changed. "But you—you he will shelter, if you repent quickly. You must stop doing evil. You must receive the light."

Karssk's angry voice assaulted her like a blast from sierent. "Who are you, woman, to say such things?"

Mela had turned up the lamp's pilot light and had unfastened the flaps covering it. Taking one step back, she took the covering off. At the same time she said loudly, "Light purges! It illumines the dark night. Don't be afraid. Come to the light."

As if from one voice came shrieks, whimpers, gasps. Karssk cursed in a voice so weak she barely recognized it. They all fled in a turmoil of churning legs and stampeding feet.

Their response had jarred her, but she recalled her own reaction that morning to a voice. How much more stunning for those in darkness, who had always feared even flickers of light, to have this sudden brilliance explode in their faces.

She lowered the pilot light and replaced the flaps, once more hiding the lamp. Lysse had already released Jesk from his bonds, and Mela turned to Delin and inserted a blade between his hands.

"You spoke with remarkable power," he said as she cut the ropes.

"I was praying every moment. I was desperate. But I was also certain that love of light was more powerful than fear of darkness."

—— Enre ——

"I hate to say this, but there must be twice as many out there as yesterday," Jesk said. "Hundreds of them working themselves into a frenzy."

They were still in the cave after two nights of sheltering in it and two days of listening to hostile voices.

"Maybe we should uncover the lamp and scatter them out of here," Jesk said.

"Maybe. But what would it really do?" Delin said.

Mela felt irritable. The days had been long and the tension high. "Most of them out there have never actually seen the lamp. Letting them all see the light—"

"But Karssk and Luemuhs saw it," Lysse said. "They're both shouting to obliterate us. You can smell the hatred out there."

"But maybe someone's ready to receive the light. Maybe I didn't emphasize enough the Maker's love—"

"No!" It was a new voice, a woman's from within the cave. It jolted their senses anew. "Don't show them the light now."

Mela instinctively reached to protect the lamp beside her. Who was this woman? She spoke Askirit crisply and perfectly, but with an accent unlike any above. Her next words came with a little snort: "But maybe you only have stories about light."

Mela toyed with the fasteners on the lamp's flaps. "We have light. We have brought it from above."

"The talk about your light is everywhere. My name is Telen, and I am Enre."

"I have spent much time with the Enre."

Telen pounced on Mela's words. "What Enre? What are their names?"

She hesitated. "I have met Varial. And I've listened to the storms with Asel, who was Varial long, long ago—both down here, and in the world above."

"Asel?" The woman sniffed. "A name one can pluck from the air. Asel was Varial generations ago. Everyone knows her name."

Mela ignored the accusation. "Asel is still alive."

The woman sighed. "This is no time for tales."

Mela carried the lamp farther into the cave. She had been

turning it up and loosening the flaps. Without ceremony, she lifted the covering off the lamp, and light flooded the cave.

A gasp came from Telen, and then silence.

After a long time, Jesk took a drink of water; his movements were the only sounds in the cave. The four friends were respecting the silence of the Enre. She was breathing deeply and, Mela suspected, weeping. All her life she had longed for and believed in light, and now she was confronted by its brilliance. All around them light illumined the darkness of the cave, but outside chants and shouts continued at an unnerving pitch.

Telen finally broke the silence. "The Culmecs will soon attack us. We must break out."

"Where should we go?" Delin asked.

"To Varial. To the Askirit strongholds in Dorte. The lamp gives us the power to restore the Askirit nation."

"But we're not interested in that," Mela objected. "We came to share the light, to lead everyone up and out of Aliare."

"Of course," Telen said abruptly. "That's always been the Askirit hope."

Mela wasn't so sure, but she had to agree when the Enre said, "The light would shock the barbarians, but it would also enrage them. They'd recover their wits and try to destroy it and us, no matter how terrified they were." Telen was busily arranging things from her pack. "They've had a lot of time to think about this."

"The tunnels behind us all dead end," Jesk said. "And we can't all sneak out."

Telen agreed, rummaging through her things. She said with relish, "We'll charge through them like a blazing knife."

"Or smashed crockery," Lysse said.

As if in response, the Enre stuffed small, stubby lizards into Lysse's hand. "There are ten of these. Your job is to get as close as you can, then loft them right into them. Can you throw?"

"Not well."

"Get close, then. Just throw them high, and then I'll come get you."

She did not explain their purpose but turned immediately to Delin and Jesk. "These were to have been meals and clothing." She put several carcasses of small animals into their hands. "Just the thing to make them think they're being attacked by keitr. Shout as if you are many men. Use the word keitr. Throw the little bodies hard at them, then imitate keitr screams."

No one objected as Telen gave many more hurried instructions. Finally she said, "Everyone at the same instant. *Go!*"

Mela pulled off the lamp's covering and held the light aloft, running after the Enre and shouting, "Light! Light!" Straight down a gully they ran, a glowing, raucous pack illuminating the night, shouting and charging at the thick knots of men.

They heard in front of them a vast, collective gasp. The reaction was like a sudden change of weather, as if the very air had stiffened. Telen was first among them with her Enre chops and thrusts. Jesk's and Delin's shouts and missiles, and the bizarre sounds from the creatures Lysse lobbed at them, created pandemonium. Confused, men struck at their companions or fled.

As instructed, Mela then covered the lamp. Telen hitched Lysse onto her back and they all stumbled along beside her as she led them to a ridge and away from the chaos.

—— Keitr ——

Three days later they had traversed long stretches through the mountains. Telen, sensing pursuit, emphasized speed and kept varying their pattern. Yet when they came upon some keitr caves and Jesk begged for time to enter them, Telen was the most receptive.

"I have six empty pouches," Jesk said with enormous excitement. "I've practiced constantly all my life, and I've made these pouches myself—all with the proper sleeves and launch hooks."

Telen inspected them carefully and pronounced them acceptable.

"All I have to do is slip in there and grab six of them!"

Mela told him definitely not. Telen said they had to rest a little anyway.

"But one wrong move and Jesk is dead. He's too young. Lots of grown men die gathering keitr."

Telen asked, "Above, men don't gather keitr, do they?"

Her tone angered Mela. "Above, there's no keitr to gather." She pulled a root out of her pocket and bit it savagely. "Jesk practiced so much only because our school for the blind studied our ancestors' culture."

"Blind?" Telen asked. "Jesk is blind?" She moved to him and touched his eyes.

"All of us are blind," Lysse said softly. "Like you, we have learned the skills and wonders of touch and taste."

Telen was clucking like an old woman hearing a crazy story. "The Askirit above sent us the blind? What a tale that is! You who bring the light to us cannot even see it?"

"We cannot see it, but we can feel its heat. We carry it in faith."

Telen threw her arms out wide. "Why didn't they send ten thousand sighted warriors? Warriors to light Aliare with thousands of lamps, to show the Maker's power!"

Delin broke in. "Auret himself came down as a broken child, a cripple."

But Telen was too amazed by the news to see any connections. "I wondered why they'd sent four striplings, but I said nothing. Yet now I learn they sent the blind! Who are these men who live above, who live in the light and are nourished by its power?"

Mela had no response, for the accusations brought back all her resentments. It was Delin who spoke again. "We were not chosen by men."

The discussion had slipped from Mela's control. With Telen saying things about Jesk's being an acceptable age to gather keitr and that the caves might make a man of him more than his teachers above were apt to do, Jesk quickly slipped away.

It was difficult for Mela to envision Jesk moving among those lethal creatures hanging near his probing hand, the slightest stumble apt to anger them. She felt responsible for him and sat braced for the sound of screams and flapping wings.

Telen was stretching a leather exercise thong in each hand. Delin walked over to her and said, "The Culmecs aren't at all the way our teachers described them."

"How did they describe them?"

"Like sensible, hard-headed barbarians. People proud of their ancestral peaks. People wearing claws and feathers to identify with the birds that flew among the formations. People spinning elaborate tales to match the fantastic shapes."

"They were once like that. But now, the evil from the abyss is rising. Only two generations ago, one of their kings sacrificed his son on the peaks. It opened the way for the powers. And now the Culmecs are consumed with appeasing the gods."

Mela said, "We felt the heaviness and oppression as we descended."

Jesk's triumphant yelp startled them out of their discussion. "A full belt!"

Delin leaped up and ran to inspect the bulging pouches around Jesk's middle. "A full belt!" he declared in the traditional response. Then he roughed Jesk up, smearing him with scent from his pack.

"Where'd you get this stuff?" Jesk protested. "It's not authentic—smells like mouse droppings."

"It is!" he said, smearing it into Jesk's hair.

"It is not!" Jesk shouted back. The two of them sang the ancient songs, and flushed with victory, Jesk let loose an imitation of an angry keitr's cry.

Telen bolted upright. "Now you've done it!" She grabbed her pack. "That could bring them boiling out of the cave."

They scurried away, and it was only after they had gone over many a ridge that Mela asked Telen how dangerous Jesk's imitation had actually been. "Were you really alarmed?"

She replied with a laugh and ambiguity: "I was hungry and wanted to get on the hunt."

They were successful on the hunt, but not in evading their pursuers. Telen kept the pace brisk, for she kept saying, "We have to get to the sea—it's the only way to break loose." Yet the four from above could move just so fast, and they feared the trails would be soon blocked.

Sweating, blistered, and bone-tired from the forced march, they very cautiously topped the final rise. To either side were sheer drops, but a wide funnel of descending trails spread down from their position. "It's the obvious place to come, I'm afraid," Telen said. "But it's the only place to get down without crossing more mountains."

She went off to reconnoiter, and after what seemed an interminable time, returned with a sobering assessment. Troops clogged the trails and more were filtering in. "These are not just stray barbarians. These are controlled by the Laij."

This revelation sent chills through Mela. The mighty Laij nation had in Asel and Yosha's time mounted the invasion that had ultimately devastated the Askirit and enslaved Tarn. The Laij used their own forms of terror, and they knew how to force tribes and peoples into subjugation and disciplined warfare. Those

Askirit who did not submit were now scattered throughout Aliare and hunted everywhere.

"We've heard the mountains are honeycombed with tunnels," Jesk said. "Could we find one that could put us below them?"

"Nothing but shallow caves here," Telen said.

They crouched in silence, listening. Mela thought she could hear the movements of troops slowly advancing up the trails.

"So what do we do?" Jesk asked.

"If anyone has one good option, speak," Telen said. "I do not." Throughout the afternoon, the sounds from below grew louder and bolder.

"One thing sure," Telen said, tapping the handle of her blade in agitation. "We have to get the lamp to Varial. These people all hate the light. They'll destroy it as soon as they lay hands on it."

Mela finally spoke up, saying quietly, "Remember when Asel and Yosha faced a similar crisis? Maachah reminded them of the Absurdity."

"And what absurdity is that?" Telen asked.

"The one revealed in the liturgy: 'The cosmos turns on this absurdity: your little prayers.'"

The Enre acknowledged the saying.

"Maachah then led them all in worship."

Telen was selecting small weapons from her pack and laying them in front of her in orderly rows. "Did their prayers, then, lead to triumph?"

Delin, who knew the story well, said, "No. They led to disaster. A total rout." He too was arranging his meager store of weapons. "But after the rout came the greatest triumph of all."

Telen stopped arranging her weapons. "I fully embrace worship and prayer," she said. "Let us begin."

When they rose from their knees, the sounds of advancing troops were unmistakable. Mela felt deep peace and power; she held the lamp in her hands like a sword.

"We have one chance!" Telen said, her voice rising with enthusiasm, as if she'd had a vision in her prayers. "I know these trails well. Two come up together, a wide one and a narrow. They do not think we have keitr. Jesk," and she reached out and gripped his shoulder, "you'll fire your keitr into the troops in the wide trail, and I will cast high, looping weapons into them. We'll create chaos again."

She paused, breathing in short bursts, excited about the breakthrough in planning. "The troops on the narrow trail will be gawking, hearing cries of keitr, distracted. I know that trail well. We'll sneak along its edge, unnoticed."

Jesk began loosening his belt and tugging at the fastener on the first pouch. "How close should I get to them?"

"We'll go together, and you'll launch at my signal."

Mela had been listening carefully to the advancing troops. She said, firmly and distinctly, "No."

Telen jerked around, then stood up. "Why not?"

"It's not likely to work. You've told us the troops are well trained. We know the reputation of Laij soldiers—they'll not stay diverted. They'd be all over us, and the lamp destroyed."

Telen never stopped with her preparations, her hands moving expertly at assembling her pack and weapons. "I've seen such tactics work."

"Not with us. You're Enre—we're blind fumblers from above. We could never merge with the troops the way you Enre can."

"Give me the lamp, then, and I will take it to Varial."

"A reasonable suggestion. But I've been charged to carry the lamp."

Telen stopped working. "Must we help the Absurdity produce disaster?" she said heatedly.

"But these men are under the discipline of the Laij," Mela said with equal heat.

"So? The Laij will smash the lamp quick as Karssk would! Don't you know gathering keitr is a capital offense? Jesk will be executed. Likely we all will, if not sacrificed on the peaks. The Laij don't believe in anything—but they let the barbarians do what they want with captives like us."

But Mela had already unfastened the flaps as she heard the troops getting closer and closer. "Telen," she said, "escape while you can."

She grasped the cover and yanked it off, striding forward briskly and shouting into the brightly lighted plateau she herself could not see, "I have a gift for your king! For the king of the Laij! It's from above, from the world of light. The most remarkable gift in all Aliare! A gift your king will insist on seeing."

Mela thought it ironic that she felt the lamp's heat on her wrist but saw nothing of the light exploding among them. She heard the expected gasps and exclamations, but she didn't count on more than a moment for the troops to recover. "You dare not destroy this gift! It's from the king above for the king of the Laij. You who are Laij officers, don't take it on yourselves to destroy the king's property! He will be astounded by this gift."

Chapter 6.

—— Slave ——

Though ropes had rubbed Geln's wrists bloody and his broken ankle made him sit painfully on one haunch, the barbarian raiders still forced him to paddle vigorously. If he slacked off, the boat would start turning and they would lash him with thick leather strips.

His hands slipped on the paddle, and he braced himself for another blow. He wished they'd quickly kill him. He kept thinking, *If only I hadn't cried out when sierent was sucking me away.*

Geln had been washed up on shore, face barely out of the water as the evening's early winds whipped at the surface. He'd known sierent would soon suck him away, so he'd cried out in fear. The raiders, always looking for slaves, had heard and yanked him into a shelter. They'd joked about his broken ankle and deep bruises as they'd tossed him on the floor like a sodden rag.

He felt little improved after weeks of paddling and fetching for them. He'd explained repeatedly how he had come from above and was clumsy because he'd never worked in darkness. They'd laughed at this and at his strange Askirit accent and ridiculous stories, calling him feeble-minded and cheerfully kicking him as he washed their clothes or scavenged shellfish.

His hands were shaking on the paddle and he considered collapsing to the bottom of the boat. He didn't care much what they'd do—beat him and toss him into the water? *Good,* he thought, *that would end it.*

Geln suddenly realized he was being spoken to. "You Askirit are strangely religious. You worship light, but you fling keitr at us and throw captives into the abyss."

He's afraid, Geln thought, and he surmised they were approaching Dorte, where Askirit warriors might be waiting to defend their last stronghold. It was far different from when the Askirit ruled the vast kingdom of Tarn and were known as the world's terror. In those days, no one would disembark on their shores uninvited.

But that had been Tarn, before the Laij had invaded and devastated the Askirit kingdom. Now Geln's captors feared the Askirit remnants much less than their enemies controlling Tarn. The men's whispers couldn't conceal their excitement. This was their life—to raid, to capture slaves, to grab goods and take their chances against defenders. They acted as if they were on a pleasant hunt, sniffing the tang of danger but feeling little terror, quietly readying their sheafs of spears.

The thin shafts were bundled in eights to be launched with an atlatal. They'd be flung high and fast to separate in a spreading volley, for in Aliare's darkness, accuracy was always a guess.

The boat grounded noisily on the rocks. The raiders barged out and dragged the small craft onshore, heedless of Geln's weight within it. He lay down in the bottom, listening to their scurrying, trying to ease the wet ropes' tightness on his wrists.

Whatever happened on this raid mattered little to Geln. His inner emptiness accentuated his horror at being trapped in the darkness. Even if he fled his captors, he knew he'd never find his way back up. And, up there, where could he go that he wouldn't be found by the greater terrors?

He heard the man nearest the boat adjusting his atlatal, smoothing the leather under the butt of his sheaf of spears. Geln listened for other movements. Finally a cry of terror rang out a short distance away. A few more moments and he heard another cry. Then, nothing. Only the nearby raider's nervous shiftings.

Thlatch! From a short distance away rang out the sound of leather released; instantly the man nearby bolted up and flung his sheaf of spears at the sound. He'd barely gotten them off when a keitr flapped open its wings close by and screamed.

He'd heard descriptions of a keitr's fury, but the sound so close to his own ears made Geln shudder. He jammed his body low inside the boat. The keitr struck the raider, flapping its wings against him. Its claws scrabbled at his body and it made frenzied "shrik-shrik-shrik" sounds as it bit the side of the man's face.

Geln stopped breathing and hoped he was not even twitching. He couldn't remember if keitr sought a second victim after a first and wondered at how such a little fact had suddenly become so significant.

In just an instant, the keitr broke off and he heard its wings flapping away and the raider's legs kicking against the ground. Then all was silence.

The Askirit cautiously took a long time to approach the boat. As soon as he heard them coming Geln called out, "Help me!"

They located him and cut away his bonds. The leader of the four men, Bika, helped him from the boat, saying, "Your accent is like none I've ever heard." His hand courteously scanned Geln's face, checking his features. "I know Askirit these days come from everywhere."

Clearly the officer was suspicious of him. Geln knew if he said he was from above he would create only more suspicion and perhaps derision. Yet if he lied, he'd be quickly caught by a false detail. "The raiders were looking for a small village," he said, focusing the talk on them, recounting their conversations.

"Raiders are parasites," said the man half-carrying Geln up the trail. "They only destroy."

"How did they capture you?" Bika asked.

Geln hesitated. "I was almost drowned. I was about to be sucked into sierent when I cried out and they found me. They've used me worse than fish bait!"

The man supporting him said, "Not surprising. They're loyal to each other, but to slaves—"

"How'd you almost drown?" Bika asked.

Geln took a very deep breath. He felt vile and exhausted. "You're determined to find out everything, aren't you? But if I explain, you may decide I'm deranged."

They laid him on the thick aceyn, the fibrous sea plant which through the eons had extended its tough carpet over the barren rocks. He fingered the tight tangles in which birds and small mammals found their insects and worms. In school he had learned much about aceyn, the plant by which the nutrients of the sea ultimately fed much of Aliare.

He asked for water and took a long, slow drink before talking. "I've lived all my life above—in the light. I've seen kelerai, and I've watched the birds soar and glimmers of light in the sky. I've seen lightning and fire. But not long ago I entered the rifts of Korbas, and I was swept into a river and down into Aliare."

Interrogation

"So maybe you are deranged," Bika said after they had eaten. They were deep in a cavern listening to the roaring winds of sierent. "Many minds snap in Aliare. Many go insane and say they're from above—even that they're Auret." The officer noisily bit down on a spicy root. "Are you Auret?"

Geln didn't care for this game. He had nothing to offer this man. "Of course not."

"You're hiding things. Why shouldn't I consider you a spy?"

Geln considered himself worse than that but said simply, "I am Askirit, an officer in the king's army above." He wearily told the history of Asel and Yosha and all the Askirit who had found their way to the light.

"Stunning information, if you're sane." He offered Geln a piece of the root. He bit down and welcomed the spicy mist that made his nostrils tingle and his eyes water.

"We serve Auret," Bika said. "We know something about your tales. If they're true, we must learn from them." He waited long moments, then asked, "Have you learned from them?"

"Of course."

"Above, do they tell the story of how the madman Belstin recognized Auret and worshiped him?"

"I've heard the story many times."

His interrogator held out two pieces of flint and struck them sharply so that a shower of sparks flew into the air. It was the first light Geln had seen since descending and he immediately understood why the people in the nightworld hungered so for it. He wanted the officer to strike the flints again, but instead Bika asked, "What's the difference between that light, and the light above?"

Geln sighed. "That cannot be answered with words. Above, light reveals. You see a green frog leap into blue water. You see the beauty of blossoms and the ugliness of a wound. You see stars in vast splendor and mites crawling on a leaf."

Bika told him to describe the Askirit kingdom above, and he did so, saying nothing about himself, concluding with, "The king above has no enemies, so the kingdom has grown soft, and sometimes corrupt."

The officer snapped his knuckles against his own palm. "Rycal leads us here. He allows no corruption."

Rycal? Had Geln heard correctly? Rycal had been the king who'd long ago lost Tarn to the Laij. His name was synonymous with "traitor." Above, no greater insult existed than to be called a Rycal.

"Wouldn't he be older than Yosha? Could Rycal still be alive?"

The man did not answer. Instead he began tapping the handle of his blade. Geln asked yet again if he could sleep, but Bika said, "Tell me what you know of Yosha."

Why was he so suspicious? Geln decided it was his own manner as much as his unlikely story. He was not only exhausted but morose. Bika would figure a rescued slave would be full of gratitude and that a man from above would show some spark, no matter how weary. But Geln was a burned-out shell. He came across inauthentic because he was inauthentic.

The officer forced him to explain more about Yosha's reign with Asel. Inadvertently, Geln mentioned Varial's name and the man instantly said, "Varial is often here on Dorte. She's never found the way to the light."

Geln hated this verbal sparring. "Asel was Varial down here. You know that. When she found the way above, she established the new Enre. She was Varial for many, many years. Now a new, younger Varial leads the Enre above."

The officer kept pressing him on this, and somehow as they spoke of Enre and Varial the word "Purgation" came out. Geln blanched at letting it escape his lips.

The officer instantly asked, "What Purgation? Were you there?"

Bending his knee to get at his aching ankle, Geln moved it closer to his hands and eased the bandages around it. He wanted to lay his head on his knee and sleep, but he mumbled, "Perhaps I was there—I hardly know. My mind is like the froth of sierent."

"At whom was the Purgation directed?"

Geln felt panicked. If he kept talking he'd soon be admitting his attempt to kill Yosha and the sand shriikes stalking him. If they learned enough, they might cast him into the abyss. At best they'd kill him quickly.

Yet what awaited him after death? Creatures from the abyss worse than shriikes? Would he be thrown to the furies? Or dragged to the Maker's judgment—holy light scalding him with its awful purity, and his mother and Varial and all the psalm-chanters condemning him to eternal agonies?

No way out, he thought, *no way out.* He clenched his mouth shut and tried to shut down his mind.

—— Rycal ——

They let Geln sleep most of the morning, then inspected and bound up his broken ankle. They laid him half asleep on a litter and began carrying him toward the hills.

Men's whispers showed they were fascinated by his story. Madman or messenger from above—either way, his presence created constant talk, for their passion was finding the way to the light.

He heard Rycal's name mentioned. When he asked about him, he was told he was actually the old king's grandson. "But wasn't Rycal the king who lost Tarn? Wasn't he a traitor?"

"Yes. But Auret forgave him. And he had much to forgive his grandson as well." Yet the man went on to speak of Rycal with awe, describing him as a powerful commander but also a remarkably intuitive sage. "He knows the core of a man as soon as he meets him."

They stopped after a long climb. Bika strode up and helped him stand. "Touch the wall." Geln reached out and explored the rough, broken surface. "This is the wall of shards and death that our ancestors scaled and shattered."

He knew the tale of Dorte's being freed. As they made their way to the top, Bika added details new to Geln and at the summit said, "This is the Place of the Sledge. The place of abominations. But the people rose up, and the powers were cast down. Now we celebrate here."

People were carrying and dragging things, chattering and eating freely. He heard birds and small animals. He was handed some roots, which he bit into with relish, and raw meat which he ate with difficulty. From all around them came sounds from stringed instruments; men and women began humming.

Two men lifted his litter to a high point where the breezes were strong; thousands of voices rose in songs of praise to the Maker. They sang of the wonders of Aliare, of the purity of light and the joy of seeking it.

Most astounding to Geln were the songs they sang of Auret—songs he had never before heard. Above, in Asta, everyone believed Auret was forgotten down here. But acclamations of Auret's love and stories about him were sung more heartily than he had ever heard above.

He hated hearing them. He'd always hated hearing about Auret, but hearing this down here confused and drained him.

The singing and playing continued until, as sierent's early winds began, small drums beat out a rhythm and people's feet moved with it.

Larger drums boomed as sierent's winds grew stronger. People moved energetically with the sounds, shouting after each loud beat. At first Geln didn't catch the words, but then he heard phrases about Auret facing the dark powers, Auret laughing, Auret forced into the abyss. The sounds were wild and dramatic, the passion strong in the voices and the stamping, twisting bodies.

The winds' velocity increased. Geln lay wondering at their disregard of sierent's dangerously growing intensity.

When the winds grew fierce, buffeting their bodies, one huge drum sounded, reverberating so massively that Geln could not imagine its size. It thundered above the rhythms of the smaller drums, combining with sounds of roaring winds and bodies in motion to express the wildness of the drama the voices were shouting out.

Three strokes of the massive drum signaled a mighty shout from everyone: "All power to the broken one! Auret has conquered!"

Then came a mad scramble for shelter, a wild dance of a scramble, as if the music were still playing and the tearing, loud winds were accentuating that music, the blasts nearly sucking them away as the dangers of running for shelter concluded the celebration of the great risks Auret had taken for each of them. Geln's litter was grabbed up and jostled away among the hurrying crowds carrying and dragging their burdens. Winds lifted the litter under him and he had to grip its sides tightly until, gusts blasting at his face, he was at last rushed into a cavern.

They paused for only a moment, then went deep into intersecting tunnels and entered a room, where he learned they hoped to meet with Rycal.

Their long waiting was suddenly interrupted by animated voices. One boomed out loud and resonant, full of laughter that filled the room. A whirl of sweaty, muscular motion clapped Bika on the shoulder. "Magnificent!"

Bika said something about the thunderings of the huge drum, and Geln thought, *This must be Rycal. He himself must have been striking the drum.*

The big man was exuberant, smacking the big bone-and-leather drumstick against his palm. Large, hollow balls hung from his hair with pebbles that clicked as he jerked his head around. "Light shrivels the vermin from the pit," he said, his vast, incongruous laugh echoing from the walls.

He was oblivious to Geln's presence on the floor. Bika finally said, "You may be interested in someone we rescued. He's Askirit, but with a strange accent."

Rycal ignored him. "Do you know what the celestial ones are

doing right now? Joining our celebration. But the furies hate it. They have nothing to laugh about!" He spoke like a child who'd hooked a flopping fish too big for his strength, yet his voice was resonant and old.

Bika spoke of Geln again. "He claims he's from above."

Rycal turned and walked toward his litter. Less than halfway to him, Geln heard his quick, sure pace suddenly stop, as if he'd stubbed his toe. "Ugh!" he grunted, making a loud, gagging sound of disgust.

Slowly he stepped closer and poked Geln's leg with his foot. He stood in front of him sniffing and making grinding sounds with his teeth. Finally he demanded sharply, "What carrion have you been rolling in?"

Geln was nonplussed.

Rycal turned to Bika and said, "This man's a used-up sack! Corruption and dry-rot!"

He turned back to Geln and blew air loudly through his teeth. "You smell like a corpse."

And with that Rycal with his retinue swept out of the room.

—— The Wounds ——

Geln lay on cold stone, his hands tied behind him. He had been stunned by Rycal's reaction the night before, not like a man slapped in the face but like someone with a hidden, gangrenous wound ripped open to reveal its stench.

I'm putrefaction, he thought, *food for the furies.* The fear from his belly was crawling up his throat.

He felt a guard's foot against his side. Someone loosed his bonds, then handed him some food but kept a spear poised at his chest. As he chewed, the man touched Geln's throat with its point and lightly swept it across his skin in a little arc. "Condemned," he whispered.

If only death would obliterate me, Geln thought. But he felt the hunger of the next world's darkness waiting.

As he swallowed his last bite of raw meat, a curious thing began. A voice within was urging, "Why be so afraid? I've found you again. It's only little me."

What was this? The thing was not vengeful or controlling but sadly whining, even obsequious. "I can't hurt you," it said. "It's only little me."

Yet this "little me" was reminding him of his old dreams of power. "Your destiny is down here. You can still shake the world."

He sensed, for the first time since fleeing Yosha's tent, trickles of life. The dull sense that he should resist this voice leached away.

"Don't worry," the thing reassured him, "it's only little me."

His mind churned about great forces and murderous deeds. "Succeed down here and you'll get all your old power back . . . and much more. . . ." He was enormously relieved to feel any kind of life, any hopeful whisper. Yet he also felt repugnance, for now he had experienced being the hunted, the spiritually disemboweled.

Bika's quick, authoritative steps entered the space. "Get him ready," he said, making a clicking sound with his tongue to emphasize speed.

Geln hurriedly swallowed the last of his meal as they bound his hands again. Bika told his men that he'd expected an order to simply drop Geln into the abyss, but that Rycal had sent for him. Holding his fists horizontal in front of him, he slammed together the hollows shaped by his thumbs and forefingers, producing a loud thud. "Maybe Rycal wants to do it himself."

The man pulling Geln to his feet grunted approval. They hustled him out of the caverns into the open air. Considering Geln condemned, they were rough and caustic.

"What did you do up there in the light, to get thrown down here?" Bika assaulted him with the question, like a blade hacking at filth on a shoe bottom.

With his bound hands and painful ankle, Geln was lurching forward, trying to keep up. "I wasn't thrown down. I was escaping sand shriikes—things that could snap you in two."

Bika spat. "Never heard of 'em."

Geln was force marched up steep trails into the mountains, stumbling so much that finally one man on each side gripped him roughly by the shoulders, yanking and dragging him upward. Where the trail bent around a mass of stone, they slowed, moving ahead with extreme care.

When Geln felt the stone beneath sloping down, they halted. "Careful," Bika said as they pushed him down to his knees. "Don't let him slide into the hole."

Geln knew this had to be a "snakehole," found throughout Tarn and Dorte, shaped as if giant snakes had tunneled them into the stone. No one knew their true origins, only that they dropped all the way down to the abyss.

Rycal came from afar, talking loudly, making at one moment a growling sound, the next laughing and mimicking an off-key note. But when he was close to them he fell silent, and all Geln could hear were the pebbles in the hollow balls clicking as he moved his head. Slowly he sat down across from Geln, on the other side of the hole.

Suddenly a bird burst out with a cheerful, melodious call, and Geln remembered that a bird often rode on Rycal's shoulder.

The wind teased their hair and the men nervously shifted positions at the hole's sloping edges. Bika quoted lines from the liturgy about thrusting evil away from the people. As he spoke, the men behind Geln pushed him several paces down and closer to the hole.

Across the gap, another man repeated Bika's words, then added, "The abyss is always hungry for its own."

The bird chirruped its loud, happy song again. Geln braced his feet against the slope.

Rycal asked, "Have you heard of how Auret threw the furies out of a child?"

Geln didn't know if the question was for him. No one else responded, so he said, "No. I haven't."

"The story is what brought me here this morning. It's been spinning in my mind."

Strong fingers still gripped Geln's shoulders; he was grateful for them, feeling how close the slippery edge was.

"The child was as dead inside as you. But no one threw him into the abyss." He was tapping out with his fingertips the same rhythm as the evening of the drums.

Geln desperately thought, *The hands on my shoulders are not only a support, but my only chance. These men are fidgeting and nervous as mice. If I yanked at them just right, they might be the ones to fall.*

"The child didn't need to be cast into the abyss," Rycal said. "Instead, Auret touched his dead soul. He gave him life. So I thought, even though you carry death's stench, maybe you could be touched."

Geln's mind was awhirl with ideas of jerking the men forward, and in the confusion of their screaming descent, surprising Rycal and tripping him in as well.

"But now things have changed!" Rycal declared.

Changed? What had changed?

From Rycal's throat came a grunt of disdain. "Don't you realize that if I could smell the decay of your soul, that I'd know you were consorting with liars and fiends?" He rapped a leather stick against the stone. "You belong to the abyss. Go to it."

Horror drenched Geln. Not just horror of the abyss and the tightening grip of the men's fingers on his shoulders, but the realization that the voices had used him again. That wanting to trip Rycal into the pit was as evil and absurd as the mission to kill Yosha. That the things hunting him and hungering for him had once again seduced him.

In contrast, he remembered the stunning light that had kept him from murdering Yosha.

In utter despair, even as he felt strong hands lifting him forward, he screamed out a name. "Auret!" he cried, the sound ripping out of his throat like sierent screaming at night. "Auret!"

Suddenly, as if his own screams were violently assaulting his senses, he was stripped bare of illusions. He saw evil and his own choices, saw that he had surely chosen the abyss again and again. "Auret!" he screamed. "Auret, save me!"

Chapter 7.

——— Mud ———

"Delin, what are you doing over there?" Mela asked. "You've been quiet all morning." Closely guarded by Laij troops, they were confined to a small stretch of shore on the rocky coast.

"Playing in the mud," he said cheerfully.

She walked over to him and her feet sank. "The stuff's still mucky," she said, feeling it ooze around her toes.

"You should have walked in it earlier. I had to dig way down to get something thick enough." He was trying to make mud sculptures but was having difficulty with the substance. The storms of sierent scoured clean every peak and rock, but it also churned up mud and debris from the sea and capriciously deposited piles of it along the shoreline. "I was hoping to get just a little clay mixed in, but it's just grainy mud."

She heard him place a figure up on a rock. "Can I touch them?"

"Might collapse if you do—but I'll just make more."

She reached out gingerly and found a simple figure with arms flung high, and from each hand a string of tiny birds connected wing to wing in cross patterns soaring upward. Nearby was a similar figure, and another.

"Hope," he said. "Hope in the darkness."

The birds fell off one of the figures when she touched it, and she said, "Hope despite disaster."

"Maybe." He brought another figure to the ledge.

Lysse mumbled something about being tired of waiting for the Laij officer and Delin said he had no desire whatever to meet him.

"Let's get it over with!" Lysse snapped with uncharacteristic shortness.

They'd been dreading his appearance for days. Mela's demands that she take the lamp to the king required a decision by the region's top general officer; she was told he would be furious at being summoned. "He might loose a merret at your throat," an officer warned. "Tresk won't like being told what to do with your lamp!"

The Laij had used merrets to conquer Tarn, and the comment made the deadly little beasts keep scurrying into Mela's mind.

Midafternoon, Mela was still in the mud with Delin trying her hand at making some figures when marching feet sounded. She stood up and bent over the water to wash off the mud.

The leather-clad feet slapped in unison against the wet rock, then suddenly stopped at the captain's command. The officer curtly ordered the prisoners to stand to attention.

An older, much deeper voice than the captain's demanded, "Which one is Mela? Speak up."

Mela took one pace toward him. "I am."

The man moved toward her and she noticed slight rubbing noises. She knew them to be signals of very high rank—flat lattice-cut bones sewn into the thick pleats of his uniform just above the knees and encircling elbows and wrists, making faint but distinct sounds as he moved.

He stopped a mere hand's width away and boldly explored her face with his fingers. His great bulk breathed in short, controlled bursts. "What's this about a gift for the king?"

She described the lamp and its remarkable light.

"Light? We hear rumors of that vile stuff sifting down through the cracks!" The grizzled veteran cursed the light. "It's a fantasy used to inflame the people."

Mela insisted light was not imaginary; that in fact everything in Aliare was sustained by the waters from above, and that all life above came from light. "We are ambassadors from the king above."

"The king above?" Tresk made his tongue rattle like the death sign. "The king of the Laij has kings waiting on his tables—and under his tables." He spat out his words like darts. "I hear you've brought troubles here."

"We've brought only the light. A lamp of peace and hope." She felt her voice had come out like a little squeak against his powerful accusations. How did she ever get down here? How could she even speak to this man? How could she stop the roiling in her stomach?

The officer put his huge palm on the top of her head and pressed his fingertips down against her hair. "Peace," he exclaimed, rocking her head back and forth. "You've got the whole region in turmoil. Rumors of light and the roof of the world splitting. The Culmecs are furious you've insulted their sacred peaks."

Mela made an incredulous popping sound with her tongue. "Sacred peaks?" Her neck muscles felt tight from resisting the pressure of his hand. "Peaks defiled. Debauched."

He squeezed tighter, then pushed her away. "You condemn yourself with your own mouth. The Culmecs say the peaks must be appeased with the bodies of the violators." He turned to his troops. "Where's the lamp?"

They walked a short distance to the eight men guarding it. Mela was allowed to take the lamp into her hands. "Should I take off the covering?" she asked, unfastening the flaps and turning it up full. Tresk, towering over her, grunted assent and she uncovered it.

Mela sensed his body jerk and heard a little rasp in his throat. Then after a long time came a whisper so quiet she could barely hear his words: "No wonder they summoned me."

They stood motionless in the light, the only sound the huge

man's quickened breathing. It was Mela who broke the silence. "It's light from above. A sign for those who seek the light. There's a way to reach it."

Tresk stiffened. He said in a level, sobered voice, "I see why everything is in upheaval. When light shines, it dominates the senses." He took several paces back. "Cover it up."

Slowly she did so. As she fastened the flaps, she summoned courage to say the dangerous, hard thing. "The light is for peace. But darkness hates the light. Aliare is judged guilty. Guilty of loving evil. Laij, Askirit, Culmecs—all must repent."

The big man made a loud whack by striking his leather stick against his thick pant leg. "Child, what do you know of evil?"

His sarcasm felt like his heavy hand gripping her head. She felt like shriveling under him, but she swallowed and used an answer from the sages: "Light stuns evil. That I know."

"You know nothing of evil," Tresk insisted, snapping his troops to attention by two slaps of fingers against palm. "But you will soon learn."

—— The Center of Camp ——

By midafternoon the next day, anxiety was draining their spirits. Even Delin had become morose; sierent had swept away his figures and all the mud, leaving—in its capricious way—only rushing water and slippery rocks. Soldiers exchanged watch with sharp barks and commands, but except to hand them food, they said nothing to the captives. In the distance, the sounds of the main encampment rose like the sounds of a city.

Abruptly, Mela was summoned; she stood to her feet.

The main camp was even louder than she'd imagined. She was marched past a cacophony of sounds and smells: sweaty men hauling boat sections and shouting instructions and warnings; Laij instructors drilling barbarian recruits; select troops training the merrets. She was placed between two guards and told to wait.

A few paces away, she could hear Tresk talking to a man. She knew little of the Laij language, but she concluded they were discussing loading the boats. When he turned and moved briskly toward her, she again heard the faint sounds of bone against bone from his uniform, warning that this was a very senior officer.

Without greeting her he said, "Do you know why we've diverted thousands of troops to this place?" His voice sounded to Mela like gristle being chewed and cracked. "Rumors are everywhere. People from tribes and cities coming here—the region's in an uproar, warriors arming themselves."

"But they aren't just rumors."

Tresk bent over her, very close to her face. "I'm telling you all this so you'll know I'm very, very serious about learning the truth from you." He called out a command and a soldier came carrying his pair of merrets covered in their case. "Tell the young woman your training procedures."

The soldier explained in particularly grisly detail how the ground-burrowing merrets, terrified of their natural enemies, could be trained by scents to burrow in a set direction and erupt suddenly from the ground to go for someone's throat. The soldier ended by saying crisply, "It claws its way from feet to throat faster than a snake in water, rips out the windpipe and is gone."

Tresk dismissed him, then said to Mela, "I will tolerate no lies. Where are you really from?"

"Above. Where I learned all those facts about merrets from those who fought them!" She was shaking with both fear and anger. She jutted out her jaw. "You insult me by trying to frighten me. When I chose to descend into darkness, I considered myself already dead."

Tresk sniffed and said she could take it as an insult if she wished; he only wanted to impress on her his pressures and his necessary options. He then barraged her with a stream of questions about her birth, her people and religion, her education, and how she had come by the lamp. He said nothing about her answers until he asked about war.

"We have no warfare. The men are well armed, but we have no war as you have in Aliare."

His silence indicated he thought she was lying—about this and perhaps everything else.

Nearby Laij officers instructed recruits in the use of the atlatal with bundles of spears. "Above, we have no enemies!" she said indignantly. "When our ancestors emerged from darkness, no one else was there to keep them from claiming all the land and the sea."

"But you admitted you have a king. Kings become kings by war. And war is how they stay kings."

"But Auret made Yosha king."

Tresk cleared his throat in disbelief. "You mean men above don't seek revenge or plot to overthrow the king? That they're without greed—that the light has changed their very nature?"

It was a terrible question, for all the holy liturgy of the Askirit said exactly that. One sought the light, for it was holy, and when one found it, one lived a holy life. She longed to be able to say that the lack of warfare came because everyone above had been transformed and found peace through love of the light. But she had to say, "No. I think it is because Yosha and Asel, though very old, are still alive, and because the kingdom is young. No one has risen to challenge it—yet. But I fear for the kingdom when its founders are gone."

Tresk eased back and led her to a flat stone that served as a bench. "An apt answer."

"But there is a holy light, a spiritual light," she declared urgently. "Auret brought it into Aliare."

In the distance, men carrying a very large section of a boat were shouting, as if something were slipping. The large Laij boats had to be disassembled every night, and they listened as this last of many pieces finally moved past them.

She broke the silence by saying, "I met an Enre here in Aliare who knows this spiritual light."

"I knew an Enre once," Tresk said quietly. "She was fearless. She died with a song."

Mela wondered how she had died but did not ask. "The Maker is right now giving her new songs in the next world . . ."

Tresk growled in annoyance. "You know the Laij don't believe in the Maker. Nor in sacred peaks. We observe men's passions, weapons, delusions." He stood, his great bulk rigid. "We study them all—history, aesthetics, culture. All the belief systems. Each one came from wild men's dreams."

"So you consider Askirit barbarians?"

She heard him pull open his loga, an intricate set of wheels and beads and calibrators, and snap an extension smartly into place. She had heard of these sophisticated devices for an endless variety of computations, used by Laij officers and scholars, symbolizing Laij logic and precision. He manipulated several wheels on it, as if proving his points. "I hate to disillusion a child. Yet it's obvious you Askirit elevate myth to truth. You bend your knees and spirits just like barbarians."

Praying desperately, she stood up beside him full of spiritual energy. "We kneel that we might rise in purity and power. Otherwise we're mere slugs and lizards." She felt an urge to strike the loga from his hand, feeling that his spinning and clacking of it was just another attempt to intimidate her. "Our sages tell us that those who don't worship the light will soon worship the dark."

His voice once again sounded like the cracking of gristle and bones. "The Laij don't grovel before figments of imagination."

Flushed with the force of her argument, she said heatedly, "But there's a danger you don't see. Without worship, you become an empty skin the furies will fill."

Tresk spat in contempt. "Furies? Has anyone ever captured one, faced one, talked to one?"

"Hah!" she said. "In such a world as you've just described, are you so very sure such evil doesn't exist?"

Salamanders

The shallow cave in which Mela and her friends had spent the night was barely deep enough for shelter. She'd once again slept poorly with sierent's thunderous sounds so near, and as soon as the storms lessened she emerged on the rocks and started toward the shore.

Water rushed by her feet and winds bearing big droplets lashed into her face. She loved it, and she bent into the wind to make headway against it. Above, dawn for her had been warm rays and songbirds—but no light. Down here in Aliare, everything was wild, fresh and new, the cries of the aurets exhilarating.

This morning she had special need for the rousing of her spirits, for she had been summoned once again to report early to Tresk. She walked along the shore in the opposite direction of the guards to have a moment to herself, feeling the winds turning into breezes, listening to the many water sounds of dripping and gurgling on land and cresting at sea and crashing on shore. No wonder the Askirit had so many words for water.

Reluctantly, she turned and walked till a guard challenged her. He led her past several guardposts and then to the neck of a small peninsula reserved for the commander.

She felt her way along boulders near the shore, letting the waves crash over her calves. The trail markings were easily found, and at the last one, she heard splashes, grunts, and swishing sounds. She listened for a time but remained perplexed. The swishing would rhythmically sweep back and forth, and then she would hear a splash out in the water. Then the swishing would start up again.

Finally she called out a greeting.

The swishing stopped. "Just a moment," Tresk said, and the sounds started up again. He grunted with his efforts, and his tongue made drumlike sounds from military songs.

"Here." He reached over and put something into her hand. "See if this one's alive."

It was a salamander covered with muck. She knelt and rinsed it off; suddenly it wriggled to life, scrambled off her hand and plopped into the water.

"Almost done." He worked a few moments more, then threw something large far out into the sea.

"What was that?"

"Jellyfish. Slung it out on the rake—didn't want to touch it."

She remembered that Delin had found many dead creatures in the mud. "Why do they get trapped?"

"Foolishness. Fish that don't go deep enough when sierent peaks; salamanders that poke their noses out too early at dawn. They get whirled into the silt and muck, and unless you rake it right away before it packs down and hardens, they die." His demeanor was changed from the day before; still imperious, but not hostile.

Mela was amazed. "Why are you doing this?"

He raked one more creature out and flipped it into the water, then tossed the mesh rake aside. "Because they'd die if I didn't."

"But you could order soldiers to do it."

He started walking farther out on the peninsula, snapping his fingers for her to follow. "I've done it for years. It gives me pleasure."

She followed behind, reticent to ask more. But after stopping and indicating they should sit down, he added, "Maybe my soul demands I give some life back after killing so many."

"Your soul? Do the Laij believe in a soul?"

"Of course—by our definitions." He stood to accept food from an approaching guard. After the man left he placed the spread between them. "I did not have a very good night."

"I'm sorry I've brought you so much trouble."

He took a long drink, then said, "Trouble's an old

companion. That's not why I had a hard night." He ate silently, then said, "The light from your lamp is living in my skull."

He was yanking out extensions of his loga, rolling and spinning the tiny wheels in the intricately carved lattice frames. He kept working it, making all sorts of sounds as he clicked and slid and shifted and rolled the movable parts. She decided his movements were mostly nervous habit. "When we conquered Tarn, we believed we'd proven it all. At the end of the world, we found no unnatural terror—only a poisonous beast, the keitr. The Skull of nightmares our children had always feared was just a massive cave, the abyss merely an emptiness beneath it."

Tresk loudly snapped a hinged rod back into the loga and said irritably, "Yet stories of the abyss and the light keep growing. All my life I've squelched rumors about the light. But now I've seen your lamp."

He stood abruptly. "Have you heard of the expeditions to the abyss?"

She said she had not.

"The king grew tired of stories about the abyss rising and soldiers afraid to shelter in the deep caverns. He sent scouting parties into the pit. Sent hundreds at a time, but none ever returned. Then he sent a force of ten thousand men, heavily armed, no fools! They too never returned. So the king and all the cultured, intellectual kingdom of the Laij proclaimed it all superstition!"

Tresk had replaced the loga in his clothes and was now twisting his leather stick in his hands so that it made a squeaking sound. The waves against the shore were the only other sounds until he said, "Rumors of insurrection keep growing. Some want to kill you and destroy the lamp. Others threaten to abduct you, to get the lamp and find the way up to the light. And the Culmecs are obsessed with sacrificing all four of you on the peaks."

The morning sounds of the camp grew louder, but he seemed in no hurry, as if he were deliberating his decisions with her. "No one trusts the king to act wisely, so they want me to act before he hears of all this."

Mela had no idea how she should be responding. At last she asked, "What should you do?"

"Do? Act wisely, of course." He gave a rueful little laugh then took a long, deep breath. "But every choice will make enemies."

They talked much of the morning, and Mela was amazed at the scope of his insights but appalled that every choice could bring disaster.

He stood to dismiss her but asked if she had anything more to say. She said she did but then stood silent for a very long time before getting her words out. In a resigned whisper that came from an insistent urging within, she said, "I'm ready to be handed over to the Culmecs. With the lamp."

—— Sand in Aliare ——

Atop a sacred peak, Culmecs in a great ceremonial display of wails, chants, groans, and supplications strained to position boulders at the entrance to a deep cavern. Wearing long, trailing plumes, hundreds grappled and jostled to shove one boulder atop another, and more than once a scream rang out that a massive stone had ground its weight onto a hand or foot.

Within, Mela and her friends listened to the massive objects thudding and crunching into position. The sounds became duller as the space filled, then were like distant thunder as the entryway became a small gap and was finally sealed as piles of smaller stones were dumped into it.

The scents the Culmecs wore were still heavy in the air. "I don't like the smell," Lysse said. "Let's go deeper in."

They knew the tremendous force of sierent would tear the boulders from the entrance before the night was over. But they were sealed in till then, and the Culmecs fully expected the sacrifice to be consumed by whatever lived within.

Mela had had plenty of second thoughts about her choice to do this. Yet she had come to an inner certainty that they must confront the evil in the peaks. She had asked only that Tresk ensure they not be drugged or bound when left sealed in the cavern.

"We are to be given up to the Culmecs," she had told her friends. "But the Maker will not give up on us!" Then she shared with them all the reasons, keeping her own fears and doubts to herself.

As they went farther in, she kept reminding herself of her own words. Just as she was sensing something loose under her feet, Jesk knelt to scoop some up. "Sand. Gritty and dry—dry as the sands of Korbas."

Delin yelped and the echoes indicated the cavern widened ahead, but was flat and low. "All sorts of geologic seams in these peaks—and obviously lots of sandstone."

"Let's go no farther," Lysse said.

"We have to," Delin said. "This cavern has a weird shape, and sierent must blow way down in here. That's probably why people trapped in here as sacrifices never get found in the morning. The boulders suddenly blow away, and they get sucked into the storms." He dug with his toe into the sand but didn't strike bottom.

"But then all this sand would get sucked away, too," Mela said.

Delin hesitated. "You're right." He felt along the walls again. "The winds must rifle down those side tunnels and deposit it here. But if you're as low as the sand, you won't get sucked up."

Lysse complimented him on his theory. "Hopefully, we'll all agree with you when sierent blows away those boulders."

They sat nervously on the sand for a long time, telling each other stories as they heard the muffled winds outside. Suddenly, a screaming wind with stinging particles assaulted them, and an instant later as more boulders were swept away, heavy winds tore through the channels above them. Grit filled the swirling air and Mela pulled a cloth to her face.

Then, as suddenly as it had come, the winds died down to noisy gusts.

"It may be like this all night," Delin said. "Sierent is always erratic."

"At least we weren't sucked out into it," Jesk said.

But everyone wondered why sacrifices were never alive in the morning. Delin suggested they listen for something strange.

"A very bad suggestion!" Lysse said. "We'll all be going crazy with that shrieking wind out there. Our skin will start crawling off our bodies."

But they did listen intently, Delin and Jesk with blades the Laij had given them, Mela holding the lamp close like a strong companion. Lysse kept making light remarks, but the others were largely silent, with the wind sometimes screaming in their ears and the sand particles biting their skin and at other times the sounds of sierent distant and only bare movements of air around them.

"I do hear little creatures in here," Lysse said. "Something's scurrying over the sand."

"Be strange if there weren't," Delin said. "Let's hope it's not poisonous."

Mela said she heard nothing at all. "But I do feel oppression, as if the air is hanging on me like wet clothes."

Then they heard the squeaking of a small animal and a turbulence not far from them. Mela pressed her lips together, determined not to let a sound escape her mouth. The sounds continued for a moment, then moved away farther down in the sand.

"Something's feeding," Delin said. "Night bird or something."

"Don't lie, Delin. That was no bird!" Lysse said. "Maybe a snake, but no bird."

Mela's arms were wrapped around the lamp. At Lysse's reference to snakes and sand they jerked painfully tight. Sand shriike. The thought of a snake catching a mouse in the sand had brought visions to her mind of the creatures Asel and Yosha had encountered in the abyss. She unbuttoned the flaps of the lamp and pulled off the cover as she fired up the pilot light.

"I'm turning up its full brightness. I don't know if a lamp can thwart evil, but we know we have many promises about our prayers!" She linked hands with her friends, the lamp placed at their feet on the sand. "Cry out for mercy! Cry out against evil!" One by one they pronounced their prayers in ringing tones, blind to the light casting rays on their legs and into the sand all around them.

Morning found them exhausted, still praying and standing with the hot lamp at their feet, alive and desperate for the fresh smells and winds of the dawn. As soon as they sensed no danger from a sudden last gust, they bolted from the cavern and to the lip of the plateau now clean of boulders.

Mela felt almost giddy from no sleep, but she was also exuberant. "Praise the Maker!" she cried out.

She held high the lamp and all four shouted out praises against the ebbing winds and the sounds of water rushing in rivulets around them. "The light is greater! Light purges evil!"

They descended from the peak, crazily sliding and slipping down even more clumsily that the first time. Before they were halfway down, they heard sounds of crowds below, and as they descended farther heard shouts directed to them.

"They see the light," Jesk said. "Must be grand to look up and see the light descending from the peaks!"

When they reached a plateau not far above the people, Mela stepped to the edge and shouted down, "The peaks have now tasted the truly sacred. What was the place of defilement has become the place of the light!"

They did not descend farther, for thousands waited below and they feared being mobbed. They waited on the plateau, hearing people climbing up from many directions, and they were greatly relieved when they heard the voice of Tresk.

Chapter 8.

—— The Boat ——

Once more, Geln gripped the awl and tried to ram a thong through the hole in the leather. The wet, thick thread unhooked and squirted out of his sore fingers. "They're like eels; can't grip 'em!" Geln muttered, retrieving the end and trying to squeeze it between two fingers and a thumb. Even when he got a thong hooked on the awl and poked through, it often slipped out like something alive.

"Thongs have got to be wet," the women had told him as they showed him how to attach sheets of leather to the boat frame. The huge bones had also been wet when he had sawn and dipped and rasped them, filling the air with their dank smell till he had dropped them into the setting vats. He had helped the women assemble the lengths of bone into the boat's skeleton. Now he wrestled to attach a big flap of leather, one hand gripping it, the other attempting again to push the slippery thong through the hole.

"Work is like food," a voice behind him rang out. "It nourishes the body."

Rycal's voice. Geln hadn't heard it since, as the men were thrusting him into the hole, Rycal had shouted, "No—hold off!" They had nearly all three slipped and flopped into the abyss as they had frantically reversed momentum.

Geln responded, "Work's also stinky and sweaty." He felt flat, lifeless, as he had when the barbarians had enslaved him.

"Stinky? Wait till you get to the greasing!" Rycal was full of good humor. "You'll slop it all over every seam till you stink like a dead fish." He stepped closer and asked about the progress on the boat.

Geln felt he had nothing to lose admitting how clumsy he was beside the skilled women. "I'm not worth their time. I've broken needles and sawn bones in ragged lengths. They re-do half my jobs."

Rycal laughed. "The work is for you, not them." The bird on Rycal's shoulder sang its cheerful song and then repeated it, as if joining in Rycal's laughter.

His statement intrigued Geln. Was he more than a slave, then, someone who could learn and develop? When he'd been taken from Rycal's presence, no one had said anything about his future. His cries to Auret at the edge of the abyss had awakened new, vague longings. But they were only flickers of feeling in the numbing, odorous work.

Rycal said, "We hear rumors from Tarn that a young woman has come with light in a lamp."

The awl dropped from Geln's fingers. His ankle had become infected and he couldn't stand on it; he was gripping two ribs of the boat to steady himself, resting against the prow. He wondered how much he should reveal. "Have you heard the prophecy of the Blind Princess?"

Rycal said he had not. Geln explained it to him and described Mela's descent. Rycal was dumbfounded that a king would send Mela down without escort. They discussed it a long time, then Rycal said, "We've no prophecies about a Blind Princess. But we have one about the boy from above."

"The boy from above?"

"I'd have thought you'd heard of it. Auret prophesied the young would descend, and all the world would convulse."

Convulse? The young? Geln's hands released the thong and the awl. "But you said a boy—"

"They say the prophecy refers to 'the boy who is helpless.'"

Geln started. The phrase sounded familiar, something he'd heard in the liturgy somewhere. He had retrieved the awl from the fibrous aceyn and now rolled it between his sore fingers, saying quietly, "The boy who is helpless. No one is more helpless than I."

Instantly Rycal said, "A good beginning toward wisdom!" The man was full of energy, scuffing a foot across the beach and dislodging stones, the bird flapping off and on his shoulder. He bent and skipped a stone on the water, counting the pit-pit-pit-pit-pit-pits as it sped on the surface tension. "Six!" he declared.

Then he said much more quietly, "I was helpless once." Rycal coughed with a sound like a man rasping a boat prow. Then he gripped Geln's shoulder and helped him adjust the stick he used as a cane. Slowly he led him out on to a spit which extended narrowly into the sea. They sat down and for a time listened to the birds and waves.

Finally Geln braved the question. "When were you helpless?"

Rycal dipped his chin so that the balls hanging from his hair clicked. "It started with my grandfather. Rycal the king. I hated him."

Geln, trying to sound matter-of-fact, said, "We were told above he was a traitor."

"Hah! I hated being named for him." Rycal had been collecting flat stones and now bent to rapidly rifle one after another across the water. "Grandson of the king—I'd always been pampered and feared. But then the kingdom fell. I was only twelve. I still remember standing on a street in Aris, suddenly stunned at hearing Rycal's name spit out in hate. Rycal's name. The king's name! My name!" He paused. "They wanted to eviscerate my grandfather, throw him into the pit. I was terrified—I, his namesake, standing only a stone's throw away. So I fled."

He coughed one of his stupendous coughs again and paced back and forth on the shoreline. "Askirit hunted me. Laij hunted me. My only ally was rage." He kicked at a loose stone so that it splashed into the water. "I became a raider. But worse than a raider, an avenger. I wanted to kill every Laij, and I recruited many Askirit men to hate with me. My passion drew hundreds, but I never told them I was Rycal. We destroyed Laij towns and brought fear to every collaborator."

He stepped closer to Geln and took his hand. "Here. Touch my head."

Rycal guided Geln's fingers to its side. Behind his ear was a deep gully of ridged flesh with folds and pits and no hair. Geln traced the wound as it widened toward the top of his skull. Then, splaying his fingers, he ran them back past the ear where the gully split in two, one gouging into the jaw so that the bone jutted out in lumpy peaks. The other gully became three fleshy rivers under the hair above his neck.

"They ran us over a cliff. The Laij came in force, and with their spears they herded us over a high precipice. We fell to the rocks below."

He pressed Geln's fingers against his distorted jaw, then released them. "I lay dying in a tangle of bodies, gasping through the blood in my mouth. But I felt fingers clearing the air. I felt healing from hands lifting me to shelter. And a voice saying, 'I did this for your father's father. And I do it for you.'"

Rycal was having difficulty controlling his voice. "Auret healed me. He came when I was helpless, lying in my own blood."

He stopped talking and paced back and forth along the shore. Then he came close to Geln again. "Most of all, I was helpless in my hatred. But Auret healed my rage. He penetrated me with light and silenced the death rattle."

Geln adjusted his position, using the stick to shift himself on his haunches and stretch out his aching leg. "Auret? Was it truly Auret who bound up your wounds?"

Rycal's only answer was, "Only he can help the helpless." Then he said, "Now we carry his stories throughout Aliare."

The big man knelt down where Geln's broken ankle was

stretched out and took it into his hands. Slowly he unwrapped the old bandages, gripping the leg firmly. With seawater he washed it, and then from his pack opened something that smelled like a disgusting gland of a fish. Geln grimaced as he rubbed its wetness into his painful ankle.

"The wounds in your soul are even deeper than mine were, for you've trafficked with the powers." Rycal began binding the ankle again with fresh bandages. "But you recognize you're helpless. That's something. And you no longer have the stench of death."

"I cried out to Auret to save me."

"Auret saved you from the pit—by my command. As Auret just bandaged your brokenness by my hands, and as he surrounds you with the prayers of all of us on Dorte."

But, Geln thought, *what good are all these prayers to me? I've disfigured faces and souls, and tried to murder the king.* He remembered that stunning light, that substantial, terrible holiness that had stayed his hand at Yosha's side. "Though Auret saved me from the pit, I'm still lifeless," Geln said through clenched teeth.

"Yes," Rycal agreed. He helped Geln stand and they started walking back to the boat. "Yet, there is this: Auret specializes in rousing the dead. That's why he came to Aliare."

—— A Young Woman ——

It was happening to Geln just as he had so often dreaded it would. Sierent was already buffeting his clothes, yet he had no idea where to dash for shelter. He'd come that morning from a village high in the peaks, had taken a wrong trail and was now hopelessly lost.

Long ago, with Geln's ankle healed and the boat finished, Rycal had sent him out alone. "Go to the wilds," he had ordered. "Go smell the freshness of morning in the villages of those who believe. Listen to their stories of Auret. Hear their prayers for you. The furies won't find you; all Dorte is praying."

Some of the villages were near the peaks, others in valleys or by the sea. Some were Askirit, others of diverse tribes and customs, but all believers. At the touch of Rycal's seal, each welcomed him, each placed him at the center of a circle to touch him and cry out with loud prayers. Each told him the stories of Auret and how he fulfilled the ancient prophecies. Then they'd fill his pack with food and his ears with descriptions of trails and shelters to the next village.

Each time he'd feared he wouldn't make it there, yet each time he had. His hearing was becoming a little sharper, his sense of touch and smell and direction better. He sensed the presence of birds and animals before he heard them clearly. He'd been learning to survive in darkness—until this one wrong turn.

The winds were now so strong he gripped a spire of rock with arms and legs and, in desperation, cried out for help. He knew he should be seeking shelter instead of hanging on, for he would soon be torn away anyway and lofted into the storms. Yet he had no idea where to go.

He cried out again, and then again and again, clinging like a wet rag in the burgeoning winds. His pack kept lifting off his back then thudding back against it. A powerful gust struck him from the side hard against the spire, hammering at his grip.

His voice became hoarse, yet he kept screaming for help.

Suddenly tough little fingers dug into his shoulder and wheeled him about. The hand of a child, he thought, but then an urgent shout in his ear, "Come!" and he realized it was a woman. Her small, strong hand twisted his body from the spire to which he clung while at the same time she signaled something to him by three quick chops to his wrist. He didn't know what it meant, but he scrambled after the sounds of her feet.

But almost immediately, though he was rushing in their direction, the sounds disappeared in the roaring winds. He stopped, both terrified and feeling like a fool, crouching with nothing to hold onto, teetering in the storm. Finally he dropped to hands and knees to keep from being lifted off his feet.

"Help!" he screamed.

The small hand once again gripped his shoulder, and the voice fiercely insisted, "Come!"

This time she ran forward with one hand clenching his wrist. His feet whirled under him on the slick rocks, slipping and skidding as she yanked him forward with urgency little short of panic as the winds battened them downward, then sucked upward. Suddenly they were plunging into an opening, and with surprising quickness the winds ceased buffeting their bodies and became just a loud noise behind them.

They stood drenched and gasping. Geln's knee and shin were bruised and bloody, and he bent to examine the damage.

"What's the matter with you?" she demanded.

"My leg," he said. "When I fell—"

"No, that's not what I meant!" she said hotly, as if to settle an impertinence. "What were you doing out there? And why'd I have to come back? That was too close!"

Geln sat down heavily, the wet leather of his sleeves splatting against puddles on the rock floor. "Thank you for saving me," he said, swallowing down resentment at her accusations.

"What's the matter with you?" she repeated, only a trifle more kindly. "We just about got a free ride to the world's roof."

Geln smiled wearily. He pulled off his pack and his outer jacket with its many pockets and started to pull out his supplies and food. "I'm very clumsy," he explained. He held out to her Rycal's seal. "I don't move very well in the dark. It's because I'm from above."

Her hand was under his, poised to grasp what he was

handing her, but at his words her hand stiffened. Very slowly she took the carved oval, fingering its surface as she pulled it from his fingers. "I've heard of you."

"What have you heard?"

She pressed the seal back into his hand. "Everyone has been at prayers for you." Her tone was no longer angry.

"But what have you heard?"

"That perhaps you are a sign. Perhaps the helpless one."

Geln was still shaking from his experience, but he began uncovering some of his food from the last village and offered her some. She thanked him and turned to fill two cups at the trough which brought a narrow stream of sierent's waters into the cave.

"You know my name. What's yours?"

"Asel."

His eyebrows shot up. "Asel! How could you be Asel? You're not that old." He guessed she was slightly younger than he.

"Asel brought the light to Dorte. Many girls here are named for her. Actually, I'm Asel-ri, which means 'Asel who is swift.'"

"You are swift! Are you Enre?"

It was the right question. She spoke intensely, rapidly: "I always wanted to be Enre! But you have to be chosen as a baby. You have to train from the time you start crawling. But not only did I want to be Enre, I wanted to be Varial!" She stopped herself and laughed. "But I suppose that's not unusual for a girl named Asel. We all want to be like our namesake."

"You act like an Enre."

"Thank you." She sounded pleased. "So there are Enre above?"

"Yes."

"I've done everything possible to be like one. Every time an Enre has been within a day's walk, I've sought her out and plied her shamelessly with questions. I constantly practice their ways, the skills in water and for warfare. But most of all I seek the light, as all Enre seek the light."

Her fierce commitment reminded him unpleasantly of his experience with Varial and the Enre on the rifts. Yet he also desired his deadness within to be replaced by even a flicker of what blazed in this young woman.

He stood and refilled their cups, holding them under the little cascade made by a short drop in the trough. "Still sounds strange to my ears, a young woman named Asel." He walked toward her with a full cup in each hand. "Perhaps it's not done above because up there everyone knows Asel's still alive."

The young woman bolted to her feet. "Alive?" Her hand shot out to his arm and spilled a little water, but she was oblivious to it.

"She and Yosha are both still alive."

Her fingertips kneaded his shoulder in excitement, jiggling more water on his foot. "We heard Auret had shown them the way to the light. But still alive! Some say once you reach the light you never die. This means they're right!"

Geln handed her the cup that was still full, then squatted with his back against the wall. He said quietly, hating his own words, "Yosha and Asel are both very, very old. They'll surely die soon."

Her foot scraped sideways beside his knee. "But it's something Auret himself promised," she said, none of her exuberance gone. "Auret said, 'You'll live in the light forever.' Forever! Not die in the light!"

Geln didn't respond for a time but listened to the screams of sierent at the entrance. He didn't want to speak again but finally said, "Asel and Yosha have lived remarkably long. But people die there all the time. Kings die. Priests die. Even Enre die."

She slid down beside him and exhaled heavily. "Your words about Asel fired me with hope that all the promises were proven. That our greatest hopes were reality."

"But they are!" he found himself saying. "A much greater light exists." He remembered the light staying his hand at Yosha's bedside. He'd sensed powers in the songs sung in Rycal's villages.

"We'll enter worlds after this one. You're right—the liturgies are full of promises that we'll live forever. But that light is far more than the rays that bathe the world above."

Geln was amazed at the words tumbling out of his mouth, amazed that he, entangled in evil, was instructing this spiritually intense young woman.

"I wish for one moment I could speak with Asel," she said. "I wish I could see her face and ask what light she had found."

"The Roundup"

Geln responded to many of Asel-ri's questions about life above, but when she pressed him about Yosha and Asel, he avoided direct answers. "It's your turn to talk. You've said you like to tell stories. Tell me one."

Asel-ri took from her clothes a small stringed instrument and handed it to him. It fit easily in the palm of his hand, a tall triangle bone frame with a long string in the center and three of shorter lengths on each side. He put his fingernail under the longest string and produced a mellow, pleasant sound.

She took the instrument back and strummed it to accent her words. "This is a children's story," she admonished, "so pretend you're a child."

"One day in a city not far away—a sparkling city by the sea—the children were rounded up.

"Oh, not children like you, of course! No, they were rascal children. These were the ones who slip up behind you and steal your pack. The ones spying for nasty men. The dirty, hungry ones grabbing your food. You know who I mean.

"Well, yes, in other ways they were children like you. But no one wanted them. No one cared about them. Everywhere in the city—a city of many tribes and many tongues—people shouted at them when their stinky bodies got too close. When one of them grabbed a bag of roots or a sack of fish, they'd scream for help.

"But not today.

"This was roundup day.

"They'd nabbed and herded the renegade waifs into the shallow pit at the center of the city. The children lay quiet as captured birds—like quivering birds when a snake encircles a nest. For the great men of the city were bunched around the pit as tight as the coils of a serpent.

"The men of the city could make a good profit today.

"The children would make good slaves, though their masters would have to beat the rebellion out of them. Slaves for Laij ships. Slaves for rich women. Slaves for soldiers.

"One after another child was yanked out of the pit by the men who had rounded them up. They shouted out what was for sale—boy or girl, skinny or fat. 'Come touch them!' they pleaded.

"The buyers shouted that the children were wretched and worthless, hardly worth the price, and as they haggled, none of them heard the distinctive clack of Auret's canes.

"Auret was a cripple, you know. The click, pause, click, click, pause of his sticks and the scuffling sounds of his twisted feet came up quietly behind them. He found the leader, an Askirit wealthy from running the roundups, and with his cane he poked him hard on the neck.

"'Stop this.'

"The big man whirled on him like a lizard at an insect. 'Stop what?'

"'I have a place for the children. Don't violate the Maker's laws.'

"The man cursed mightily and pushed the cripple away.

"Auret located the big waterpot waist-high at the entrance. With his cane, he tipped it over so that it crashed among the men

bunched around the pit. Crockery and water splattered everywhere.

"The hubbub ceased.

"Auret said in a loud voice, 'Don't make them into slaves! I
have a place for them.'

"The man who had pushed him said, 'Arrest him!'

"The cripple said, 'Arrest me for obeying the Maker? You
know the laws. Don't violate them.'

"Men angrily yelled at him to get out. Auret was wearing a
full belt of keitr. He loosed the belt, then snapped it over his knee
in the military manner. At the sound, men around him shouted in
fear, 'Arrest him!'

"But Auret commanded, 'Leave this place. All of you.'

"Soldiers came running.

"Auret opened a pouch, pulled out a keitr in its protective
inner sleeve, loosed its edge, then flung the creature at the men.

"Instantly the keitr screamed. He threw out another, and the
keitr sent soldiers and buyers and sellers alike scurrying madly
away.

"'Children!' Auret shouted in his strange, thick voice, 'if you
want to live, don't run! I have a place for you.'

"The keitr returned to the pouches of Auret, having killed
no one, for he had power over all elements and all creatures. To
the children Auret said, 'You are free now to be obedient.'

"But they were full of wildness and sins and had long
rebelled. So Auret touched every one of them, and prayed for
them and healed them. He spoke to them of many wonders. They
followed him to a little village, where those who believed made a
place for them—a little village where people abhorred the selling
of children."

Then, Asel-ri recited what was always said at the end of the
stories of Auret:

> "From the light above, he came to us as a child.
> He who lived in the light, and was the light,
> came as a cripple.

"Imagine that!

"Auret touched those in darkness,
and he healed all he touched.
He heals all who seek the light and who seek him.

"Imagine that!'

Geln had heard many stories of Auret, but never this one. "Is the story true?"

"It was told by Rycal himself. He met one of the children many years later."

She took a drink from the cup, then related more stories. Some she sang and some she told, using the little instrument in the pauses and for emphasis. She sang of how Auret had walked the bridge with the fatal gap, and she told how he had touched a traitor and healed him.

He thanked her, and then she stood and said, gathering up her things, "We're trapped in this cave, for it dead-ends not far back. I will sleep there, and you will sleep at the entrance."

"But the roaring of sierent will keep me awake. Even here it's loud."

"It's the proper thing to do," she said, brooking no argument. But to assure him of her friendliness, she reached out and touched his face.

Startled, he pulled back.

"What's the matter?"

The impress of her fingertips on his burned skin felt like something stuck on his face. He didn't know what to say.

"May I touch your face?"

He was embarrassed. He mumbled a yes, then felt her hand touch his cheekbone, then move to his forehead and across his eyes. His mouth pursed in embarrassment as she courteously explored all of his face. When she had finished, she said nothing about the scar of burned skin on his cheek that rose like a three-fingered hand toward his eye. Instead she said, "Why is your face so tight and your lips all scrunched up? I wasn't going to pinch you!"

"The scars ..."

She reached out and gently touched his burnt skin, saying, "How did it happen?"

"As a child, I fell into a fire."

"Perhaps it is well we have no fire here, if it does this to a child."

She was tenderly stroking his scar; tears began wetting his cheeks and her hand. It was the first time in many years a woman had touched him, and he was thinking of awakening at night with the terrible burns and his mother rocking and soothing him, saying, "My poor, burnt baby. I love you. Burnt baby, don't fear."

He swallowed hard and stepped away from her, ashamed at the flow of tears. But she said matter-of-factly, "I've never felt wounds like that. Remarkable, the skin's thinness and the puckery folds by the bone." Then she started putting her things into her pack.

Slowly he wiped his face with a cloth. "Have you heard anything else about me?"

She finished her little task, then stood with her pack. He rose and faced her, and finally she said, "I've heard that the powers had you, and that they want you again."

He grunted affirmation. "Anything else?"

"That perhaps you can be raised from the dead."

—— Dawnbreakers ——

The howlings of the storm kept Geln awake, and its violence once again emphasized his helplessness. But for once it didn't make him despair. It made him think of the helpless children being touched and healed by Auret.

Rycal had said, when he'd sent him into the wilds, "You don't have to do anything there. But you do have to meet someone." Then he warned, "He comes unexpected. He comes as fire, for he is fiercely hostile to all that ravages you."

Geln felt he was a scorched soul, yet he clung to Auret's words from one of the stories: "The Maker prefers mercy over vengeance."

All through the night his torments whirled in him like the screeching storm outside. He remembered the stories of Auret he'd heard in the villages and above as a child. He recited in his mind again and again the promise Asel finished her stories with: "He heals all who seek the light and who seek him. Imagine that!"

But his imaginings did nothing.

A voice within asked, "Are you really willing? Do you want to be healed?" He moved his lips with the word "yes," but nothing touched his spirit.

Finally, when night was almost gone, he fell asleep.

A short time later he felt Asel-ri's fingers on his cheek. They raced across it lightly like little fluttering wings as she announced, "We must greet the dawn."

The winds were still howling outside, but she grasped his shoulder and led him closer to the entrance. "They're already dying, and I want to feel their full force on my face." She shook her head, making her hair fly to the side, and something struck him softly on his chest.

"What's that?"

She laughed. "I purposely flung my hair around so you'd feel it." She held out for him what was attached to her hair—a carving of a bird in flight, about the size of her hand. "I'm wearing four of them."

She stepped into the wet, forceful winds; bracing himself, Geln followed. It bent him back, but he heard her wide-armed dancing into the wind. And as she did, he heard the whistling sounds of birds.

The wind was rushing through the carvings in her hair as she spun about, making the sounds of the birds of dawn. The birds called aurets.

As the winds died down a little, she said, "Listen! Can you hear them? The dawnbreakers! The aurets on the coast?"

His ears were not nearly as sharp as hers, but when the winds died down a bit more he did hear their cries as they rose from the coast to announce the dawn. "The carvings in your hair do make sounds like theirs."

"The wind hits them at many angles, so the sounds are imperfect. But with the singing in my hair, I feel I'm a dawnbreaker too!" She spun around with arms outstretched, and she called out,

> *"Praise to the Maker!*
> *Rejoice!*
> *Shout glory!*
> *He makes wonders everywhere!*
> *His majesty fills our spirits!"*

The fresh smells and winds were awakening Geln. The sounds of the aurets were getting louder, whereas sounds from the carvings in Asel-ri's hair were ebbing away as the winds became moist, pleasant breezes.

"Do others wear carvings like this?"

"Only women—to greet the dawn. You men should have such a custom."

He spread wide his arms. "It's enough to simply stand and listen to you and the aurets. To feel the winds and droplets sting my face." As he spoke, he realized he did feel—that deep in his chest and gut were not dry sand and deadness but new moisture and life.

Everywhere around them water cascaded from the rocks, ran in fast rivulets down gullies and dripped loudly off boulders above them. "I was amazed yesterday," Geln said, "how at dawn the streams are wide and tumultuous, even up in the peaks. But at evening, they're just a trickle, even as the new winds of sierent begin."

"There's a trail here to the sea," Asel-ri said, starting off ahead. They soon reached it and stood listening to the agitated waves crashing against the rocky shore. Far above them now, the aurets still were announcing the dawn as they rose to the peaks.

As their cries faded, he was startled by her making a loud sound remarkably like the cry of the auret. "You didn't need those carvings. You do a wonderful imitation."

"The carvings are the custom. Do you know the myth of the dawnbreaker?"

He knew it well, for it was recited above at every funeral. The myth that the first person created was so awestruck by the magnificence of dawn that he was changed into the bird—the auret—which announced every dawn thereafter.

"I love to think of Auret as the Dawnbreaker," Asel-ri said. "It was his mother, Chaisdyl, who named him Auret. She said he was always like those little heralds of the dawn, always giving her hope."

"Giving hope. And raising people from the dead."

She repeated Geln's words by racing her fingers over his wrist in Yette. "Rycal keeps saying Auret's so full of life that it rushes from him like a geyser through the least opening!"

He reached to her hair and touched one of the carved aurets, tracing its outstretched wings with his forefinger. "Last night," he said, "I must have opened something."

Chapter 9.

—— The Path for Two ——

At the command to halt, Mela numbly sank and dropped her pack. They'd been force marched for days, and she was still bewildered at the quick turn of events.

The massive crowds that had met them after their triumph on the peaks had grown in fervor and numbers. Men and women from all tribes and even Laij soldiers pressed to see the lamp and to hear the tales of Auret. Tresk had gone everywhere trying to manage the chaos: trails filled with pilgrims, soldiers agitating for information, recruits near rebellion.

Mela had then received a terse command from Tresk to travel on this long journey into the mountains. "Now we wait," an officer named Belen said as he offered her some water. "We're right at the edge of the Path for Two."

He had described the path to her as they'd climbed. Two high mountains in their bizarre configurations were nearly joined at one point, and in fact, a thin span between them had not yet been worn away by sierent. "This they call the Path for Two. The legend says only two may walk it—a third would make it collapse."

A breeze was cooling the sweat on her face and arms. Turning toward it she said, "I hear an Askirit army is approaching on the other mountain."

Belen knelt beside her. "They know about the turmoil. The Askirit say they're coming in peace, but who knows? Thousands of them invading just when they know we can't control anything."

Mela asked why they had chosen this mountain.

"Tresk's idea. Here, the armies can face each other without fear of attack. Neither side can swarm over the path—it would collapse."

"I've heard that every night sierent wears it yet thinner."

"The risk is not the path. Tresk is taking a terrible chance. We're under orders to annihilate every armed Askirit—not negotiate with them. The king would be furious."

By the time Tresk arrived with additional troops, Mela had been listening for a long time to the sounds of an army assembling on the other side. Tresk issued orders, then his huge bulk hovered over her. She stood and greeted him.

"You're the reason they're here, you know." His voice was not unkind but tight.

"We brought the lamp for peace. I'm told they come in peace."

"Maybe ..." He twisted his leather stick, then rapped it against his boot. "They know we're vulnerable. It's their first chance to upset the Laij kingdom. All the tales about light are Askirit. They know they can inflame all Tarn."

An officer reported on troop arrivals, and another gave intelligence on Askirit movements. Tresk kept making calculations on his loga, spinning and snapping it. He said to Mela, "Most dangerous of all, it's Rycal who leads them."

She had been told about Rycal, grandson of the king. "I hear that he too tells stories of Auret. That he seeks the light."

Instantly Tresk said, "Didn't all the warring Askirit kings say that?" She wondered if she detected fear in his voice when he added, "The Askirit hate me. I once forced Rycal himself over a cliff."

Mela's foot was carefully braced on the precarious trail. "I'd heard about his fall, but not that you were the commander."

He started to leave and Mela said, "I'm told Auret brought Rycal back to life again."

"That's the legend."

As formal shouts of peaceful intentions were exchanged across the thin linkage, Mela thought the sounds could as easily have been spears or keitr. Around her, Laij soldiers fidgeted uneasily. This was the first time armed Laij and Askirit warriors had ever met other than in battle. She heard Tresk muttering something about having "killed Rycal once" as he stepped out onto the Path for Two.

Like points of spears probing each other, the two men with armies at their backs spoke with elaborate politeness, carefully selecting each word. Then she heard Rycal say, "How long we have hated each other. Yet now the light has come."

Tresk, wary, said, "You Askirit have always talked about light. But you've made converts by the teeth of keitr."

Rycal murmured agreement. "Just as the Laij talk of knowledge and send merrets at our throats."

A bird, halfway out on the narrow path between Mela and the two men, was scratching for insects in the cracks. Suddenly, oblivious to the drama, it startled everyone by calling out loudly as it flew off.

Tresk said, "Sudden moves—like that bird's—are what I've always expected from anyone who speaks peace. You talk peace, but you wear a full belt."

"You're equally armed."

"You've flooded all Tarn with your tale tellers—spreading stories that incite the people."

Rycal objected that he no longer sought insurrection. "The story I tell most is how Auret found me shattered. He gave me back my life. And he said this: 'The light is coming. The time is nearly here.'"

"We've always fought such tales. They've always been used for Askirit conquest."

"But now you've seen the light with your own eyes. You know the Laij, with all their learning, were wrong about light. And you know also that there really is a way out of darkness."

—— Mela and Geln ——

Each time a whistle signaled that two men had crossed, two more stepped onto the thin bridge. Geln was appalled he would have to follow, especially as he got closer and heard each pair step off briskly to maneuver a very long stone's throw. The Path for Two could not be walked two abreast. One walked behind another, hands groping to touch uneven edges.

Rycal had given the order to the Askirit troops to move across, and they were moving with all deliberate speed before sierent began.

"Front or back?" the man beside him asked.

"What?" Geln was deciding whether to crouch with his hands on the edges or go on his hands and knees. He was willing to hump like a worm if that was what it took.

"Do you want to go ahead of me or behind?"

"This is crazy," Geln said. "I can hardly walk on a flat surface down here. How am I going to cross?"

"Don't you have your stick?"

Geln was holding one, but he had never learned to use it. "I'll probably trip over it. Maybe I should crawl over."

"Maybe you should."

He ended up in front, the man behind him firmly grasping

his belt as he slowly felt his way on all fours over the narrow way. Yet when he made it to the other side, he felt relief both at making it and at hearing others describe how low they'd hunched.

The Askirit were nervous walking among the Laij with full keitr belts. Warily, they moved down the trails, keeping tightly together lest this odd development suddenly turn into a trap.

As Geln descended, he heard a girl's voice not far off. He followed the sound, which came from a plateau beside the trail.

"Mela?" He knew that the bearer of the lamp was reputed to be with the Laij.

"Yes?"

Belen ordered him to keep moving but he said, "I too am from above. Give me a moment with her."

The officer made a clattering sound of derision, but Geln said, "Mela, on the sands of Korbas I was with the troops who guarded Yosha when you entered the rifts. I watched you and your friends say goodbye to your father."

Mela's breathing quickened. "It can't be!" she said to Belen. "Yet his accent is from above, and he says what's true." She turned to Geln. "How can it be?"

Geln stepped closer and reached out courteously to touch her arm. "Above, people speak of the Blind Princess. Here, they talk of another prophecy—the coming of the boy who is helpless."

She laughed. "Are you a boy? You sound more like a young man."

"Yes—but no one in all the world is more helpless than I."

She sensed he was in no way jesting. "But how did you come down—"

Geln was jostled by passing soldiers and they cautiously stepped farther back. "I was driven into the rifts."

"By what?"

He hesitated, then said, "Sand shriikes."

He expected her to doubt his statement, but she murmured that she understood. "In the peaks, we were stalked by the things ourselves."

Geln and Mela talked until Belen insisted they follow the others toward shelter. On the trail Mela told of the crowds agitating to learn the secret of getting to the light and insisting on hearing the tales again and again. With Mela, Geln felt reconnected and filled with questions and ideas.

Yet she was blind. She sensed everything differently. And talking with her about the past and future was a bitter mixture.

At the mountain's base, they followed others into a great cavern and into a place reserved for leaders of both sides. There, as they broke open their packs and began eating, she asked Geln, "What happened when you first fell into Aliare?"

He told Mela about his slavery and being taken to Rycal. He described his emptiness and helplessness, his search among the villages of Dorte, his rescue by Asel-ri and his new sense of healing and energy. On the way here, he and Rycal had told tales of Auret from village to village even as they dodged Laij patrols. "Remarkable, how people responded. Everywhere they insisted on hearing everything."

He began to tell her about visiting Wellen, Yosha's home village, but he suddenly had to stop talking. He remembered the ancient king with tears sending Mela down into the rifts. He saw himself in Yosha's tent raising the cloth over the king's face to murder him. He felt speechless and helpless.

Mela asked, "What's wrong?"

"Pray for me."

They sat in silence. He prayed desperately that if his guilt was truly forgiven, he would be released from the accusations drilling into his spirit.

Finally he continued his story. "Wellen, you know, was Yosha's childhood village. We met a boy on the shore there, and Rycal left me with him for a while. He was about ten and he knew all the legends about Yosha. He even kept little pools of selcrit in case leviathan crashed onto the shore. He was ready to risk his life as Yosha had. The boy took me up into Kjotik's Jaw, high above the village, where Yosha would listen to the sea and resolve to act on the promises. I tried to inhale great draughts of his courage!"

"I pray you will have Yosha's courage."

Her words hit him like a sharp command. He knew he had to reveal the depth of his complicity with evil, and he told her everything, even his gripping the wet cloth at Yosha's bedside.

"The sages were right," she said, unsurprised. "The depths of evil can never be plumbed; yet the light is far, far greater."

Belen interrupted them, then led them through long, connecting tunnels. As they rounded a turn, Mela could hear the animated voices of both Tresk and Rycal coming from a large chamber. She and Geln were led in as the two old enemies were discussing the danger of their men spilling out of their shelters in the morning, tempted to settle old scores.

"Not many years ago I'd have eagerly welcomed war," Tresk said. "But now, war stinks in my soul, like a corpse dressed up for celebration."

Rycal grunted agreement. "Believe me—we may have full belts, but we haven't come here to launch keitr." He yanked his belt off and flipped it over to Tresk. "Here. Take it. Just don't open a pouch!"

Tresk laid it in front of him and felt its contours with his hands. "My men have thrown many of these into the sea. But I've never touched one myself." He reached over and, with a clack and a snap, he handed Rycal his loga. "Ever touch one of these?"

Rycal said he had not. He toyed with the device as they discussed the coming dangers.

"Euphoria may be the deadliest enemy." Tresk said. "Soldiers who think their hard times are soon over. Villagers who think they'll soon rise like birds to the light. All their giddy talk and songs could quickly turn into blood and screams."

Rycal said, "I understand you're in a very delicate position."

"Not delicate. Maddening! All those fools in the ranks and

all those civilians chattering on the trails little understand the fury of the king."

Mela said in a quiet, respectful voice, "Perhaps we should take the lamp to him. If the king of the Laij saw with his own eyes, as you have ..."

On hearing her voice, Rycal stood and strode over to her. "The girl with the lamp. The Blind Princess!" He gripped her shoulders in salute and touched her cheek with a highly respectful swirl of his fingers.

"I am only an envoy."

"You've brought us the light! You've forever changed the world." He took both her hands in his. "And you have the tales of Auret on everyone's lips."

"I've heard you've done much the same."

Rycal turned back to Tresk. "Might the king listen to you, who command so much of his army?"

Belen said, "If I may speak for my commander. He allowed you to come armed, which is against orders. He must not only deal with the turmoil here, but the rumors against him in the capital."

"I let you come," Tresk said, "as the only chance to avoid war." He had retrieved his loga and snapped it into a new position. "Passions are building everywhere. They believe the light awaits above. They fear the abyss is rising."

Rycal agreed. "They sense something fearful coming up. My men won't sleep in the deepest caverns."

Tresk took a deep breath. "Is Auret more than a legend? Does some Maker care about what happens here? Who knows? But this I do know: everything in Aliare is changed."

"Can the king be convinced?"

Tresk drummed his tongue like a marching platoon. "After the king lost ten thousand men scouting the abyss, he closed his mind like a trap." He snapped the end of his stick against a rock. "Rycal, you understand how the Laij kingdom was built on logic, and on power. The king knows the Askirit religion is the only force that could topple him. Anyone with a whiff of rebellion—or with talk of new realities let loose in the world—he wants annihilated."

—— The Scent of Life ——

Midday on cliffs above the sea, long lines from all tribes pressed forward to hear the tales of Auret and news of the light. At the front of each line glowed a bright lamp, for Jesk and Delin had successfully worked with both Laij and Askirit to make lamps which burned oils harvested from the sea.

Geln described the scene to Mela beside him: dark shapes of people moving toward them and features of faces close by, long shadows cast and barely discernible movements of the sea's waves behind them.

"You talk like my sister Ashdel describing kelerai. Everything sensed through the eyes, but no comments about sounds and smells."

"True. And all these coming are euphoric about light, but they don't see clearly. What strange ways they describe things."

Varial and Rycal joined them and Varial said, "The crowds keep growing, weeping and asking forgiveness for their hatreds."

"Day after day they come," Mela said, standing beside her lamp, which burned brighter than them all. "Auret's love is so different from everything else they've ever known."

Rycal held his hand by a lamp and let its shadow fall on the ground. "The Spirit is at work. They speak less now about climbing up to the light and more about the Maker's holiness."

Mela put her hand on the warmth of her lamp. "Here in the darkness of Aliare is more communion with the Maker, more tears of repentance and of joy, then I ever heard above." She dipped her fingers in a shell filled with scent and sniffed its fragrance. "Perhaps I can finally sense just a very little of why Auret doesn't just break open the crust of the planet and bring everyone up into the light. Maybe I can finally understand why the planet was long ago judged and so many people cast into darkness."

Rycal stepped up to a slightly higher ledge, lamp in hand, and his voice boomed out that he had a story to tell. He placed the lamp at his feet and started:

"In the time when Tarn was fresh-conquered by the Laij,
The time when Asel and Yosha had just wed,
A hundred prisoners—Yosha's men—were led into Aris.
Bound one to the other, they were marched to the city.
Condemned, they were led to the judge to be marked for death.

"You know the scent. The Laij handle it like a live pectre!
Soldiers soaked each man till he gagged of it,
Till he was saturated with the permanent scent of death.
The hundred men with burning eyes they sealed in a chamber,
Sealed to wait for dawn in thick odors, the signs of execution.

"At dawn, soldiers came to march them to the cliff,
To publicly cast them down to rocks and sea.
They found the chamber empty!
They found instead a new scent.
A scent pungent as the fruits and blossoms above.

"A shout went up in Aris: 'The prisoners are among us!'
The people said, 'Whoever heard of men marked for death—
men scented for death!—walking with the aroma of life?'
The judges said, 'Hunt them down!
Kill anyone in all Tarn wearing the new scent.'

"But the men escaped. The death scent was swallowed up.
The aroma of life filled the people with yearnings.
And how was the chamber of death emptied?
They say a cripple entered there,
Auret, the broken one."

Rycal then said to the crowds, "You, also, are marked for death. The scent on you can never be washed away. Except by the life that swallows death. Except through Auret's scent. If you want to live, come. . . ."

Mela worried each time Rycal told this story, for the Laij could take it as a political invective against them. And the ceremony now starting was clearly a statement of new loyalties. All who wished to identify with Auret and the quest for the light would receive his scent on forehead and hands.

It was a seditious act. She was especially concerned Tresk not think they were betraying his trust.

That's why, as the people came up to receive the scent, she was astounded when she heard Tresk's voice beside her responding to Rycal's invitation.

"The scent of Auret, the scent of life," Rycal said.

"The scent of Auret, the scent of life," Tresk repeated as Rycal smeared on his forehead and hands the fruity aroma made in the Askirit villages.

"Take the fragrance of life everywhere," Rycal said. "Seek the light."

It was over in a moment, but Mela, even as she placed the scent on other hands and foreheads before her, knew that something profound had taken place.

Tresk left immediately to confront the growing tensions, for many resisted the new "religious fervor." On his return, he summoned Mela and Rycal to his quarters by the sea.

Before even greeting them, he told them he had received an

imperial summons. "We must act decisively. We must be gone before the king's troops arrive." He was like a great bird fluttering and straining to break a tether, saying in a rush of words, "All my career I've made excuses for the king's arrogance. And now half his army wants to follow a girl and a lamp to the fabled world of light." He paused, then said, "I'm ready to follow her too."

Here it is, Mela thought, *the scene played out in the pageants above in which thousands streamed out of Aliare and into the light.*

Yet she knew she couldn't actually lead anyone out.

She told them so. "The roof above the peaks is full of cracks, yes, but which is the right one? The rope we left is by now shredded by sierent."

"But isn't that why you came?" Tresk asked. "To invite us into the light?"

"Of course! But the Askirit searched for centuries and never found the way, until Auret showed them." She was praying desperately. She knew they could at least try it, yet something was whispering within her.

She was envisioning something very different from the pageant image of thousands happily coming up out of Aliare. Instead, she saw the Laij and Askirit and tribes—many still hating each other and bent for vengeance—swarming up out of the belly of the planet, expecting paradise. At first they'd be welcomed. But then war would start. And their undeveloped eyes, seeing only distortions in the painful brightness, would make them inept. They'd be attacked and enslaved.

She thought of the time Yosha and Asel had emerged into the light. Their eyes had to be touched by Auret. These longing to climb to the light would need not only their eyes touched, but also their souls—first of all their souls.

She had reached an inescapable conclusion, but felt she could hardly voice it. Yet they waited for her until she said, "Yosha and Asel learned the way was through the abyss."

Rycal and Tresk greeted this with incredulity. Rycal shook

his head so forcefully the hollow balls in his hair clicked. "We can't do that! Asel and Yosha went down the trail from the Skull. That's close to Aris—we'd all be in the king's hands."

"Yes, I know. That's why something within tells me I must carry the lamp to the king."

These words were even less acceptable. Yet Mela said, "Perhaps if the king saw the light for himself, we could fill him with dreams of reaching the world above."

Tresk laughed dryly. "No one fills the king with dreams."

They argued, but Mela said adamantly, "What rings in my ears is this: 'The way to the light is not through the peaks. The way to the light is through the pit.'"

—— Fire ——

In light flickering throughout the great cavern, men and women were noisily assembling hundreds of lamps. Geln was amazed at the sounds coming from the festive workers: teeth, tongues, and throats mimicking amphibians and insects, creating thumping rhythms interspersed with strange reports and familiar Askirit tunes—the variety of sounds as remarkable to Geln's ears as the light to the eyes of these subterranean people.

"Mine's going out!" a man said as his lamp guttered in the oil. Before Geln could reach him, the flame expired.

On hands and knees, Geln jiggled the dead wick till it was slightly higher in the oil, then relighted it. He knew enough about common lamps to guide their production and now looked around the massive cavern with satisfaction. Leather bags of oil lay in piles beside row after row of new lamps, a score of which were lighted, casting giant shadows from the workers.

Their haste came from knowing the king's ships were

coming and that they had very little time to prepare their escape through the peaks. Their high spirits came from handling the lamps and talking about climbing to much greater light above.

Geln marveled at the skill of the artisans. Askirit women shaped bones into precise forms, tribesmen cut thin shale. To discover effective wicks, they wove aceyn and grasses and insect wax into countless combinations.

A Laij soldier interrupted and announced in Geln's ear that someone was outside for him. "Askirit girl named Asel-ri."

Geln turned quickly on his heel. "She dragged me out of sierent," he told the man.

The Laij soldier led Geln to the darkness just outside where Asel-ri stood by the boulders used for rest times. When the Laij said, "Here she is," Geln regretted that in his haste he'd forgotten to pick up a lamp. What might she look like?

But her first words after they greeted each other made him wish he'd also cleaned his hands. "Smells like very old fish around here."

He'd gotten used to the smell and had forgotten it. "Let's go down to the sea." He skipped giving her the traditional greeting with his oily palms.

They maneuvered down the short trail and at sea's edge he rubbed his hands briskly in the aceyn. She laughed at his concern. "Fish oil doesn't bother me."

He courteously touched her face, then she his. "All Dorte is emptying," she said, telling of widespread revival of desire for the light. "We've all followed Rycal here. It's time for the promises to come true."

"Come and see the lamps ... if you can stand the smell."

They walked back up the trail, she surefooted and quick, he far less skilled yet keeping up. But when they turned the corner in the cavern entrance and the light became a glowing nimbus before them, she suddenly moved very slowly, and in the light he became the one sure of his steps.

"Is that the light? So big? It fills my sight."

Geln knew the only light she had seen before was from sparks struck from flint and small luminous creatures. The glow from the cave filled the air before them.

They walked into the full glare. Even to Geln, it seemed dreamlike, the workers casting shadows in their movements, lively sounds echoing everywhere off the curved walls, smells of fish oil and the cutting of bone heavy in the air. Asel-ri had stopped beside him, her fingers digging into his elbow.

"What do you think of the light?"

Her fingers tightened yet more. Geln picked up a lamp with his free hand and held it high in the light. He saw she was breathing rapidly with eyes tightly shut.

He studied her face, narrow, dark, attractive, squinting as if fighting the rays illumining her. He'd learned that the first experience of light often disoriented the people of Aliare, that it distorted their sense of perspective. "Does the light hurt your eyes?"

"It frightens me." She threw out her arms as she had at dawn when the cries of aurets were in the air. "And it exhilarates me. It is terrible!"

He grasped her shoulders and turned her toward the entrance. "Here. Look this way; it's not so bright." He held the lamp in his hand low behind him.

She opened her eyes slowly. "No wonder so much is sung about the light," she said. "No wonder there's so much yearning." She turned very cautiously to face the brighter light. "It's as if sierent is thundering into my eyes and right through me."

He led her to where they were assembling the lamps and knelt beside one. "Look at the flame. It's like a living thing. But don't touch! It burns."

She stayed her hand but held it close enough to feel the heat. "Remarkable." She touched her warm hand to her face. "Light searches out every word," she quoted from the liturgy, "and makes ashes of evil."

He lifted the lamp in his hands and looked at its flames, then at the activity throughout the cavern that he alone could see clearly. "How ironic, that I—the helpless—should be the one person in all Aliare with eyes that truly see." He raised the wick and the lamp burned brighter. "Yet perhaps I also see clearest the stench of our rebellions. And the depth of the Maker's love."

Asel-ri was turning both her hands beside the little flame and spreading out her fingers. "Is this what burned your face?" She pulled back her hand. "It feels warm, but a little closer and it hurts."

"Fire can be terrible." He looked at her calm face in the shadows, savoring his own feelings of gratitude. Then he said, with such cheerfulness it seemed to contradict his words, "I'll never know why Eshtel didn't crush me like a poisonous beast."

Geln and Asel-ri walked beside the workers, talking above the din of their hummings and clackings and whirrings and chatter. "The lamps aren't difficult to make," he explained. "I'm sure it was often attempted by those who first fell into the darkness. But they had no flame to light the wicks, and it was too damp to create a flame."

Asel-ri asked about Mela's lamp. "Why did she leave us?"

"Everyone said she was crazy. Going to Aris like a fish swallowing a hook. But she believed she was commanded to give the king a chance to see and believe."

"Now that we have the light," Asel-ri said, "war is crazy! Why is this armada coming to fight? They'll drag Tresk and anyone siding with him to the torturers instead of just getting us all out of the darkness."

"But we'll be out of here before the armada arrives." He explained this was their last day of work, that they would leave at dawn. "Who knows if we'll make it? No one has ever gotten out through the peaks."

Asel-ri leaned forward, grasped the handle of a burning lamp, then stood and lifted it. "That's true. But we'll have the lamps to light the way."

Part Three

The dirtiest hand
can never soil
the tiniest shaft of light.

—FROM THE ASKIRIT RITUAL

Chapter 10.

—— Audience with the King ——

The sounds and smells of subterranean Aris were, to the four blind envoys, not so very different from Aris above. It was ruled by the Laij but filled with diverse languages. Shouts and movements of commerce, the smells and sense of crowds around them were like a city above.

Except for the missing smells of hot food.

"What I long for are stews cooking and breads baking," Lysse said.

Belen hurried the little procession toward what was once the Askirit temple. He was nervous and shared his commander's dismay at their decision to come. Both Rycal and Tresk had warned Mela that she and the others were reporting for their own executions. Yet in the end, they'd put the four into the hands of a cadre of select Laij officers.

"Tresk!" The call rang out as they were speaking to the guards at the temple. The voice carried authority and an edge of exasperation. As the man came toward them in quick, measured steps, she heard the same high-rank sounds rustling from his clothes that Tresk's always made.

Belen snapped to attention. "Tresk is ill. At his orders, we have brought the four envoys and the lamp."

"Ill?" The roar of disdain from the general officer made Mela flinch.

Belen said evenly, "We received that word from the commander's quarters."

The officer cursed and struck his palm loudly with his leather stick. "Don't give me that! The king has already sent an armada of ships to quell this madness."

Belen avoided responding by saying, "May I introduce Mela and the other envoys?"

The commander observed protocol by turning to them. Mela and the others found Belen had been right to predict they'd be shown every courtesy. "It will be like tribes that treat condemned prisoners like royalty—till their last meal."

They were ushered into the vast open courtyard of the temple and invited to feel the rounded walls of precisely cut stone. Mela remembered the story of how Yosha came here after the Laij had conquered Tarn. When he had felt the carvings of faces looking up toward the light, all had been gouged and disfigured. Now, smooth stone covered all the ancient work of the Askirit artisans.

They stepped close to the pool the Laij had built. "I wish you could see the movements of all the luminous sea creatures," Belen said. "A feast for the eyes. To us, the pool rivals those in Kelabreen, which took centuries to build."

The general officer asked, "Is it true you're all four blind? How strange, that messengers from the light cannot see."

Mela said, "We are like you. We hear and feel and taste. We sense the smallest nuances—the smell of a rose that's red, or yellow, or pink—we know the difference. We know the smells and feel of green grass and open fields."

Lysse said, "And we've listened to kelerai as it explodes each morning, shaking us alert, filling the air with sweet scents, making us praise the Maker."

"The Maker?" The commander's voice was gravelly and firm. "Some say that at seditious gatherings you've marked thousands of agitators with the Maker's scent." He said it calmly, as if his accusation were small talk. "Rumors about you are impossible to verify. We're certainly glad you're here, so we can learn the truth."

They climbed up many flights of smooth stone stairs and finally arrived, tired and perspiring, at the entrance to what was once the Tolas, the holiest place in the Askirit kingdom. Now it was the high throne room of the Laij king.

As they stepped forward, Mela heard a little gasp from Belen, who'd never before entered the throne room. "What do you see?"

"More than I'd imagined." His voice was subdued. "Diffuse light everywhere. Small pools with swimming, phosphorescent creatures. On one side, gems of many colors with moving creatures casting faint, white light on them. On the other side the reverse: sparkling white gems and creatures of spectacular colors. All soft, dim light that lures you forward."

They made their way up a rising aisle that wound around enclaves of scholars and courtiers. Scents wafted in from all directions, and musicians and singers softly complemented the images and aromas. They kept rising, always rising, every enclave and scent and sound they walked through designed to awe them, to slowly escort them up to the throne, where an array of sea creatures radiating light swam in a pool at the king's feet.

At a signal, as the envoys reached the throne, scholars, officers, musicians all fell silent and turned toward them.

Mela had been told that at each of the king's hands would be an olek, the Laij national symbol. She heard the big birds now, about head level, making throaty kelking sounds.

"So, you are envoys from another king?" The voice above them was high pitched, reminding Mela of the noises of a seal. "I understand he has sent me blind children."

Mela tried to read his inflections, to sense how sarcastic he meant that. She said with great deference, "We are blind, but we are of age. We were chosen by the prophecies."

The king sighed theatrically. "Is your king a fool, like the Askirit kings who lost Tarn?"

He lifted one of the birds onto his wrist, and it made its deep sounds in a long cadence. "Do you know why the olek is our national symbol?" He paused a moment, then answered his own question. "Because it's smart. Everyone tells stories of how cleverly the olek gets its prey or escapes capture. It's the smartest creature in Aliare. Except for the Laij."

He laughed at his own jest, then held out the bird on his wrist toward them. "You might think the merret would be our symbol—they're fast and lethal. But the merret is stupid. They do our work for us." He laughed again. "The olek would know it was being used. Just like the Laij know ..."

He put the bird back, then said loudly, "I'm not stupid! You've seduced my own officers and corrupted my army. You've filled the world with seditious tales. Envoys? You're spies and insurrectionists!"

Mela's throat tightened with terror. Yet she also felt anger. "We have come from the light only with a message of peace, and a lamp of hope."

"Askirit talk! Why should I receive envoys from your king when we have kings serve at our tables?" He leaned down and asked, as if to a little child, "Tell me. How does one get from here to the world above?"

Mela sensed he was waiting like a hunter who'd laid a trap. But, regardless, she said, "The way to the light is through the abyss."

His laugh was a knowing cackle, as if he had been very clever to pry it out of her. "I'd heard that was the way!" He laughed again and shook his head at the richness of the joke so that the necklaces at his throat jangled.

Mela said angrily, "The world above is real! It has not only light, but the warmth of the sun's rays and the riches of forests and fields. It's a world beyond darkness, a world—"

"I'm content to conquer one world—Aliare," he interrupted. "The abyss below, the roof above. It's enough. Another king can conquer your false imaginings."

Mela thought of the ten thousand troops he'd lost exploring the abyss and realized he was not content but fearful. Though he'd throw away legions of men on foolish campaigns, he understood little beyond this suffocating throne room.

Simply and firmly Mela said, "We have no wish to conquer your kingdom, only to freely share the light."

The king abruptly stood, and his movements made his thick garments sound like whirring insects. "Show me the lamp."

With fierce prayers lofting, Mela undid the flaps and turned up the pilot so that the flame leaped into life. It flooded the throne room with bright light and shadows.

She heard behind her gasps and many movements and whispers. But in front of her the king said nothing. She recalled Belen's prediction: "The king has been told the lamp is a great wonder. He will refuse to be amazed—no matter how much it stuns him."

The king stood in silence for a long time. Finally he sat down again. He called an officer to him and asked if the lamp could be used as some sort of weapon. They talked for a time, then he turned back to the envoys. "Too bright! Too bright! I find the light very disagreeable." He was staring at the shadows made by the birds. "I hate all those ugly, dark movements. Turn it off."

Mela lowered the flame.

"Ugly rumors," he said. "Cracks in the roof above. Death crawling up from below. And now this. Just a brighter light than our eels and fish, but mumbo jumbo to incite anarchy."

Mela fastened the flaps. She sensed she had nothing to lose and boldly said, "The Maker long ago judged the world above. He scourged its rebels. But now his arms are open, inviting all to come to the light. The Maker never, never removes his hands from what he has made! He will not leave Aliare in darkness."

The king ordered an officer to take the lamp from her.

"Learn its use. We will place it so that its glare can shine in the eyes of those who kneel before me."

Told to show the man how it worked, Mela re-opened the flaps and taught him to work the pilot. They left it lighted next to one of the birds.

The king said, chuckling, "We'll turn it on for those who want to worship the lamp. They can revere it as it illumines my face."

Mela envisioned supplicants kneeling and worshiping the light on his face. Some day, when its fuel was gone, the lamp would splutter and blink out.

She savored his eventual dismay, but was caught short by his abrupt announcement. "We've extended to you diplomatic immunity. Now, return to your king. The four of you will be escorted to the Skull and to the descent to the abyss." He chuckled again, as if he had trapped her once more. "If you see some of my ten thousand men while you're down there, tell them they are absent without leave."

The king then began laughing at his own words, laughing so hard that one of the birds rose up and flapped its wings. The flame of the lamp was tossed back and forth crazily by the draft, making the light dance and cast eerie shadows on the gems and sea creatures and the royal, laughing face.

—— The Planet Shudders ——

Geln and Asel-ri worked with the others from dawn through the day assembling lamps, placing the thin shale wafers into interlocking bone frames and handles, then setting the wicks. Mid-afternoon they took a break and carried two lighted lamps to the boulders outside.

"Fresh mycea and fish," he said, holding out a small basket.

Mycea was eaten like a plant with fish or meat and tasted like a spicy, substantial root. Yet in reality the creatures were extremely thin, giant ovals that during the day rode the sea. Each evening they came rippling in to affix themselves to cliffs and rocks to ride out sierent. Fastening themselves tight as skin, they couldn't be pried loose. At dawn, they'd peel themselves off the cliffs and ripple back out to sea, only their curled-up sides differentiating them from the sea itself.

Geln heard the crunch as Asel-ri bit down on a slice of the fibrous mycea. They were cut into long, thin strips, which made a thick bed for the chunks of fish. He reached into his own basket, felt the pleasant crunch under his own teeth and asked, "Ever ridden a mycea as it comes in?"

She stood and held out her arms as if balancing herself on a moving boat. "Of course. They're like skin on the water—makes you feel as if you're riding the sea."

"They're the best surprise I've found in Aliare. Nothing like them above."

"In our bay at home, they come in by the hundreds—so many I can jump from one to the other as if I'm running across the water." She smiled. "But eventually I always fall through. That's part of the fun. You hit a curl at the edge, water rushes in, and down you go."

They agreed that when they finished eating and the first breezes of sierent began they would go down to the shore and await their arrival. "I'd love to carry a lamp and actually see the waters moving under my feet."

But they had barely finished eating when a brisk wind suddenly swept down on them.

"A wind like this in the afternoon?" he asked. "I thought that never happened."

"It doesn't," she said, standing up against the stiffening wind, her hair blowing out behind her. "It never, never happens."

The shifting winds quickly became stronger. Then came windswept water, as if sierent were beginning in earnest.

Geln held up his lamp, but the winds blew out the flame. He began sprinting for the cavern, and Asel-ri ran after him, water and wind now whipping against them, slowing their progress.

Buffeted by walls of winds, they were actually blasted backward. They dropped the lamps and crawled forward on all fours. By the time they were at the entrance, they felt they were moving through deep sand. Gripping each other's hands, they thrust their bodies forward until they felt other hands pulling them into the safety of the cave.

Everyone was astonished, saying the phenomenon was impossible, even as they helped drag in those who had been outside.

Geln and Asel-ri sat drenched on the cave floor beside the rows of lighted lamps, silent with wonder. Asel-ri said, "Never, never has sierent come so early, so suddenly."

He held his dripping hair in his hands, staring down at the puddles reflecting the drips amid shadows from the lamps. "Anyone not near shelter would have been swept away."

"I wonder if the king's armada was at sea."

"Probably. Something fundamental has shifted in this unstable world."

—— Many Hands ——

The trail down to the abyss had become a narrow chimney. Above Mela was Lysse, below were Jesk and Delin, all four with feet and hands grasping for holds on either side. Delin called out so that echoes rocked down the canyons of stone. "Nothing but air in front of us. If you fall, don't fall forward."

His words struck terror in Mela, because Lysse was slipping above her. Stones fell on her head and shoulder and Lysse cried out that she was falling. Her knee struck Mela's hand, ramming it against a sharp ridge. Half an instant later her full body landed, wrenching Mela loose and propelling them down. They fell heavily on the young men, dislodging them, and for a long instant they were in a free fall, hands and feet flailing to grasp something solid. They landed in a tumbled melee.

"Who's hurt?" Delin asked immediately, dragging himself free of the tangle.

Mela felt her hand and tried to move her fingers; she thought one might be broken. She was bruised and her hip and forearm scraped. "I'm okay." She stood, as did the others. "They could at least have given us a rope! We're going to kill ourselves."

"We never asked for a rope," Jesk said wryly. "Pretty stupid of us."

Mela took his comment as criticism and said she should never have insisted on going to the king. "We'd be up in the peaks by now if I'd listened to Tresk and Rycal."

Delin put his arm around her shoulders. "Every one of us agreed with you."

"But it was my conviction!" She was angry at herself but grateful for his touch. "I was exuberant about what had happened in the peaks and to the thousands taking the scent. I thought the momentum would go right on to the king, and then to all Aliare. But now I feel like a dry, dirty pot left on the fire."

Delin made his fingertips move like waves over her cheek, which in Yette represented soothing waters. "Get off the fire. You had to take the lead. Don't be sorry for obeying your call."

"Then why do I feel so rotten about it? Why are we down here, when we're supposed to be bringing people up out of darkness?"

Next morning, Mela was slowly, very slowly awakening, trying to stay within her dream. Something hopeful from it was lingering. She didn't want to let it go, yet the sounds of her friends rising were prodding her awake.

She stood and stretched, remembering, and all that morning as they continued their descent, she kept trying to bring the fragments of it back. It wasn't until midday, as they were resting after a meal, that she said anything about it. Lysse asked why she'd been so quiet.

"I had visitors last night."

Her words got everyone's attention. "In a dream," she explained, and everyone eased back again. "I remember only pieces, images of this very tall man with wild hair but smooth, loose clothes standing in the wind beside me, saying that someone is coming for me."

They asked questions about the man, but she couldn't describe him further. "He kept pronouncing, like a prophet in a desert, 'Beloved child.' He kept saying those two words, then finally said, 'Beloved child, he is coming for you.' The man was leaning into the wind with all his might as it whipped at his hair and clothes."

She stopped talking, and she was embarrassed to tell the rest, but her friends sensed there was more and pressed her. "The man also said this. 'He is coming, no matter what the cost. You, Mela, are the beloved from before you were born. He will battle the powers to reach you—because his love for you is stronger than all the powers in Aliare.'"

When her words met with silence, Mela worried that her friends thought she once again was thinking too highly of herself. But finally Delin made the little sound of awe with the tip of his tongue against his teeth. "May he come soon."

Jesk's tone was more urgent. "When you said you'd had visitors, I thought you meant whatever's following us."

"What?" Mela had heard nothing. Yet she soon learned that the others had become increasingly aware of sounds around them.

"Something's here with us," Jesk said. "Sounds like lots of them to me—whatever they are."

As they edged their way down, Mela became aware of scuffing sounds and falling stones above and below. She even thought she heard breathing just above her. She tried to sense how many directions the sounds came from and decided Jesk was right about there being "lots of them."

They sat down to eat back to back, unable to stop listening to the sounds moving all around them. "Wish I had my keitr belt," Jesk said.

"For once, I wish you did too," Lysse said.

"At least there's no sierent down here," Delin said. They knew that deep in the bowels of the mountains, no winds or deluge would reach them.

"I miss sierent," Mela said. "It lets us know when it's day and night. And I've caught Asel's love for its fierceness, and the freshness of the dawn."

A dislodged rock nearby startled her. "Was that one of you?"

As if in answer, she heard scrapings and shufflings coming from many directions.

"They sound like men to me," Delin said. "Like slow, deliberate men." He called out to them and greeted them, and when he got no response, implored them to speak. He then stood and walked toward them, but they backed away.

All afternoon and evening fear had been stabbing at Mela. Now, as she sensed these presences so close, the fear came like heavy moisture in the air, settling over her body.

As they ate, little moans and woeful fragments of words came from all around them, and the spirit of fear floated onto them with the sounds.

"They themselves are full of fear!" Delin said, as if just discovering it. "They carry their fear within, breathing it out like clouds of hopelessness."

They had stopped eating. The fear kept wafting among them, prickling their skin, penetrating their spirits. Mela was sitting with a slab of root in her hand, toying with it, when she heard movements right beside her and then a limp hand placed itself on her forearm.

She stifled the scream in her throat, jerked herself to her feet and yanked her arm away. "Let's get out of here!"

"Where would we go?" Lysse said. "If we run all night, we'll only feel the fear more." She sounded as if she were stuffing down her own panic. "We need again the Absurdity of our little prayers!" She said this last as if she were straining to believe, clinging to a thin strand.

They all prayed aloud, words against the breathing of the crowds of passive, agonized men all around them. And as they prayed, Mela suddenly thought, *These must be the king's men! The thousands sent down to explore the abyss.*

Men—mere men—made into Tremblers. Asel long, long ago had met them in Dorte when, enslaved by the furies, they had dragged the Sledge of the Dead. This realization only increased the fear pumping through her. "You're right, Lysse. There's only one weapon against the powers of the abyss."

Yet their prayers mixed with their fears like clear water polluted by decay. They clasped each other's hands and prayed aloud, but their hands trembled. They felt that soon they would be Tremblers themselves, that they would merge with the men wandering and moaning here above the abyss.

Yet they kept praying, their weak little words rising and dissipating in the air, but touching, they hoped, some mysterious levers above.

The night was more than half gone when they heard shouts and commands in the distance, and sounds of feet, purposeful and quick. As they drew closer, the Tremblers pressed close around them, heaving out great sighs of terror.

Then Mela recognized Geln's voice calling out her name.

She called back in response, and he shouted as he moved

down the gully behind them. Then he was crashing past the Tremblers and broke through to them.

"Geln, I thought you'd be in the peaks! How'd you find us?"

As he embraced all four of them, he simply said they'd come with a hundred lamps and a thousand men and women. "After all," he said, "since you were convinced the way out was through the abyss, you were probably right. You are the Blind Princess."

The Weight of Darkness

The voices and faith of those carrying the lamps charged the atmosphere with hope. The four friends wept in relief as they embraced the newcomers. The Tremblers stood rigidly upright, like soldiers called to attention. A few were jolted out of the oppression that bound them, but most stood hopelessly in place.

Geln lifted his lamp high near the face of a man rigid except for his shaking arms. His pursed lips quivered slightly as he made quiet mewing sounds like a bereft child. His Laij uniform was as filthy as his skin, but Geln put his arm tightly around both shoulders and his hand on his neck, saying, "He came for the worst of us, for cowards and rebels. Auret redeems us from darkness and death."

Then Geln stepped away from the man, raised his head and said distinctly, "Spirits of fear, flee from the light!"

With buoyant faith the many lampbearers touched their hands to the heads and shoulders of the shaking men and prayed for their release. Slowly, very slowly, as they persisted in their prayers and singing and in their worship and praise to the Maker, Tremblers were released into ordinary men.

The first sign was a man's blinking in the light, and then weeping as his spirit was finally melted loose by the presence of so much good will and love. For more than a day they sang and ate and clasped hands in solidarity until the last Trembler returned to reality.

"But why did you come?" Mela asked Geln again, after all were freed from the fear and were feeling the enormous sense of relief and victory. "I thought you were going to the peaks with Rycal and Tresk."

"Somehow, I knew that I too was required to go to the pit. When sierent came early, all Aliare was shaken. I took it as a sign."

Asel-ri, standing beside Geln, said, "It came so suddenly that anyone far from shelter was sucked away. And the king's armada was obliterated."

"Not an entirely bad thing, considering their mission," Delin said. He was holding his hands up to a lamp, feeling its warmth. "Perhaps this is the start of the prophecies that someday all the world will convulse."

"Thinking about that very phrase made me come to you!" Geln said. "It made me realize my only safety is being where Auret wants me. The peaks, the world above, nowhere is safe unless the Maker leads. But with him, I'm safe in the abyss."

The mellow light of lamps, the meeting of the two parties and the deliverance of many hundreds of Laij scouts made them talk and laugh with a lightheartedness completely at odds with their predicament. When someone wondered what they would face in the depths of the abyss, Geln said, "At least we have the lamps. When Yosha and Asel went through, they had only their prayers. We will have both our prayers, and the light in our hands."

They descended as a great force of energy and light. Even the Laij soldiers, still dazed by it all, were following them, some enthusiastically, some fearfully, but all willingly. The five who had been born above laughed about many absurdities, not only that all depended on little prayers, but that this weaponless little band was descending to the depths of evil with songs and laughter.

Delin and Jesk complimented Geln on his courage for coming and on his persuading all these people to follow him.

"I simply invited them to join me." He handed his lamp to Jesk to hold as he lowered himself down a steep decline.

"Take some credit," Delin said. "Not many could have gotten them to come. Don't let humility fog the facts."

Geln laughed. "Rycal's been telling me about humility. That it's simply seeing myself as I am. 'Taste humility,' he says, 'and you simply see clearly what you are. And that starts the music— when you can laugh at yourself.'"

They descended deeper and deeper. No one realized that after the third day, their talk had changed. No lightheartedness, no laughter, only fears of getting blocked and what they would do if unknown forces came against them.

They said little about the changes in their spirits, but many felt smothered.

Then the flames in the lamps started flickering. After carefully inspecting them, Delin said, "It's not the oil, and it's not the wick. We have to shield them from the slightest draft."

Yet the drafts didn't damp the flames; the air itself somehow flattened the flames against the oil and sent up black smoke.

Cautiously, they descended farther, shielding every flame in every lamp. But as each arrived at a deep basin, the flickering flames disappeared.

"Don't bring any more lamps down!" Geln commanded. "They're getting doused."

Yet when he moved his hand toward the lamps, he still felt the heat from the flame. He turned the wick all the way up, and it burned even more, but he saw nothing.

All those near Geln turned their lamps up fully, yet they gave no light.

The energy and faith Geln had felt was leaking away. He looked at the light of the smoking lamps above them and the thick darkness below. He'd imagined going through whatever was down there with lamps in hands and high spirits of mutual purpose. Now he could barely stand thinking of groping his way down into the heavy darkness of the pit.

"Do we leave the lamps here?" Jesk asked. "No sense carrying them."

"Maybe we should go back up," Asel-ri said. "Or find another way."

Her words warmed Geln, but Mela said, "Yosha and Asel went through the pit without lamps."

As soon as she said it, Geln agreed they had no choice. He rammed his fears down his throat. "We need to keep moving."

The soldiers wanted to go back. Said one, "The air's so thick it coats your tongue."

Another spit loudly. "It's not anything natural—it's the dark seeping into our souls."

"The ravenous dark!"

Yet in the end, no one was bold enough to break off from the rest. They left some of the lamps still burning above them, but they carried most of them, hoping they would shine again.

—— Desert ——

The formations became more slippery, the boulders larger, and the sense of oppression weightier. "We'll all be Tremblers soon if we don't keep to our prayers," Lysse said.

They came to an abrupt downward slope. Delin yelped to get an echo, which indicated it was a long way down.

"Wish we had a rope," Jesk said.

Sticking very close together, grasping wrists and ankles, taking it foothold by foothold, they laboriously descended. Finally Jesk, his hand gripped by Delin, said, "Let go," and he skidded down onto a flat plateau.

Delin jumped down beside him, and almost immediately those close behind were tumbling with relief from the slippery slope onto the massive open space. Geln was one of the last to slide down and the instant his heels dug into the surface, his mind received an unacceptable message.

This can't be sand, he thought. He knelt and picked some up, letting it flow from his palm, feeling he was once again fleeing across the sands of Korbas. "Sand!" he exclaimed.

Mela heard him and quickly worked her way to him through the milling, noisy soldiers. "We have to get off this! It's full of death," Geln said.

"We felt such sand on the sacred peaks. But our lamps and our prayers protected us."

Geln dug his toe down to test its depth, his body insisting he clamber back up on the rock formations.

Delin and Jesk had gone exploring and returned to say they seemed to be at the bottom of a canyon thick with sand. "An opening in the mountain probably lets sierent swirl sand into this hollow," Delin said. "Even the air is gritty down here."

"Must be what Yosha and Asel spoke of," Jesk said. "The great floor of the abyss."

"Do you know what lives in the sand?" Geln asked abruptly.

"Shriikes," Delin said, sounding unperturbed. "We figured that's what were up on the sacred peaks."

Geln thought Delin would be far more perturbed if he'd ever been hunted by them. Jesk, with equal calmness, quoted an old saying: "Deep in the abyss, sand shriikes always feed and wait.

They wait for you and for me." He said it as if telling a story about far away, not with sand under his feet.

"They are also feeding up on the sands of Korbas," Geln said testily, "breaking into our world."

They wondered how the eggs could have gotten to the peaks or to Korbas. Had a possessed bird flown them there? "Or, do the shriikes reach a stage where they themselves can fly?" Delin asked. "I've heard they might."

"It can only whirr itself aloft for a little ways," Geln said, "but its heavy body drags it back down till it squirms forward again."

"How do you know that?"

Geln's mind was on that moment he'd looked up at the oval red eyes and the gigantic snout. Delin had to repeat his question.

"I saw them on the sands of Korbas." Geln was digging a heel into the sands, listening for sounds of movements. He forced himself to say, "I was in league with them once."

Despite the shame, he'd said it. Yet the confession hanging in the air seemed too fantastic, words of spiritual madness.

Mela broke the charged silence by saying with conviction, "Yet you have repented. You have been born fresh in Aliare. Rycal is certain of it, and we are certain you too are beloved."

Her last word struck him with enormous force. Forgiven, perhaps. A fresh start, perhaps. But beloved? Actually beloved by Love, when Geln had chosen so much hatred?

Mela said that the Maker's mercy was greater than the accusations of his own heart, and then she quoted a proverb:

"In the deepest darkness,
One finally begins to see."

And she repeated the prophecy Geln had thought about so many times:

"The blind,
The crippled,
The helpless.
These three will convulse the world."

—— The Greater Weight ——

They walked forward, in the weighty darkness of the canyon, on and on over the heaped-up sand. They followed the steep canyon wall, yelping for echoes yet always finding the canyon going on forever in front of them.

After nearly half a day, they finally heard sounds other than their own plodding feet and subdued voices. More Tremblers. Their familiar moans rose all around them, like the sound of a soft alien rain.

Mela fought the fear settling on her as they moved among them with their pathetic little shivering mews, walking and whimpering along with them.

"Here, then," Delin said, "are what's left of the king's ten thousand. Shall we greet them for him?" He burst into a song of praise to the Maker, and others joined with him. They sang until their voices grew hoarse and then they hummed. Yet the Tremblers were so many they were being swept along with them. Mela felt as if she were in water struggling to move forward.

Then Geln said, shouting over the shoulders of Tremblers jammed tight around him, "The sands are swirling." He fought his way to Mela and put his mouth by her ear. "Smell the sour odors. If ever you've prayed against evil, pray now."

A man not far from Mela began whimpering, and she was close enough to realize he was already deep enough in the sand that his head was at the level of her waist. The sand was churning, and the sour odor assaulted her as she envisioned him being sucked down. In front of her she heard the sound of wings.

Remembering Geln's descriptions, she cried out in fear. Moans around her grew louder as the whirring of great wings sounded above and around them. Mela, transfixed in terror, stood feet apart, arms outstretched, praying desperately. She was consigning herself to the will of the Maker and believing Auret, yet feeling neither she nor anyone on the sand was in any way beloved.

She heard Geln cry out, "The forces of light are greater than the pit! Call out to the Maker!"

At that, the sounds of wings and the moans and cries around her were suddenly overwhelmed by a stupendous crack that numbed her ears. She fell to her knees as the atmosphere changed like a substance struck by lightning. All the fearful powers tormenting shriikes and men were, she thought, abruptly fleeing in agony.

Light flashed around Geln as the thunderous crack bent him double. He looked up to see the planet rent, with light so bright he shut his eyes. He slowly opened them to see wide shafts of light from far above slicing down through the pinnacles and sheer cliffs. Far in the distance, water plummeted in cascades, sending mists toward them full of shimmerings and colors.

At the same time, from beneath came masses of roiling brightness bursting out of the sand. And then a shout. A shout shaking the foundations of Aliare. A shout fulfilling the prophecy that even the furies in the pit would hear the shout of victory.

Glory! he thought. *Splendor and Glory!* Thousands of luminous beings filling the air with living light, dispersing thunderbolts of light more weighty than the dark, more alive than the dark, lifting his spirits so that he felt aloft and soaring with them.

But he also saw many around him fleeing, clambering up the

canyon wall, scuttling into hiding places. They cried out with equal terror as they'd shown on the churning sands.

Geln ran and grabbed a terrified man by the shoulder, saying, "Don't fear. It's glory! It's Auret himself, come as he promised!"

But the man wrenched himself away like a jackal escaping a lion, and Geln was sent sprawling.

A hand gripped his. A powerful arm lifted Geln to his feet.

He looked up and saw the face of Auret in all his glory.

It seemed that all the light penetrating and filling the depths of Aliare somehow came from him, from those blazing suns of eyes and the fierce holy love radiating from his face. Geln thought, *All the luminescents of the sea, all the creatures of light and the suns and stars all have their origin here, in this living one.*

Auret's hand touched Geln's cheek. His voice sounded like kelerai at dawn. "You are forgiven. You are healed." Auret's fingers stroked over the angry burn marks under his eyes, and Geln felt tears flowing as he reached up and touched with his own fingers the healed skin of his face.

Mela heard the joyous voices of celestial beings and sensed glory all around her. Then, she heard Auret's voice, and she felt his hand on her eyes. "I have always loved you, Mela. Again and again, you have heard my voice and followed my call. You have returned my love."

He removed his hand, and the first thing she saw since she had been a little girl was the glory of his face. She was filled with awe and unspeakable rapture. She felt suffused with light, as if she were light itself, one petal of the beauty of his holiness.

Auret took her face in both his hands. He looked deeply into her eyes with such love that the cosmic light radiating into her did not overwhelm her but made her break out in a massive smile like his.

Slowly his smile eased and he said, "Mela, beloved, you now have sight. Yet you must still exercise faith."

She closed her eyes and, as she knew it would be, he was gone when she opened them. Yet above her were wonders she had yearned for so long to see. Light streamed down through the gorges with celestial creatures radiating their own brightness. She was startled to realize the sand on which she stood was a deep amber, its mica sparkling in the light. She thought, *When one has eyes to see, even the abyss is beautiful!*

Curtains of purple fringed with green danced in the distant mist above the gray crags. A movement of color at her feet caught her eye; it was a golden toad with bright blue markings. *Even here,* she thought, *there is color, the irrepressible beauty of the Maker's creation.*

Above, bright motions seemed like a snowstorm of energy, yet also like soft, gentle flakes of light. She lifted her arms and burst out in praise: "Great is the Maker! Joy! He has come as he promised!"

Geln was surfeited with light above and all around him. When he heard Mela's joyous voice and walked toward it, he saw a light.

The light came from her face.

He stood before her thinking, *She's so small, so reckless to have come down here and taken all those risks, so small and yet so powerful and her face shining like Auret's face.*

Mela was first to speak. "Your burns are gone. He touched you!"

Geln reached out to her face. "And now you see!"

They spoke of glory and unveiled splendor. Their friends joined them and they joyously sang in the light until all the celestial hosts had gone and the only light was that streaming down through the great chasms far above them.

Chapter 11.

——— The Tree ———

Pulling herself up on moist handholds, Mela said to those behind her, "Watch out—I could fall on you."

"Better not!" Lysse warned. "We're all hanging on these little niches ourselves."

"You should see the light up here! Must be near the surface."

They had been climbing for days, bright rays streaming past them, lighting the abyss below into mottled patterns of colors and shadows. Mela thought the sounds of the hundreds of climbers below her were like those from a forest full of birds: murmurs and exclamations and gasps of wonder at how the light kept revealing new shapes and scenes.

Now Mela scrabbled her way a bit higher and suddenly found herself on a gravelly, gentle slope. "It's wide and open. Come on!"

A wedge of brown topped Mela's vision. As she climbed, it grew into a slab of gnarled bark, and soon she saw the bottom of a huge tree with its roots exposed. They clung tenaciously to the freshly sheared slabs of stone and dirt. A bit closer and she was looking up at a magnificent conifer, straight as a mast, dark green against a bright blue sky. A good half of its base jutted out over the new rift, a tangle of roots, rocks and dirt. Yet on this precarious base it stood steadfast.

She ached to merge somehow into all the colors so new to her eyes. She stared at everything so long without taking a breath that suddenly she had to gulp some air. Climbing higher, she could see the great new rift she stood in running jagged into the distance.

She grasped one of the lower roots and, as she worked her way up, saw a figure sitting at the tree's base. His chin jutted forward and his head was cocked the other way, as if anxiously peering down the fissure.

When she dislodged some stones, he stood and looked in her direction. He was big, muscular, like her father. As soon as he moved toward her, she recognized it was he. Then he spoke her name, half question, half welcome, all anticipation and wonder.

His saying "Mela" lifted her to her feet and she scrambled toward him.

"Father!"

He came to her with eyes open wide, jaw slung low in disbelief. His arms clamped her tight, and they held each other for a long moment.

"You see me, don't you!" He stared into her eyes.

She nodded, feasting on the sight of his astonishment.

"I had only such a little hope for you, though I prayed always. At these new shakings of the world, these strange reports of glory bursting out of darkness, I couldn't stay home. Perhaps there was still a tiny chance you'd come up alive. So I came here to watch and pray."

She gripped his arms. "You look as fine and as full of love as your voice has always been to me. You don't know how many times as a little girl, and when you visited the school, that I yearned to see your face."

He smiled a great, broad smile. "And how I've longed to see your face again. It's beautiful! Even more beautiful now that your eyes are alive." He was shaking his head in amazement. "And yet I can barely look at its brightness. You've not only come back alive, but with such energy, and your face full of glory!"

"It's as if I'm looking through the Maker's eyes, with love for every person and every creature."

They stood beneath the boughs of the great tree as hundreds exuberantly climbed out all along the fresh rift, raising their arms in wonder to the day, to the sights they had always heard about but never seen.

A creek close by looked magical to her, gurglings over rocks and living curves and frothy shapes. She sat at its banks and stared, transfixed.

Her father put some flowers in her hair. She picked one out and studied its redness. "So red, and the grass so green. I hardly remember the green. And every stalk so distinct and perfectly shaped. To feel and to see it at the same time!" She looked up. "And the birds. I never realized how high they fly."

Mela's once-blind friends joined them, greeting her father with whoops and hearty embraces. The big older man scooped Mela and Lysse and Jesk all up at once in an awkward but hearty grasp, and they all laughed as they tumbled out when he tried to swing them around.

The voices of the thousands now in the fields around them sounded like a festival. Delin said, "Not one of them had ever before seen more than a spark, yet now all of them see the world's wonders perfectly. Each one has been touched by Auret!"

"And we're doubly fortunate," Lysse said, "for smell and touch and sound are still far more powerful to us who were once blind." She gripped a limb of the tree and pulled herself up a ways, showing the strength of her newly healed body.

They watched the ever-growing crowd touching leaves and the trunks of trees, looking up at the sky and mountains and sea. "Everyone's face is alight with wonder," her father said. "Yet why, Mela, are you the only one with such glory on your face?"

"I don't know, Father."

But Delin said, "She loved Auret more fiercely than us all. She believed in the Maker's promises when no one else did. And she led us to take every risk to obey him."

—— Seeds in the Dust ——

Geln watched a young woman, rich dark hair highlighted in the sunlight, as she walked across his mother's yard. Delas. How many years he had missed with his sister Delas.

He thought of her little-girl stories of monsters and her always wanting to follow her big brother. He thought of his deserting her again and again for the powers that raced his blood and seduced him.

She emerged from the shed with a little sack, roosters and hens noisily flocking around her. She threw handfuls of seed in wide sprays into the dust, talking to the chickens scratching and pecking at her feet as if they were obstreperous children. For the first time, Geln could see the resplendent roosters through new eyes, appreciating the majestic humor and beauty of the saucy creatures.

Delas didn't spy her brother coming up the path till the roosters alerted her. Limp sack in one hand, the other poised to cast the seeds, she turned her head and froze. Her hand very slowly lowered and released the seeds into the dust as he walked toward her.

"You are like Geln," she said at last, "but you are not Geln."

He stepped a little closer. "I am. And I've finally come home."

Never removing her eyes from his, Delas flipped over the bag, held the bottom between her fingers and flung the remaining contents so that the fowl raced toward it. "Your face is not the same. You have no scars. Even the way you stand is different."

He touched the skin under his eye. "The burns are gone, from Auret's touch." He reached out slowly and embraced her, his hand in the thickness of her hair. "Little Delas. I have much to be forgiven."

A woman's voice rang out. "Who's here?"

Their mother stood at the door staring suspiciously at the man embracing her daughter.

Geln turned toward her, full of peace within, yet still feeling stabs of guilt. As he walked the short distance, he watched her expression change to bewilderment mixed with hope as she took in the mystery of this familiar stranger walking toward her.

When he stood close, looking down at her with none of the arrogance she'd known so well, she said. "You look like a little boy I once knew." Both her hands went to his face, covering his cheeks and temples. "You've been made new."

He nodded. "It was your audacious prayers that kept me from being devoured." He told her of Auret's touch and the glory in the abyss.

"We've heard many rumors. That all Aris is in an uproar. That thousands have escaped from below and are singing for joy." She kept rubbing her fingers over his healed skin. "And many say the whole world is shaken. That it's truly the end of the world."

Her hands were tight on his face. He bent down and kissed her. "That may be. But, Mother, of all people, you have nothing to fear from that."

—— The Pendant ——

The jubilation of thousands of men and women being welcomed into the light didn't last long. More quakes in the unstable planet frightened the nation. Yet the world held together, and the next year was troubled mostly from ethnic animosity and the dashing of high expectations.

Rycal and Tresk had nearly starved on the peaks, surrounded by the king's troops. Then the light and the glory had exploded around them, and they had led tens of thousands to the surface.

They arrived weak from hunger, expecting to find not only light but joyous welcome and food. Hadn't the king sent his envoys for them? But the king's officials were dismayed at the numbers.

Barbarians and Laij they flatly refused to help at all. Indeed, they attempted to enslave them. They distrusted the strange accents of the emerging Askirit.

The king himself, who had never faced a challenge larger than ordering festivities or making proclamations, worsened every conflict by signing harsh decrees. The kingdom began falling apart.

On a rainy day in early spring, the king was assassinated. No one in the kingdom wanted his son to take his place.

Since Mela had emerged from Aliare, many had secretly spoken of her as Auret's new chosen one. Some resented her part in bringing so many thousands up from below, but as the turmoil increased, they too joined the movement to make her queen.

She resisted. She declared she had no skills in statecraft, and she knew of no prophecies about a Blind Princess becoming queen.

Yet barbarians and Laij bands had now fled to the mountains and were conducting bloody raids on villages. Rycal and Tresk and statesmen from Aris came to her village.

Tresk said, "These are the world's last days. Can we allow chaos when so many have come up to the light? In the darkness, we looked up, and we saw his glory. Our eyes were healed. You're the only one who can bring his healing here too."

"But my face no longer shines," she said. "And many others would love to rule." She was sitting on the ledges near her father's home, looking out over the sea. "My little prayers here may be more powerful than making hollow decrees in Aris." She turned and faced her old friends. "I have no calling and no skills."

But her objections were easily countered, for Rycal's and Tresk's wisdom could be joined with that of others. "In fact," Rycal said, "you're the only one the entire kingdom would follow.

The people say you have not only the blessing of Auret, but that Asel on her deathbed predicted you'd lead the nation."

"A story none of the Enre tell," Mela said.

"But both Asel and Yosha affirmed your call into Aliare. And if Auret called you to descend to the pit, don't you think he might also trust you to be queen?"

Mela sat on a horse in the darkness, the sounds of many other horses and riders behind her. At the first rays of dawn, she kicked her horse forward and began the great inaugural procession.

She had chosen both this time and place. Not Aris. Not the King's House. Instead, the magnificence of the Maker's creation of kelerai. The sky was brightening as she felt its first rumbles. Then came a powerful reverberation, followed by another. The horse moved forward cautiously, tentatively.

They rode on an open plain, and when kelerai burst through with a roar, the horse stopped, trembling. From the procession behind her came exclamations of wonder like her own, and before her the triumphant calls of birds rising. The blues and whites of water rushing upwards filled her sight. She still loved the smells and sounds, but now she also could see the colors and all its magnificence.

"Kelerai," she sang. "Kelerai. Kelerai." Others joined in the traditional song as Mela moved her horse forward, the mist wetting her face.

She led the procession of white and black horses with bells on their bridles and brightly colored plumes, wagons with ladies dressed in gold and men in blue and scarlet. She wore the woven clothing with rustling, ridged sleeves that had signified royalty below and had become part of regal clothing above. Winds blew spray from kelerai on them as they slowly mounted a long hill, then arrived at a meadow overlooking the sea on one side and the city of Kelerai on the other.

The procession took a long time to assemble. She had wanted a simple coronation, and Lysse had agreed, saying, "Let's make it a small delight." But others insisted the ceremony was not for her but for the people. Tresk said urgently, "The people must sense grandeur, coherence, ritual, and festival. All four! Without them, you cannot rule. Horses and trumpets and processions aren't frivolous—not to people with a planet shaking beneath them."

The ceremonies began. Standing near in places of honor were the three friends who had gone into the darkness with her. Leas was there, and her father and Ashdel, who was embarrassingly obsequious to Mela now.

Afterward, she remembered little of the Enre blessings or Cheln's presenting her with the royal intaglio or Geln's oath of fealty from the army. What she remembered most were the challenges from Rycal and Tresk.

Rycal looped the thin chain over her head so the ancient Askirit pectoral hung below her collarbone. "Touch it."

Her ribbed sleeves rustled as she fingered the carving of serrated wings rising, with rays of light at the top.

"Touch its sharp edges."

With her fingertips she carefully stroked the edges sharp as knives.

"You must uphold the cutting edges of the law, even when it divides your own flesh. Even when it destroys those you love." She touched her thumb to the tiny cuts on her fingertips.

"Touch also the wings. Wings of hope."

Tresk hung a newly fashioned pendant on top of the other. It depicted a burst of light from a dark center, flames rising and curling. "You carry a holy trust. Renounce your own desires. Rule for the Maker's glory. As you obeyed him in the darkness, obey him in the light."

The inauguration ended with the usual feasts. Yet Mela declared she would not rule from the pretentious King's House. She would make that magnificent building and land a school for the blind and deaf and maimed. The resources once used for feasts and servants would be used for food and teachers.

And she had her way when she said she would travel from village to village as Yosha had, and that her royal home would be the little school at Kelerai.

"No!" her own father had objected. "It's too dangerous now. Kelerai has become more powerful. Not only would the school be too humble, it would shake you every morning. At the next quake, it may crack apart."

"Perhaps," she said, smiling broadly. "But how appropriate—for the royal house to be drenched and shaken by kelerai each day. And for the queen to stand at the edge of the world's instability and still believe.

"Yes!" she declared. "Let that be the royal house."

Chapter 12.

—— Birds in Flight ——

A year passed, and Mela's reign brought relative harmony. Many began to wonder when she would marry and begin a royal family. But the young queen said, "Not with the planet's instability, and the urgency of spreading the light and the glory."

Two things changed her mind. One was a comment by Rycal that she would as likely reign for a lifetime as for a day. The other was Delin.

Leas had long ago called him the school's only genius, but everyone now called him wise beyond his years. It took only small sparks of romance between them to ignite their very deep friendship into growing love.

Mela insisted her wedding not be an affair of state, despite many entreaties, and now she made her decision stick. Near her father's home, in utter simplicity, she stood with her friends on the shore, the sound of sea birds around them and of villagers looking down from the cliffs above.

After her father blessed the union and Lysse sang, the priest placed a small bird into Delin's hand, another into hers. It quivered in her fingers as she looked down at its blue feathers and yellow markings. In the depths of Aliare, wedding birds would be sacrificed, and the bride and groom would mingle the blood on their hands as a sign of commitment.

But here, at the signal, Mela held out the female bird to Delin. As he reached out and took it while handing her the struggling male, she caught a whiff of melne, the traditional groom's scent. She smiled at him as she took the bird and they said in unison, "We pledge our holy love forever."

It was well known that the wedding birds mated for life. Mela and Delin held up their arms and released them into the air, then watched them fly off together toward the mountains.

After the ceremony, as they were talking to Jesk and other well wishers, Mela heard the giggles and laughter of children. "They're not supposed to be down here," Delin said.

Mela moved toward the small figures. "Come here, children." But they stopped their giggling and sat motionless. She moved easily along the water's edge toward them, swinging her arms, none of the thick flanges of royalty on her sleeves. When she reached them, she pulled the smallest one into her arms. "What's that on your ankle?" she asked, knowing it was a wedding anklet of little teeth that clicked at every movement.

"To celebrate," the little girl said shyly.

Mela shook the child's foot so the anklet clicked. "Let's go," she said, leading the children and the wedding party up to the village. From a distance, they could smell the feast and hear people shaking percussion pettetels and striking sietelens—hollow bones with rounded bones within that sounded a skody-bok-bok-bok, skody-bok-bok-bok.

Leas said to Mela as she put on an anklet, "The bridal scent becomes you." She thanked him. "I hope you received my gifts of special scents."

She laughed, lighthearted from the silliness of the children. "Would I tell you if I had?"

"They're authentic."

"You'll never know, will you, if I used them." She wrinkled her nose at him and smiled. "Or if I have prepared any scents at all for my wedding night."

—— A Little Lamp ——

Geln followed Asel-ri up a steep trail toward a waterfall. They had wed the same day as Mela and Delin, for Asel-ri had fancied the idea. She also had fancied the idea of making her honeymoon much like that of her namesake many, many years before.

"I couldn't find a cave behind a waterfall as Asel did," she'd told Geln. "But I did find a very secluded cavern near one." She led him to the fall, and started under it.

"I'll get wet!"

She turned around smiling and touched one finger between his lips, the playful way of saying "baby" in Yette. Then she pulled him under the fall and into a cave in the forest. Inside, she unfastened her pack and disappeared with it down a tunnel.

Geln was delighted Asel-ri insisted on all the old traditions, including the bride's making secret and personal preparations for the wedding night. The anticipation had driven from his mind the pressures of his work with Rycal and Tresk settling conflicts over taxes and laws.

Asel-ri called to him, and he entered the darkness of the tunnel. After groping his way for a short space, he saw a small, mellow light. He smelled spices and saw Asel-ri in the shadows. As he drew closer to her, he realized the aromas of various spices came from several directions.

She was lying on furs and rushes. He knelt beside her with his knees on the thick fur. Asel-ri was so innocent, so committed, so joyous in her giving of herself, he felt his past accusing him that he was unworthy to touch her. He drew back just a trifle.

"What's the matter?"

"Nothing." Most of all, he did not in any way want to spoil these moments she had worked so creatively to make perfect. But then he felt compelled to say, "My dark past makes me wonder how I can touch one as holy and innocent as you?"

She laughed. "I am only human!" She took his hand and pulled it firmly to her face. "Your past is long, long ago. It is forgiven. Even the scars of your face are healed."

"Yet—"

"We are none of us innocent." She stood up. "None of us is holy, except for his holiness in us." She held a small pouch in her hand and took from it two strips of a soft material which had been touched with the personal scent she had chosen. She placed the strips into his hand as the aroma filled the air.

Reaching out, he found the ringlet of hair over her ear and tied the perfumed material to it. Then he tied the other strip on the other side.

She reached out and kissed him.

He opened his own pouch and and handed her the tiny bag of scent he had chosen. She squeezed out a little, then dabbed traces behind his ears and on his throat. "Here we have it best of all," she said. "The sensuousness of touch and scent from below, and the soft light of the little lamp revealing us to each other."

"From the Maker comes touch and sight," Geln said. "And breath and hope, food and work. And the wondrous desires between a man and a woman."

—— Delin's Skills ——

Mela and Delin rode a short distance the afternoon of the wedding, then left the horses with guards. Delin led the way over and around formations with sparse shrubs until they reached a hilltop and Delin indicated they should sit down.

"Why here?"

"Look down where the trees and grass form a triangle. You might see something if we wait long enough."

They waited a long time, but nothing appeared.

"Our wedding day is almost gone. Shouldn't we go?"

"In a while."

The sun was low in the sky when she saw movements, gold patches shifting at the top of the windblown grass. She stared until she made out that they were the backs of lions, two of them, heading toward the triangle Delin had pointed out.

"Lion country. I've been scouting and found their den. From here, we're safe."

"They could be up here in a moment!" Mela said, as if that were a wonderful thing. "I've not seen a lion since I was a little girl with blurred sight." She was squeezing Delin's arm and turned to look into his face. "You could not have found a better gift."

The male stepped out of the grass. "Does he remind you of the lion you saw?"

"My sight then was blurred. With that great golden mane of hair around his head, he looks magnificent...."

"I always like your voice when you talk about the lion. That's why I wanted you to see one today."

The lioness emerged from the grass and the male turned his head toward her, then up toward them. "I feel he's looking at me," Mela said, "singling me out...."

The lions disappeared into their den. Mela followed Delin along a trail that brought them to a high hill thick with trees overlooking the sea. Delin had offered to prepare their shelter for this night, and she'd acquiesced. But it was nearly dark and the climb was steep.

"Are we going up here to watch something else? We need to get to the shelter."

"Look closely, as you did for the lions."

When they neared the edge above the sea, she saw a structure had been built among the trees. It blended with two hemlocks tipped slightly into space and connected with lesser trees at the cliff's edge.

Through a carved door they entered a spacious, airy lodge, with a full view of the sea and the shore below. It made Mela feel as if she were on the limbs of the trees looking down at the red sun setting on the water.

"Is this what you've been doing all this time?" She looked from the sea to every corner of the shelter. "I've never heard of anything like this. You really are a genius." She poked him playfully.

"I only thought it up. Others built it."

They watched the colors moving on the water. Mela said, "I thought Askirit lived in caves! You spoil the queen."

When it was finally dark, Mela opened her pack. "You've given two remarkable gifts. But now, as a traditional Askirit woman, it is my turn to prepare."

"Did you bring scents?" He smiled, for they had joked about how both Leas and Asel-ri had been anxious Mela prepare just the right ones.

She pulled out several packets of soft leather. "I've been told these are so sensual, it's unfair to a normal man."

He looked at her face. "I'm normal." He kissed her, then held her at arm's length in the lamplight to look at her. "I was blind from birth. I never imagined I would see the sun on the water below, or my own woman in all her beauty."

—— Other Worlds ——

Geln sat looking across at the peaks of the island Asel had long ago claimed for the Enre. It had been here Yosha and Asel had come to die, insisting they be left alone together in Asel's beloved aerie.

Mela had asked to come, to pay her respects, and to give them proper burial. The two Varials had led them, the first persons to invade the sanctuary. But when they entered, they had found signs of neither death nor life.

Geln heard a movement beside him and was startled to see a man about his own age coming toward him. He greeted Geln, a mysterious smile at the corners of his mouth. He looked familiar, and Geln said so.

"Yes. We've met before. In a tent."

Geln's brows furrowed, and his eyes tightened to study the face. In it, he saw echoes of the aged face of Yosha. "You look like the king."

"I am. I'm Yosha." He touched Geln's shoulder and puckered his chin in amusement, as if to assure him he had nothing to fear.

Yet Geln asked forgiveness and started explaining what had happened to him after he'd fled the tent.

"I know all that. You don't need my forgiveness. You already have his."

Mela stood where she had once listened to the storm beside the old figure of Asel. A woman's voice behind her said, "You're remembering days of storms and fears."

She turned to face a young woman. Mela asked, "Were you one of the Enre who was with me here?"

The woman's face broke into a wide smile. "I am Asel. And I'm pleased you are now queen of the Askirit."

Mela studied her face but could see little resemblance to the aged woman once here.

"You see," Asel said. "The promises were all true. The wrinkled skin is gone, and the shaking steps and trembling hands."

Yosha had entered and strode to Mela; he wrapped her in an embrace. "When you went down into the rifts, my old eyes wept. But now we all rejoice."

Mela stepped back to look at Yosha's face. "But are you dead? Are you in this world, or another?"

"We are eternal—but no more so than you. We go from world to world, as you will."

Asel held out her hands. "Auret came to us here."

They spoke of the glories they had seen, and Geln's wife Asel-ri had no questions for her namesake but studied her young face and listened in wonder. They were full of anticipation as they spoke of the future. "We deserve none of all this," Yosha said. "It's all the Maker's lavish gift."

They talked about Aliare and that even in the deepest darkness the Maker's glory came. Mela said, "The abyss was a wonder, when it was redeemed by the light."

"Even the clumsy shriikes whirring off," Delin said, "just natural beasts in the light, red and silver scales glittering."

Yosha said, "Our trek through the abyss was all darkness. But a time comes when all is exposed to the light."

They talked about the unstable planet beneath them, and Yosha said, "This old world is worn out. Only the faithful can stand on a shuddering world, ready for the birth pangs of new realms."

Mela touched her slightly swelling belly and said that she felt torn by such words, for the baby within her might have no future.

"The baby is eternal!" Asel said heartily. "That's a future!" Then Asel put her hand on Mela where the roundness showed and said, "Your children will bring you great joy. And you will know grief beyond imaginings." She briskly ran her fingers over Mela's palm with the Yette sign for vitality. "But you will bear a wounded child of strange powers who will bring unprecedented glory into the world."

* * *

Geln had just raised a dipper of water to his lips when he heard Mela's voice beside him. "It was all true. All of it actually true—the prophecies, the promises of life going on forever."

He drank a little and replaced the dipper. "And even I, the dupe of the furies, have tasted forgiveness."

"And Asel and Yosha transformed. How will we bear all that is ahead?" Her brows were raised, her head cocked a little, but a smile lighted her face.

"We will be asking that forever. And I suspect," Geln said, matching her smile, "that we will never cease to be astounded."

Glossary

aceyn—fibrous sea plant carpeting the rocky shorelines in Aliare

Aliare—the night world beneath the planet's surface inhabited by Askirit, their enemies the Laij, and various tribes

Asta—the world above

aurets—birds in Aliare that symbolize morning; also called dawnbreakers

Enre—ancient Askirit religious order of women warriors

grel—an edible root

kelerai—spectacular, massive geysers that erupt each morning in Asta; when capitalized, a small city near the phenomenon

Kjotik—sea monster; another name for leviathan

leviathan—huge sea monster that sometimes preys on Askirit villages

keitr—poisonous batlike creatures in the nightworld, gathered by the Askirit from caves and fired at enemies with deadly effect

loga—primitive calculating device used by the Laij

merret—small deadly beast trained and used by the Laij

mycea—flat, plantlike sea creatures used for food

niroc—mammal whose bones are used for nails and tools

olek—large bird of prey; the national symbol of the Laij

osk—sea creature with large bones used for many purposes

pattetels—Askirit percussion instruments

pectre—tiny, extremely poisonous insect

peshua—fish with small useful bones

pevas—percussion instruments used in Askirit worship

porsk—an edible but carnivorous plant with dangerous tentacles *selcrit*—small stinging shellfish

shriikes—metamorphosing beasts that drag their prey deep into the sand

sierent—the daily, immense upheaval of the underground waters; the time period people in Aliare call night

sietelens—percussion instruments made of hollow bone

Varial—leader of the Enre

Yette—the Askirit tactile language consisting of intricate motions of fingers on another's skin

BE SURE TO READ HAROLD MYRA'S
CHILDREN IN THE NIGHT

If you enjoyed *The Shining Face,* be sure to read its "prequel," *Children in the Night.* It tells the early history of this fantasy world's matriarch and patriarch, Asel and Yosha. The third volume of this trilogy, *Morning Child,* should be available in 1994.

Children in the Night is an epic fantasy of yearning, horror, myth, and wonder. It is the story of good versus evil in a subterranean world of perpetual night, in which the young man, Yosha, and the young woman, Asel, with strange and simple ingenuity, confront the forces of darkness. Startled by the miraculous cripple who fell from the world above, they begin a quest for the mysteries and power of the dawn. Ten years in development, *Children in the Night* is Harold Myra's most intriguing and complex work of fiction to date.

———————

"Beware this novel . . . an all-ensnaring tale"
—Calvin Miller, author of *The Singer Trilogy*
"Harold Myra's masterwork"
—Jerry B. Jenkins, author of *The Operative*
"I have discovered a couple of new imaginary heroes that fall comfortably in the ranks of Frodo and his friends"
—Dana Key of the rock group DeGarmo and Key
". . . flexes our imaginations to enter into the huge mysteries of good and evil"
—Eugene Peterson, author of *Reversed Thunder*
"*Children in the Night* surprises the imagination, feeds literary starvation, and soothes the soul."
—Karen Burton Mains, author of *Friends and Strangers*
Winner of an Angel Award and runner up in both the Readers' Choice and Critics' Choice categories of the Christianity Today Book Awards.

ALSO BY HAROLD MYRA:
THE CHOICE

The Choice is a book of marvels. It describes the enchantment of Creation, the agony of the Fall, and the wonders of life beyond death. Seldom does fantasy fiction get this good—or this close to the truth!

In the tradition of C. S. Lewis's *Perelandra, The Choice* is Harold Myra's fictional exploration of the nature of innocence, temptation, and disobedience. The novel follows Risha, the first woman, as she encounters her Creator, her mate, the creatures of the Garden, and the lures of the Serpent. In Risha and her husband, Kael, we can see ourselves—psychologically and spiritually—as we are and as we might have been. And we see the glories to come when we pass from this life into new worlds.

———

"What an achievement!"
—Tom Howard

"Beautifully, imaginatively told"
—*Christian Herald*

"This book will stir your imagination"
—*Youth Profile Magazine*

"Tightly knit, skillfully crafted, and imaginative"
—Harold Lindsell

"I hesitate to employ such hyperbole, but there it is: *The Choice* is a masterwork"
—Connie Soth, *Arkenstone*

Winner of *Campus Life*'s Poetry/Fiction
   Book of the Year Award